Praise for
Tamar Myers's Pennsylvania
Dutch Mysteries

"A pinch of acerbity, a scoop of fun, and a pound of originality . . . a delicious treat."   —Carolyn Hart

"A piquant brew, bubbling over with mystery and mirth. I loved every page of it."   —Dorothy Cannell

"As sweet as a piece of brown-sugar pie."   —*Booklist*

"Snappy descriptions . . . humorous shenanigans."
                                    —*Pittsburgh Tribune-Review*

"A hoot. Guaranteed you'll be laughing by the third paragraph."   —*The Charleston Post and Courier* (SC)

"Think *Mayberry R.F.D.* with Mennonites. Think *Murder, She Wrote* with a Pennsylvania Dutch accent. Instead of Jessica Fletcher, think Magdalena Yoder, a plain-dressing, blunt-speaking middle-aged innkeeper who frequently rescues the incompetent chief of police by solving his cases."
                                    —*The Morning Call* (Allentown, PA)

"With her sassy wit and odd habits . . . Magdalena is a delightful main character."   —*The Champion Newspaper* (Decatur, GA)

"Masterful."   —*Kirkus Reviews*

Butter Safe Than Sorry

A Pennsylvania Dutch Mystery with Recipes

Tamar Myers

AN OBSIDIAN MYSTERY

OBSIDIAN
Published by New American Library, a division of
Penguin Group (USA) Inc., 375 Hudson Street,
New York, New York 10014, USA
Penguin Group (Canada), 90 Eglinton Avenue East, Suite 700, Toronto,
Ontario M4P 2Y3, Canada (a division of Pearson Penguin Canada Inc.)
Penguin Books Ltd., 80 Strand, London WC2R 0RL, England
Penguin Ireland, 25 St. Stephen's Green, Dublin 2,
Ireland (a division of Penguin Books Ltd.)
Penguin Group (Australia), 250 Camberwell Road, Camberwell, Victoria 3124,
Australia (a division of Pearson Australia Group Pty. Ltd.)
Penguin Books India Pvt. Ltd., 11 Community Centre, Panchsheel Park,
New Delhi - 110 017, India
Penguin Group (NZ), 67 Apollo Drive, Rosedale, North Shore 0632,
New Zealand (a division of Pearson New Zealand Ltd.)
Penguin Books (South Africa) (Pty.) Ltd., 24 Sturdee Avenue,
Rosebank, Johannesburg 2196, South Africa
Penguin Books Ltd., Registered Offices:
80 Strand, London WC2R 0RL, England

First published by Obsidian, an imprint of New American Library,
a division of Penguin Group (USA) Inc.

First Printing, February 2010
10 9 8 7 6 5 4 3 2 1

Copyright © Tamar Myers, 2010
All rights reserved

OBSIDIAN and logo are trademarks of Penguin Group (USA) Inc.

LIBRARY OF CONGRESS CATALOGING-IN-PUBLICATION DATA:

Myers, Tamar.
Butter safe than sorry: a Pennsylvania Dutch mystery with recipes/Tamar Myers.
p. cm.
"An Obsidian mystery."
ISBN 978-0-451-22910-6
1. Yoder, Magdalena (Fictitious character)—Fiction. 2. Pennsylvania Dutch Country (Pa.)—Fiction.
3. Hotelkeepers—Fiction 4. Mennonites—Fiction 5. Bank robberies—Fiction. I. Title.
PS3563.Y475B87   2010
813'.54—dc22   2009033379

Set in Palatino Roman
Designed by Alissa Amell
Printed in the United States of America

Without limiting the rights under copyright reserved above, no part of this publication may be reproduced, stored in or introduced into a retrieval system, or transmitted, in any form, or by any means (electronic, mechanical, photocopying, recording, or otherwise), without the prior written permission of both the copyright owner and the above publisher of this book.

PUBLISHER'S NOTE
This is a work of fiction. Names, characters, places, and incidents either are the product of the author's imagination or are used fictitiously, and any resemblance to actual persons, living or dead, business establishments, events, or locales is entirely coincidental.
    The publisher does not have any control over and does not assume any responsibility for author or third-party Web sites or their content.

The scanning, uploading, and distribution of this book via the Internet or via any other means without the permission of the publisher is illegal and punishable by law. Please purchase only authorized electronic editions, and do not participate in or encourage electronic piracy of copyrighted materials. Your support of the author's rights is appreciated.

This book is dedicated to my dear friend Kay Chalk.

ACKNOWLEDGMENTS

A special thanks to the Wisconsin Milk Marketing Board, who graciously consented to the use of the recipes in this book. For lots of other delicious (and free) recipes with butter, consult their Web site at www.eatwisconsincheese.com.

Butter Safe Than Sorry

1

Finally, after almost two hundred years, my hometown had its first bona fide hooker. Of course I don't approve of a woman selling her body for sex—or even for a great deal of money—but I must confess that I found this particular situation rather titillating. After all, Dorothy Yoder was the wife of Hernia's most notorious lecher. But apparently Sam wasn't enough for her, so she tried selling herself to a handsome young tourist and got herself arrested. I mean, really, it had all the ingredients of a poorly written novel, a medium with which I am well acquainted.

To be painfully honest, when I first heard this news, my feet began a happy dance of their own accord. Since dancing is a sin, and I could not stop my tootsies from moving, I had no choice but to hop on my husband's bicycle and take a couple of spins around the farmyard. For once, hallelujah, Hernia's confirmed floozy wasn't my sister, Susannah.

No siree, Bob. This time Hernia's strumpet without a trumpet, her trollop who packed a wallop, was none other than *the* Dorothy Yoder, my cousin-in-law, a woman who had never been nice to me! Oh how the mighty had fallen—both literally and figuratively. The day after her fiftieth birthday, Dorothy—who'd managed to consume four entire sheet cakes and three half gallon cartons of Breyer's Butter Pecan Ice Cream—was being transferred to a new, and larger, bed, when the main cable broke. Dorothy was not severely injured, but apparently jolted enough to consider a very dangerous surgical option over dieting.

Two years, and many cosmetic surgeries later, seven-hundred-pound Dorothy was a svelte size sixteen and looked twenty years younger than her husband. As our town's only grocer, married to the daughter of a wealthy man, Sam had long perched on our highest social rung. But when Dorothy got her looks back—her words, not mine—she started wearing clothes that revealed her décolletage and emphasized her still-impressive derriere. Not only that, but she got her flaming red hair cut and styled, and started applying more makeup than even a fallen Methodist has a right to. Trust me, I am not exaggerating—not this time. For her maiden outing as the painted Whore of Babylon, Dorothy had a professional apply the goop and glop, and when she returned home, her three daughters didn't recognize her and tried to have her arrested as an intruder.

Schadenfreude, that peculiarly German, but oh so useful, word described my feelings perfectly when I heard this. The reason that Dorothy has never been nice to me is because her husband, Sam, carries a torch for Yours Truly. Sam's torch is like one of those trick birthday candles that can't be blown out—no matter what. Sam delivered my son on the floor of his so-called grocery store (Yoder's Corner Market), but even seeing my "business" at its worst, so to speak, was not enough to dampen his ardor.

I should hasten to clarify that I have absolutely no interest in Sam and have never encouraged him. We are, in fact, first cousins on my mother's side of the family, and whilst I am not biologically related to the woman who raised me, that doesn't matter: Sam was, is, and will always be, an annoying cousin who must be endured—somewhat like toenail fungus when prescription ointments won't work.

Thus it was a bittersweet thing to find Dorothy hanging about the store when I popped in that Friday afternoon with my son, Little Jacob, in tow. The woman was wearing a moleskin leopard-print dress and six-inch spike heels. Her eyeliner was so heavy, it looked like she'd glued slivers of charcoal to her eyelids. As for her eye *shadow*, I guessed the metallic silver was supposed to match her lipstick, shoes, and shoulder-length bangle earrings, but frankly, it gave her an eerily reptilian look.

"Is that a real woman, Mama?" Little Jacob asked the second his eyes adjusted to the dim light.

"'Out of the mouths of babes,'" I said, quoting Psalms 8:2.

"What did that child say?"

"I'm sure he was admiring you," Sam said. He dotes on Little Jacob and often gives him candy or other treats. I wouldn't mind that so much if the sweets weren't stale.

I gave Dorothy a placating smile that was at least partly genuine. Despite the animosity she feels toward me, I feel nothing more than pity for her.

"You always were beautiful, Dorothy. But if you want my opinion, this is a classic case of less being more."

She teetered closer for a few steps, her eyes flashing with rage. "Well, I *don't* want your opinion, Magdalena."

"But you look like a hoochie-mama, dear."

My four-year-old son doesn't let anything slip by him. "Mama, what's a 'hoochie-mama'?"

"Hmm—remember the pictures I showed you of your aunt Susannah?"

He nodded. "She's the lady in the hooch, right?"

"Right."

"Oh, I get it! So that's why she's a hoochie-mama, right?"

"Well—"

"Like this lady, right?"

"Not ex—"

"Cousin Sam, can I have a cookie?"

Sam gave the love of my life three cookies and then got back to me ASAP. In the meantime, the huffy hoochie-mama snarled at me and showed her claws, but mercifully retreated to watch television at the back of the store, where Sam maintains a little "break room" for himself. The redundancy of such a place makes as much sense as a fish wearing a life vest. At any rate, Sam wasted no time in pouncing.

"Couldn't stay away from me, could you, Mags?"

"I came to buy lined poster board for Little Jacob's kindergarten project. Do you have any?"

He shook his head. "You're the tenth person today to come in here and ask for some. It's for that for family-tree project Miss Kuhnberger assigned, isn't it?"

"Yes."

"She does that every year, and every year you poor parents have to drive into Bedford just to get some poster board. You'd think that old bat would catch on and change her lessons plans."

"Or"—I leaned forward conspiratorially—"some aging lothario whose wife looks like she's about to step out on him would catch on to a solution just as obvious and stock poster board each fall."

Sam rolled his watery blue eyes. "My vendor doesn't carry it. And since I'd make only about a nickel a sheet on it anyway, it wouldn't pay me to put in a special order with another vendor. But you can take back your insinuation."

"My insinuation?"

"That all Dorothy needs is a little loving on the home front and everything will be hunky-dory—as you are so fond of saying."

"Mama, what's 'hunky-pory'?"

I jumped. The trouble with children is that when not in use, they can't be folded and put away like TV trays—not that I've tried very often, mind you. Lord, if you're listening, I'm not complaining, seeing as how I fully expected to be as barren as the Gobi Desert, or at the very least give birth to a miniature version of myself, which would be punishment for all the times that I indulged in the sin of self—

"Mama!"

You see? Children can be so impatient at times!

"What?"

"What is 'hunky-pory'?"

"It's 'dory,' dear, and it means 'fine.' Now see if you can find the can that has the most numbers after the dollar sign. That's the one Cousin Sam is going to give us for free."

"Okay!" Off he skipped, as gay as a Broadway producer and twice as happy.

"Cous," Sam said accusingly, "it may be all be hunky-dory on her end, but not so on mine. You have to remember that I'm the one who had to bathe and dress her when she was too big to get out of bed. And I was the one who had to empty her reinforced, jumbo-size bedpan. How do you recapture romantic feelings after twenty years of that?"

"Marriage counseling?"

"Ha! Where would I find a marriage counselor who would have even an inkling of what I've been through?"

Much to my surprise, I actually saw his point. In the same vein, I've often wondered how a celibate person could offer marital advice—well, I still do. There is, I think, only so much that one can extrapolate from the experiences related to them by others.

I shrugged. "Have you tried the Internet?"

"Mama, what's 'twapolate' mean?"

It was Sam's turn to jump. "Hey, buddy, back so soon?"

Little Jacob nodded and proudly held forth a large jug of

maple syrup. This wasn't that sugar water over which a maple leaf has been waved; this was the genuine stuff, the real McCoy—literally, in fact, since the sap was harvested and boiled down by Gerald McCoy and his three teenage sons.

Since it takes forty gallons of sap to produce one gallon of maple syrup, the real deal costs a pretty penny, to be sure. In fact, I never serve it to my guests, although I do make it available if they're on my special luxury plan (at only two hundred dollars more a day, they hardly know what hit them). At any rate, Little Jacob was holding forth a half-gallon jug, for which Sam was asking $39.99.

"I want this, Cousin Sam," he said.

Sam tried to pat my son on the head. "You gotta pick something else there, buddy. How about a candy bar? You want a whole candy bar to yourself?"

"I don't want no stupid candy bah," my son said, proving that I didn't give birth to a cabbage. "Candy bahs cost less than a dollah, but this costs a pwetty penny. Wight, Mama? Besides, Mama says that yoh candy is stale."

"Hey, Mags," Sam said, "what's with this otherwise precocious kid not saying his 'R's? Isn't he in kindergarten already?"

"Sam," I growled, "he's right in front of you."

"Yeah," Little Jacob gwowled, "I'm wight in fwont of you."

"Well, then, kid, I think you're too old for that."

"Butt out," I said kindly. "It really isn't your business."

"Mama, this is getting heavy," Little Jacob said.

"Then set it down, dear."

"But I want my money fust."

"You heard him, Sam. Pay up."

"If you make him say his 'R's."

"I most certainly will not."

"Well, then, he can hold it all day, because I didn't say *when* I'd pay."

"You're being ridiculous, Sam. I wouldn't make him say his 'R's, even if I could. I mean, what if he decided to move to Boston someday. Would you not want him to fit in?"

"Mama, I can't hold it no mo-ah!"

The heavy glass jug slipped from my dear son's tiny fingers and shattered on the hard wooden floor of Yoder's Corner Market. I'll say this for good-quality maple syrup: it's a pleasure to lick the stuff off bare skin. I even licked some off my clothes and, when Sam went to get a mop bucket, I had a quick go at the nearest shelves.

Of course I was the one stuck with mopping the floor and getting the sticky-sweet stuff out from between the floorboards. In the meantime my cutie pie watched television in the back room with Cousin Dorothy. I worked quickly, as I do not approve of TV, convinced as I am that Satan lives in each and every set, and especially in wall-mounted megasize screens. As if to prove my point, when Little Jacob emerged, he said he'd been watching Opwah, and how come boys didn't have va-jay-jays too?

I also had to bathe Little Jacob, and redress him, and do likewise for myself, so it was late afternoon by the time we got into Bedford, our nearest real city. With a population of nearly four thousand people, this bustling metropolis offers just about everything a good Christian could want—and then some. I was able to purchase poster board without any trouble and make it to the First Farmer's Bank five minutes before they locked the doors.

As I stood at the island counter tallying checks for deposit, Little Jacob played on the floor at my feet with his own "checkbook." This is a mockup that I made out of old canceled and voided checks just for him. It's never too early to teach a child how to run a successful business if you ask me—even if he can't say his "R"s.

"Mama," the little fellar in question said, whilst tugging on my skirt, "I see a wobba."

"That's nice, dear."

"Now I see two wobbas."

"A wobba what, dear?" I asked absently. "A wobba band?"

"No, silly; they ah wobba men. But now I see thwee of them."

"*Shhh*, honey, Mama's trying to hurry."

He continued to tug on my skirt. "One of them's wobbing that nice lady behind the countah, Mama. You know, the nice lady who sometimes gives me candy. The kind that isn't stale."

"*What?*" I looked up from my work.

There were three people in the reception area, other than the two security guards. All three of the customers were Amish men, but all three were indeed armed, and one did have a gun pointed at the back of Amy Neubrander's head.

2

Of course the scenario I beheld was impossible since Amish men don't carry guns, and they don't rob banks, and even a person with just one drop of Amish blood could not point a gun at another human being. I know this is so, because my own ancestor, Jacob Hochstetler, made the difficult choice that he and his family would be massacred by the Delaware Indians rather than defend themselves. Needless to say, some of them survived, but you get my point; the Amish are the epitome of the phrase "a gentle people."

So if what I saw was an impossibility, then I was either experiencing a psychotic break or the world had just gone to Hades in a handbasket, and neither prospect was good for my Little Jacob. When you're a mother, it's all about the children, isn't it? The thing is this: Amy was somebody's child as well. The poor girl was barely into her twenties—if that. She might have been still in her late teens.

And what about the two security guards? one might ask. What were they doing? Why, absolutely nothing! They were standing as stock-still as the cylindrical trash containers on either side of the doors.

Amy seemed remarkably calm. "It takes two minutes for the SWAT team to get here," she said in a loud clear voice, "and I pressed the alarm a minute ago. If you leave now, you might still have a chance to get away."

The Amish do not value education; in fact they eschew it as worldly and dangerous. They are, however, as a rule not unintelligent. In contrast, these three were as bright as the warts on a pickle—and I say that with all Christian charity. The men looked at one another, at Amy, around the lobby at the security cameras, at the security guards, at me, and then back at one another.

The one standing closest to me called out to the others, "Do you think she's telling the truth?"

"Only one way to find out," said the man who had the gun pointed directly at Amy's forehead.

"Shoot the witch," growled the third man, "and let's get on with it." Of course, being a criminal, he used far stronger language than that.

"No, don't shoot huh!" Little Jacob was on his feet and halfway across the marble expanse before I could react.

They said that one's life passes in front of one's eyes in a life-threatening situation, but the only thing I had on my mind was the safety of my sweet little son. Like a hundred-thirty-five-pound projectile of flesh and bone, I flew at my offspring, knocking him to the floor. We slid the rest of the way across the room, where we crashed into the villain in front of the counter.

I still don't know if it was the impact that caused it, or if the robber was trigger-happy, but the gun did indeed go off. Fortunately the bullet barely grazed Amy, doing more damage to her blouse than her upper arm. Still, she screamed and staggered backward, eventually tripping and falling. It was at about this point that the two trash can–like guards awoke from their fear-induced coma and began to stumble about like a pair of drunks. Add to this craziness the antics of the bank manager and the two other clerks, and the lobby suddenly resembled a three-ring circus.

Apparently all this activity was just too much for the simple Amish felons, who mercifully hightailed it out of the bank without another word, and more important, without firing another shot. *However*, the police did not show up for another five minutes. In fact, when they did show up, it was only because I had called them on my cell phone.

"Nine-one-one," the dispatcher said in a disarmingly cheery voice.

"Uh—there's been a bank robbery. At the First Farmer's Bank."

"Magdalena, is that you?"

"Hedda?"

"Yup, that's me: Hedda Schnurmeister, although you used to call me Hedda Gabbler, on account of I used to talk so much, although I never did get the connection. But it's Hedda Winkler now, and if I recall correctly, you're no longer—"

"Shut up—*please*, Hedda. Like I said, there's been a bank robbery. Put me through to the police."

"Holy salami! Are you sure? How much money did they get?"

"Well, they didn't get anything because my son—you never saw a braver hero in all your born days—confronted them. But they did shoot Amy Neubrander in the left arm, so make sure you dispatch an ambulance as well."

"Hold on, Magdalena, will you? I've got another call coming in."

"But, Hedda—"

I waited two minutes for her to get back on the line. In the meantime, I directed the security guards as they tore a three-inch-wide strip from the bottom of my petticoat and wrapped it like a tourniquet around Amy's arm. As we were doing this, Little

Jacob cooed to her in a mixture of Pennsylvania Dutch, Yiddish, and, of course, English. The tyke is growing up trilingual, thanks to a Jewish grandmother and an Amish cousin who are living and working in close proximity. (For the record, neither of these women is "R" deficient.)

"Magdalena, are you there?"

"Of course. Where's the ambulance? Where are the police?"

"Hold your horses, Magdalena; I'm about to send them. You're not going to believe this, but there's been an honest-to-goodness bank robbery in this town—well, an attempt at one, at any rate. That was the bank president on the line just now. He said that an incredibly brave little boy put a stop to it. And I mean a *little* boy too—like three or four."

"He's four. He can't say his 'R's and he's small for his age, but other than that, he's completely normal."

"Yeah? How would you know?"

"Because he's *my* son, you—you—nincompoop!"

"Why, Magdalena Yoder, is that any way for a good Mennonite woman to talk?"

I am, indeed, Magdalena Yoder—I am, in fact, Magdalena Portulacca Yoder Rosen. There are those who would claim that I am anything but a *good* Mennonite woman, and that my apple has not only fallen far from the tree, but it has rolled out of the orchard altogether. Of course they are wrong.

A good Mennonite woman should be humble, and if I must say so myself, I am quite proud of my humility. A good Mennonite woman should be soft-spoken, never judgmental, always striving to be Christ-like. Well, let it be known that I offer observations, not judgments, and I am quite capable of whispering them. As for a Christ-like demeanor, let us not forget that the Dear Lord exhibited a great deal of agitation when he happened upon the moneychangers in the temple, and if this is the example I choose to emulate, who then are others to judge *me*?

Of course there remains the fact that I married outside my faith. This seems to stick in the craws of many of my coreligionists, never mind that the man I married is of the same faith as Jesus Himself, plus his mother, stepfather, and most of the disciples. The One Way contingent not only believes that the Babester will burn in Hell for all Eternity, but some of them demand that I believe that as well. A few of the more pious have informed me that I have endangered my own soul in a sort of Singe and Sizzle by Association (the Babester's words, not mine) theology.

At any rate, I have tried to be a good Mennonite woman, I tried to be a good big sister (at that, I did fail miserably), I try to be a good wife, and I try to be a good mother. However, when I saw my only child, that integral part of me who grew beneath my heart for eight and a half months, come so close to being murdered that day in the bank, something within me finally snapped.

The more vindictive in our community were overheard to say cruel things like "Magdalena's gone bonkers, Magdalena's berserk, she's stark-raving mad, nuttier than one of Elvina's fruitcakes"—the list of pejorative descriptions was longer than Cynthia Bertelsmann's abnormally long arms. Even Freni, my best friend and kinswoman, is said to have muttered, "I think maybe the little bird has flown from her clock, yah?"

Ironically, it was Freni, perhaps the least educated of my analysts, who came closest in her description. It wasn't that I was running around foaming at the mouth whilst spouting nonsense; I was doing quite the opposite. The cuckoo had flown the clock, and since there was no one home anymore, I—as represented by the clock—was shutting down.

The first thing to go was my appetite; only Freni noticed that. Meanwhile joie de vivre seeped out of me like sap from a tapped maple tree. In short order my sex drive dried up like a cut day-lily left to wither on hot pavement; only Gabriel noticed that. It wasn't until it became too burdensome to think, and therefore to talk, that those outside my immediate family noticed the change in my personality.

Again it was the perceptive Freni who diagnosed me first. "So," she said to Gabe, and right in front of me too, "about our Magdalena, I have been thinking."

"Yes?"

"She has the post-pardon expression."

"I beg your pardon?"

"Ach, not that one. The other one. The *post*-pardon."

"I see." And Gabe did. He's fifty, and she's seventy-six; he's Jewish, she's Amish; he's a cardiologist, she's a cook, but some-how the two of them ended up sharing the same brain wave that deals with communication.

"Yet it is clear that you do not agree," she said.

"Freni, it's been four years since Little Jacob was born. If it was postpartum depression, we would have seen signs of it be-fore this. I think it is generalized depression brought on by the trauma of what happened at the bank."

As they talked, they calmly peeled potatoes for supper. It was just as if I wasn't there—but I was, sitting ramrod straight on a chair in the corner, because that was how Gabe had positioned me, and even slumping seemed like it was too much effort. Thank Heaven the little one was spending the day with Freni's grandchildren on the Hostetler family farm.

"Is there a pill for such a thing?" Freni asked.

"Yes and no. There are several medications that can help, but she also might benefit from some talk therapy."

"Yah, that one can talk."

Gabe set peeler and spud in the sink and slid an arm affection-ately around my kinswoman. Normally, that would have been twice as much contact as she might have experienced during a reproductive cycle with her husband, Mose, but the Babester has killer good looks, and Freni has had a crush on him since day one.

"I know of a top-notch facility in the Poconos. She'll have round-the-clock supervision and all the talk therapy she can handle—plus, since she'll be in a safe environment, they'll be free to experiment with her medication levels."

Freni nodded, which took a bit of effort, seeing as how she has no neck. "So this is the Clooney bin of which they speak?"

"Of which *who* speaks?" Gabe demanded, his brown eyes flickering.

"Ach," Freni squawked, "folks!"

By "folks" she meant just about everyone in our tightly knit community of Mennonites, Baptists, Methodists, and yes, Amish, all of whom shied away from seeking help for so-called mental illnesses. The Lord was supposed to be able to fix what was wrong with us. Sometimes, however, the Devil got such a strong hold on a person that he or she was unwilling to shake his- or herself loose from demonic possession, and again turn to the healing power of Christ. Only then, and this happened very rarely, did one of our own get shipped off to a loony bin some-where, and usually those folks never returned.

"The word is 'loony,'" Gabe said sadly, "not 'Clooney'—although our Magdalena—at least the one we used to know—is very found of George. Anyway, Freni, we don't call them loony bins anymore; it isn't PC."

"Personal computers, yah? *This* word I learn from Magdalena, but now you make no sense." She wrested free of Gabe's com-forting arm. "This world makes no sense to me."

"Me either," said Gabe, his voice breaking.

*   *   *

I spent three and a half months in the West Pocono Home for the Emotionally Challenged. There I was deconstructed, reconstructed, and instructed in the basics of good mental health. But although I recovered to the point that I could be engaged in meaningless conversation, I felt as if I had yet to recover my oomph.

"We need to help her find a way to get her mojo back," my Beloved said on one of his weekly visits.

"Ya," my Jewish mother-in-law said. "Dis von needs her mo-Jew." Although Ida was born Jewish, she is now Mother Superior to a convent operated by the Sisters of Perpetual Apathy.

"Ma," said the Babester, "do you think you can help?"

Believe me, I heard the words. I was just incapable of protesting. When one is in the deepest of depressions, taking any action, even one as simple as speech, is an intense struggle. To step once again into a head-on confrontation with the mother-in-law from you-know-where (Manhattan) was flat-out impossible. My mouth simply refused to take directions from my brain. I may as well have been encased in Plexiglas; at least then I would have made a very comely coatrack.

"Of course, bubbeleh," Mother Superior said to her son. "Zee sisters und I vill vait on her hand und giant foot. She vill be vell taken care of. Een zee meantime you take wery good care of mine grandson—zee leetle pisher—ya?"

"Thanks, Ma, I'll bring her right over."

And he did—just as soon as he was finished retying himself to his mother's apron strings. In all fairness, gratitude will do that to one, just as much as desperation. I'm sure that if our roles had been reversed, I too might have thrown myself gratefully into the hands of a ready-built support system—or, more accurately, thrown my spouse. Somewhere. I'd rather not say where.

3

The Sisters of Perpetual Apathy operate the Convent of No Hope, which is located directly across the road from my bed-and-breakfast, the PennDutch Inn. The purpose of this new quasireligious order is to haphazardly assist others in their search for a life of meaningless existence. Complete and total apathy is the depth to which they all aspire to sink. Why make any effort, they preach, if life is just going to kick the manure out of you? In fact, why even care that it does? Just exist! Want nothing, feel nothing, care about nothing and no one, and you will be blessed with an abundance of pain and disappointment, but perhaps not quite as much as if you'd invested any hope in your life. Hope—now *that* was an ugly four-letter word! And shame on all the potty mouths who kept *that* word in their vocabularies.

Given the disastrous downturn of the economy beginning in '08, and the vast number of home foreclosures, a shell-shocked public welcomed the opportunity to go numb. "Novocain for the masses," one pundit observed, coining a brilliantly original phrase. At any rate, the Sisters of Perpetual Apathy became a huge movement with chapters in all fifty states, and even spawned a corresponding men's movement called the Brothers of Eternal and Abject Disillusionment.

The convent building is an old farmhouse where my pseudo–first husband grew up. The house was added to several times, and finally the barn was torn down and a huge dormitory wing was built. Because my current, and *real*, husband still owned the land and the original building, I was given preferential treatment and assigned a private room. I was even assigned a pair of novices to look after me 24-7: Sister Distemper and Sister Disarticulate. Their jobs were to see that I maintained a routine of personal hygiene, and remained well nourished—both physically and spiritually.

One day Sister Distemper was particularly cross with me on account of the fact that I accidentally dribbled marinara sauce down the white starched bib of my guest apron. After lunch, instead of taking me back to my room for my usual nap, Sister Distemper sat me out on the patio to wait until Sister Disarticulate took over from her at the four o'clock shift change. Frankly, this state of affairs pleased me—that is to say, as much as anything could. By then it was late spring, so the weather was pleasant and the air was filled with birdsong.

Just minutes before the good sister was supposed to take over the new shift, a very large pigeon flew overhead and dropped its enormous deposit on top of my head. The back of my head was covered by an organza prayer cap, but the bird's black-and-white offering landed toward the front; in fact, the more liquid aspect of this unwanted gift had begun to dribble down my forehead and channel into my deeply etched frown line.

That precise moment, the passage of the passerine and the passing of its poop, was like a switch being flipped in my brain. Just like that, I went from a near-vegetative state to the tart-tongued endearing old soul I used to be. I rose from the wicker rocker like a modern-day Lazarus from the dead, threw off the hideous turquoise-and–slime green afghan that had been wrapped around my shapely shoulders, and shook a slim fist at the son of a squab.

"You come back here, you rat with wings!"

Sister Disarticulate was temporarily at a loss for words. "You—you're back!"

"As big as life and twice as ugly," I said.

"Whum?" she said.

"Nothing. That's just something my first husband used to say—except that he wasn't legally my husband, which meant that we were cohabitating without the bonds of matrimony—oh dear, this must shock you, you being a nun and all."

"I'm not here at noon. I'm merely a cistern."

I ran that through my awakening brain. "But nuns, sisters—they're all the same, right?"

"Gracious, no. I'm not Catheter, nor even Despicable; I'm a Pigeon."

I pointed to my head. "Nonsense, dear. *That* was a pigeon; you don't look anything like one—well, other than your eyes, which, you must admit, *are* rather beady and your legs . . . Honestly, dear, you should either request a longer habit, or see if Mother Grand Poo-Bah can make an exception and allow you to wear trousers. If not, the next time you're in Home Depot, someone looking for broomstick replacements might lunge for your shins. In which case, if you're not appropriately clad under there, it could be somewhat embarrassing. Delores Klinkhauser forgot to wear her bloomers—"

"No, no," she cried, in mounting agitation, and then finally her words came out as sharp as the Devil's pitchfork and every bit as dangerous: "I have no religion; I'm a pagan!"

"Get behind me, Satan!"

My outburst produced a flock of curious onlookers. They pushed and shoved—in a gentle, apathetic sort of way—to get a better look at the miracle unfolding before their languorous eyes.

But as I said, the "old Magdalena" was back: she who was half full of the vim and vigor, and half full of wit. That is to say, it was time to check myself out of the "Clooney" bin.

"Pardon me, guys," I said, as I pointed in the direction opposite my inn, "but is that the Chattanooga Choo-choo?"

A dozen cowled heads swiveled as one. "Where?"

Off I shot like a hundred-twenty-five-pound bat out of Hades (the meals at the convent were completely uninspiring).

Despite the fact that I'd sprung myself from his mother's convent, Gabe was overjoyed to see me again—back as *myself*. Dear Freni nearly *plotzed* with happiness, and even allowed me to clasp her tightly in an English-style hug. And as for my little one—I *kvelled* with pride every time I saw him, and when I felt his little arms around my neck, I was in heaven. Oh, what *naches* (to borrow yet another term from my *yiddishe* mother-in-law)! We were as happy a family as could possibly be—well, barring a few minor details.

When our daughter, Alison, came home from college on spring break, she brought the evil mutt Shnookums with her. The creature seems convinced that I'm responsible for his mistress (my sister, Susannah) being in prison, so he spent the entire week either nipping at my heels or attempting to dance with my shins—if you know what I mean. Another small irritant—both literally and figuratively—was the Babester's mother, who, in her role as mother-in-law, was not so superior.

Understandably, she was a bit piqued that I had returned to play the part of her son's best friend, constant companion, and— horror of horrors—lover. She scrambled desperately to secure the knots in her apron strings, but I had an advantage she didn't have, and it wasn't up my sleeve either. I promised myself that if necessary I would resort to even going so far as to dance with my husband rather than let his mother win *that* battle.

In the woods behind my pasture flows a small creek. Each spring beavers attempt to dam it, as is their custom, by cutting down every young tree within dragging distance. I have one heck of a time trying to stop them from doing so, and invariably I give up and the varmints succeed, which means that they flood my woods and destroy even more trees. Beavers might appear cuddly on television, or as stuffed toys, but in real life they are about the size of Ida Rosen, but with slightly smaller teeth. Thus it was that I chose these animals as my metaphor for my struggle with my husband's mother.

The Battle of the Beavers, as I called it, was actually quite beneficial to revitalizing my marriage. Victory for me was keeping a smile on my Beloved's face, and I must confess that I got to be rather innovative in that department. My matrimonial vows gave me a certain advantage, which I exercised in all six of our guest rooms, the hayloft, the corncrib, the silo (it was empty), and even the six-seater outhouse (it's just for show). I drew the line at our solid-oak dining room table, which was made by my ancestor Jacob the Strong in the early nineteenth century. That massive piece of furniture is the only thing that survived the tornado that destroyed my inn a few years back, and while it could have held the weight of a plethora of polygamists, I didn't believe in mixing business with pleasure.

At any rate, I was soon back to my normal, pre–bank robbery self. The "old-Magdalena" as people started referring to me. I bit my tongue—the grooves were still there—and plowed on, taking one day at a time. The irony was that the balm to healing my soul, which had been wounded by a threat to my son, was time spent with my son. And the more time I spent with my son, and the faster I healed, the angrier I became.

Three men—at *least* three men—had come into the bank,

prepared to kill the occupants, and just to get money. So far the Bedford Police Department and the county sherriff had been unable to get any leads from the videotape. Perhaps I was reading something into the situation, but I sensed that they were mostly just happy that no one had gotten killed. The fact that the gunmen were Amish appeared to have made the police more than a mite uncomfortable. According to my sources (Freni and extended family), the interviews that they conducted amongst the local Amish community were bare-bones brief, and the officers seemed eager to believe every word they were told. In no time at all, an official conclusion was reached: the robbers were transient individuals and they had no connection to the community.

What enraged me even more is that the community accepted this verdict.

"B-b-but that's j-just ridiculous," I sputtered to my best friend, Agnes.

Agnes calmly wiped the coffee-flavored spittle from her face and set the newspaper on the table between us. "There's more," she said, "and you're not going to like it either."

"It's better that I hear it from you first, dear. Believe it or not, your voice has a soothing, almost hypnotic, effect." That was only a white fib, of the totally permissible variety, seeing as how it was not meant to hurt anyone. The truth is that I finally had reached the point where reading glasses were more than just a good idea, but I had yet to overcome the sin of vanity.

Agnes took a bite of store-bought chocolate éclair. It was a day old—given that she only shops in Bedford once a week—but so was the newspaper. Sadly, Agnes would still have eaten the éclair, had it been a week old.

"It said," she informed me, "that in all probability, the gun would *not* have been fired, and that Amy Neubrander would *not* have been grazed by that bullet, if an overzealous customer had *not* tried to play the part of Indiana Jones."

"Excuse me?"

"That's right. You don't go to movies or watch television," she said with exaggerated sarcasm. "Tell me, Magdalena, don't you ever regret letting the world pass you by? Think of all the things I've seen and done that you've deprived yourself of."

I snagged the last éclair from the white cardboard box. The score was Magdalena four, Agnes eight—not that anyone was counting.

"I hardly consider myself to be deprived, dear. After you saw that chain saw movie, you had to sleep at the inn for a week, and when you went on your singles cruise to the Bahamas, you got so seasick that you had to jump ship before it even left Miami."

"The harbor was choppy that day."

"You know, of course, that this leaves me fit to be tied."

"I was afraid you'd say something like that. Does this mean what I think it means?"

I bit the end off the French pastry and savagely sucked in a mouthful of rich, thick cream before answering. "That I'm going to go off on another half-cocked, harebrained, ill-advised, foolhardy, cockamamie investigation of my own?"

"I'd say that pretty much covers it."

"Then you're absolutely right."

Agnes nodded. "You're kind of like a pair of Teutonic plates, Magdalena; I know that they're going to be the catalyst for an earth-shattering event sometime in the near future, but there's just no stopping them. The same thing applies to you."

"That's just about the nicest thing anyone's ever said."

"So, you've agreed to take me along with you on your next wild adventure?"

"I beg your pardon?"

"Come on, Magdalena, you know that's why you're here; you didn't drive all the way out to my neck of the woods for stale pastries and scintillating conversation. Freni makes the best cinnamon rolls in the world and we could have chatted over the phone. No, you planned to recruit me as your sidekick."

I feigned surprise. Feigning, by the way, is not nearly as bad as lying. I defy anyone to find *that* word in their King James Version of the Holy Bible. Its absence is proof that it was not important enough to be considered a sin.

"Oh my," I said. "You don't think that position is still open, do you?"

"But, Magdalena, I'm your BFF."

"My *what*?"

"Best friend forever? Best female friend? Whatever. I'm both, aren't I? And anyway, I'm always your sidekick."

"Only when Wanda Hemphopple isn't."

"*Please*, Mags."

Feigning reluctant sighs comes easy to anyone who has ever had a mother. "All right, but you have to follow my lead. No thinking for yourself."

"I promise."

Rather pleased with my performance, I stood up. "Got any more coffee?"

"There's some in the kitchen."

I went to refill my cup but was back a few seconds later. "What's up with your uncle?"

"Which one?"

Agnes's two uncles live next door. Both men are in their seventies, and both are nudists, even when the weather is cool, like it was that morning. Yet despite the low temperature, one of the old coots was keeping a remarkably high profile—so to speak.

"I didn't look at his face, dear. He's the one who's outside the kitchen window planting pansies."

"You must mean Uncle Willard. You know that commercial that says if it lasts more than four hours, then you should see a doctor? That's right. You don't watch TV. Anyway, that's what he took, and it lasted more than that, so I drove him to the doctor—twice, as a matter of fact—and his blood pressure, heart, everything checks out fine."

"Ah, I'm not sure you're getting my drift. This would appear to be a hydraulics problem."

"That's exactly what I'm talking about."

"You mean they have pills for that?"

"Magdalena, have you been living in a cave somewhere?"

"That's a very rude thing to say, Agnes. You know that I don't read secular magazines either. It takes a lot of willpower in this day and age to keep a mind as narrow as mine, and I would appreciate a compliment now and then." I lowered my voice to BFCL—hereafter known as "best friend confidential level" before continuing. "Besides, you may extrapolate from my question that *my* Dearly Beloved doesn't require the benefits of modern science to replicate the Empire State Building."

Agnes giggled into her cup and turned seven shades of red. "Ooh, Magdalena, you're so wicked."

I considered my next question carefully. "How long has it been?"

"Two weeks."

I gasped as a very important detail occurred to me. "But *why* would he take the pills? He isn't even married!"

"There you go, being Miss Judgmental again. My uncle's reason for taking the pills is none of your beeswax."

"Why, I never! Just for that you may not be my sidekick—no matter how much you beg."

"That's fine with me."

I waggled a finger at her, à la Bill Clinton. "I mean it."

"So do I."

"Somebody else is going to get all the glory."

"They'll also have to put up with you."

That did it. I was out of there like fleas on a freshly lathered dog. Agnes Miller had a few things to learn about friendship and loyalty; too bad that I didn't have the time to set her straight just then. At least my soaring blood pressure could be put to good use at my next stop of the day.

It is twelve miles and half a century from Hernia to Bedford. Even Hernia's non-Amish population lags behind the rest of country in its mores and outlook, and somehow this spiritual quality is manifested in the physical. The end result is that one actually can feel the culture shock when passing the sign that says *Welcome to Bedford*. If I may speak frankly, it may as well say *Welcome to Sodom and Gomorrah*.

As I did every time I ventured into this den of iniquity, I prayed for strength and patience (not the strongest of my virtues). The latter is my least-answered prayer. I haven't the foggiest what it feels like to have it answered; I certainly didn't feel any different that day. With the economy still deep in the loo, I didn't have to worry about finding a parking space at my bank; neither did I have to wait to speak to the bank manager himself.

Mr. Pernicious Yoder III was at first very gracious and even offered me a Styrofoam cup of tepid coffee.

"Cream and sugar?" I asked hopefully.

"I have packaged whitener that tastes like chalk and a pink sweetener with a bitter aftertaste."

"Ix-nay on ink-pay, but I always carry some extra packets of Splenda in my purse. Would you like a couple?"

His nose literally wrinkled. It was like watching an albino inchworm trying to get away from itself.

"Uh—no, thanks."

"They haven't been opened, dear. Besides, I gave my purse a thorough cleaning since the hamster died."

"It died in your purse?"

"Heavens no! But that's where my son—he's only four—put it—it was his, you know—so that I would find it and make it better. Unfortunately, that was just before he and his dad were going off to spend the weekend with some friends on a male-only camping trip. The little tyke didn't know it was dead—he's not very clear on that subject yet—and that just so happened to be the weekend I decided to stay home and put up my tootsies. So you see I had no need for a pocketbook."

"Please, might we change the subject?"

"Certainly." I flashed him a much-practiced winning smile. "Cousin Yoder—"

Persnickety Pernicious held up a manicured hand. "I must insist that you address me as *Mr.* Yoder, as we have no proven bonds of kinship."

"Au contraire. I have done my homework. My adopted father and your father were double-first cousins. My adopted mother was a third cousin once removed to your father and fifth cousins two ways to your mother—just not through the Yoders. My biological father was a fourth cousin twice removed to your father as well as a fifth cousin in another line, and my biological mother showed five cousin relationships six generations back. Ergo, it wouldn't surprise me if you and I were brother and sister, by at least some arcane system of calculation, somewhere on this globe."

"Oy vey," he groaned, revealing yet another possible connection, "you wouldn't happen to have some aspirin, or other type of headache medicine, in that miniature sarcophagus of yours, would you?"

"But I thought—"

"You have a way of making a man desperate; two minutes with you has given me the mother of all migraines. Indeed, we must be related."

"Very funny." I fished around until I found a couple of loose ibuprofen. I picked off a long light brown hair. "This is the best I can do, dear. Although I could give you Sermon Number Thirty-seven—that's what my sister called it, at any rate—on appropriate premarital sexual behavior. Susannah used to claim that it put her in a coma. You probably wouldn't feel much pain in a coma."

He grabbed the pills from my hand and swallowed them without as much as a sip of water. "Thank you. Now, could you please get to the point of your business?"

"Very well." I took a seat opposite his glass-topped desk, smoothed my skirt, and silently repeated my prayer for patience. "As you know, my miracle baby and I were here the day of the robbery—"

His hand went up again. "Ah, ah, ah, it was *not* a bank robbery, Ms. Yoder. My capable guards and I *foiled* the plot quite handedly, if I must say so, despite your crude attempt at a civilian's bum rush, which almost resulted in disaster. In fact, as a result of your irresponsible action, one of my most valuable employees was gravely wounded." He removed his glasses with his other hand and massaged the indentations on the bridge of his nose. "Frankly, the jury's still out on whether or not the bank will sue on this young lady's behalf."

"*Sue?* Sue whom?"

"Why, sue you, of course."

"*Moi?* It was your guards who stood around, just staring, as immobile as fence posts until I took action on my son's behalf. It's me who should be suing you!"

He blinked rapidly, as if trying to dislodge an airborne dust particle from his left eye. In fact, so vigorously did he attend to this matter, and whilst making such contorted faces, that one might conclude that he was trying to remove a clod of dirt from that unfortunate peeper.

"Would you like me to look at it for you?" I asked.

"No. I'm fine." Eventually his eye filled with tears and he stopped rubbing. "Now where were we?"

"You had just said something ridiculously untrue."

"To the contrary, Ms. Yoder. My security guards are top notch, trained with the best—Israeli profiling methods, in fact. I'm afraid you have no case."

"Case, shmase," I said. "That's not why I'm here. I'm here to help you discover the identity of those three men, and in order to do that, I need to review the security tape."

"Uh—I'm afraid that's impossible, Miss Yoder."

"Why?"

"Well, uh—security reasons—yes, that's it."

"What? That doesn't make a lick of sense."

"Really, Miss Yoder, I'm not at liberty to talk about this further. But my final answer is no. N-O, no."

I am a modest, God-fearing Mennonite woman, but it has recently occurred to me that the Good Lord in His wisdom had a plan when He created women with external mammary glands that are visible—and generally pleasing to the eye—the year around. We are, in fact, the only species of animal in which this phenomenon is found naturally. Even the cow has to be "freshened" (give birth) in order to have her nice, full udder. (Think about it: you don't see virgin cats and dogs walking around with boobies, now do you?) My conclusion therefore is that human breasts were meant to be alluring, a definite asset in attracting a mate.

But since they didn't come with owners' manuals, one might be given a little latitude when it comes to using them, especially if the end justifies the means. That said, I undid the button at my throat—okay, I undid the next button as well. Even then one still couldn't see the twin sisters, but my collar slumped a bit, causing a crease to form across the curvature of the left sister and drawing attention to its comely, although well-covered shape. One could argue that the effect was akin to showing an ankle back in "the day," and that effect, I'm told, was exceedingly strong.

At any rate, desperate is as desperate does, so I waggled my bosoms at Pernicious Yoder III. Of course my sturdy Christian underwear prevented me from performing a truly Democratic liberal waggle; what transpired was more like a Republican joust.

"What's wrong, Miss Yoder? Are you having a back spasm?"

This time I tried a provocative thrust of my bosom.

"Heart attack? I don't know CPR, but I can get Ken from accounting."

"Isn't he the one who made it into the *Guinness Book of World Records* for having the most cold sores at one time?"

"No, it turns out that *Guinness* wasn't willing to create that category."

I buttoned my blouse all the way. "I have a right to see that tape since I'm on it."

"Get out of my office, you tramp! Get out now, or *this* tape"— he pointed to the camera behind my head—"is going to be on the six o'clock news."

4

Of course I hied my hinnie from the bank, but not without first making a couple of detours. Tramps are, after all, noted for their restless, wandering natures.

"Psst, Amy—over here. Behind the sickly ficus tree."

She paid no attention to me.

I hefted the tree. It wasn't sick at all; it was merely a very poorly made replica. Since there were still no customers to be seen, I picked up the faux ficus and walked it within whispering distance of the teller's counter.

"Psst, Amy, it's a miracle. Behold, thy tree speaketh."

At least she had wit enough to giggle. "Miss Yoder, you're going to get me into big trouble."

"I'm not here, Amy. And if you get called on the carpet for speaking to a tree, then sue the bank for discrimination."

"Just so you know, I'm not allowed to talk about the robbery."

"Why, shiver me timbers! I haven't even mentioned that. Who put you up to this?"

The poor girl glanced furtively around. "No one put me up to this—it's just ever since the robbery, I've been under investigation, and I'm not allowed to talk about it. That's all."

"Who exactly gave that order? The police? The FBI?"

If I hadn't been watching Amy's face closely through the fakeficus foliage, I would have missed the twitch in her left eyebrow that was just as informative, to anyone who knew her, as a red-lettered campaign poster.

"Your boss?" I mouthed silently.

"Bingo," she answered.

Then again, if Amy was any less skilled in the silent-clue department than I, she might have thought I was asking if Kate Moss was the one giving orders. In that case, she might have decided to give me a nonsensical answer, such as the name of an Australian wild dog. Before I could retest her, one of the security guards approached.

"What's going on?" he said.

"Nothing," Amy said. It was a wise answer, one used by millions of teenagers every day. To be sure, some of them get away with it, so why not Amy?

"What's this tree doing so close to the counter?" he said.

"Uh—well, sir, since I'm stuck inside all day, I kinda miss greenery, but when I look at this tree—even if it is fake—I feel better."

"That ain't a good excuse to be moving things around. Someone with bad intentions could sneak right up on you, and you wouldn't see them coming. On account of that, this here tree is what we call an 'unsafe situation.'"

"Yes, sir."

"Now I'm going to move this tree back to the corner where it belongs, but before I do, I want you to tell me what I just said. What kind of situation do we call this?"

"An 'unsafe situation,'" Amy said in a loud parrotlike voice.

"Good. Now let's not let it happen again."

"No, sir— I mean, yes, sir. Whatever, sir."

As the guard picked up the tree, I jumped up and put my weight on the pot. I only did so because I didn't know how fast he'd walk, and I didn't want him to bowl me over with the canopy of cheap silk and badly formed leaves.

"Ugh," he grunted, "this thing weighs a ton."

"How rude!" I thought. Of course I said nothing.

"You know," he said, obviously to himself, "this thing stinks. I really ought to take this piece of crap outside and give it a good hosing off."

Believe me, it wasn't the cheap tree that reeked, or even my purse; it was Johnny, the guard. I could see his name tag through the branches, all three of his chins, and the dark brown, almost black, ring around his collar. Both Johnny Ashton and his clothes needed a bath something awful.

Sometimes my mouth gets ahead of my brain. "Johnny, dear," I heard myself say, "a good scrub in a tub wouldn't hurt you either."

"Ma! Ma, is that you?"

What in tarnation? Could this man possibly be more simpleminded than me? I've been known to hear the Good Lord's voice emanating from all manner of objects, and I once mistook my sister for an angel, but this poor soul appeared to think that his mother's voice was coming from a tree—really not much more than a large bush—with a middle-aged Mennonite woman clinging to one side of it.

"Yes, dear, it's me," I cooed, trying my best to throw my voice, although I knew darn well that ventriloquists don't actually throw them, since voices aren't objects one can physically grasp. Instead, it's all about illusion, and focusing the attention on the dummy's lips. In this case Johnny was the dummy.

"Oh, Johnny, you have a cold sore," I said.

"I do?"

"I know *you* can't see it, but your ouchy-ouch must really hurt."

There isn't a man alive who doesn't like to have his ouchy-ouches and boo-boos validated by a sympathetic woman. It doesn't even matter if he has them or not; he can always store up the sympathy for a later date, because he can never have enough sympathy.

Johnny traced his lips with his middle and ring fingers and then halfway around his mouth seemed to find a tender spot. "Yeah, it hurts like the dickens, but what can I do? I gotta come in to work, so I got no choice but to suck it up."

"That's my John-boy!"

"Ma! I hate it when you call me that."

"You do? I'm sorry, son. I forgot—you know with the excitement of seeing you again."

"Ma, how come I can't see you?"

"Now, think about that; where am I?" Oops, that was indeed a stupid question to have asked. Even George Bush might have thought to walk around my bush and would thus have exposed me.

"You're in Heaven, Ma, aren't ya?"

"Why, indeed, I am. Which is why you should be keeping your eyes on the ceiling, Johnny, because Heaven is *up*—unless, of course you live in New Zealand or Australia."

"How come Heaven ain't up for them as well, Mama?"

"Oh, my sweet son, where did I go wrong? Did I fail to send you to Sunday school?"

"No, ma'am, you sent me every Sunday—even when I was sicker than a dog."

"Well, then, we know that Heaven is not above Sydney or Melbourne, because when the world ends, Jesus will come floating down to earth on a big white cloud that will be seen by Christians all over North America, but due to the curvature of the earth, the poor folks in the antipodes will not be able to see the cloud. *That's* how we can deduce that Heaven is not located above them."

"Ma, you always did talk so fancy. Can you see angels?"

"I most certainly can. In fact, I'm looking at one right now. She's a very special angel who is allowed to come to earth on special assignments. In fact, she is going to pop into your bank at any moment and ask a very big favor of you."

"But, Ma, I don't want to birth no babies!"

"Hush up, John. *Believe me*, the last thing the Good Lord wants is for you to reproduce. My message to you today is that when that aforementioned angel—in the guise of a very comely woman—suddenly appears before you and asks you for that favor, you are to reply in the affirmative. Is that clear, Johnny? Answer me quickly, because my allotted time to speak to you is up and I must go."

"But, Ma, if she looks like a woman, instead of an angel, how will I know if she's the right one?"

"Because she'll appear in the bush you're clutching with both hands—as if it were a harbor buoy and you were a drowning man. Oh, oh, gotta go—good-bye, dear!"

For the first time Johnny Ashton began to see my bush and its many branches. At the same time I made a great show of shaking said bush and moaning, as if I had just fallen into it, before crashing out the other side. It was a pitiful performance, but by the same token, it was quite up to the performance level of my audience.

"Ah—unh—what a landing," I groaned.

Young Amy raced to my side. "Are you all right? Let me help you up, Miss— Uh, what does one call an angel?"

"Your Flyness," I said without missing a beat. I am, after all, known for being rather droll.

"Ma said you wouldn't have any wings," Johnny said, "but you really do look very humanlike. What do you eat?"

I pretended to recoil in horror. "Oh, Johnny, dear, what a horrible thought. We don't eat! If we ate, then we'd have to eliminate. You wouldn't want to have to imagine an angel on the potty now, would you?"

He blushed. "Sorry, ma'am. I ain't such a good thinker."

"That's all right, dear. Did your ma tell you that I have a very special favor to ask and that you are obligated to say yes?"

He nodded vigorously. "Yes, Your Royal Flyness."

"Good. I like your insertion of the word 'Royal' by the way. Now to the favor: I've come to get a copy of the security tape for the day the bank was robbed."

"Which robbery would that be, Your Royal Flyness?"

"There's been more than one?"

"Ma'am, Pennsylvania is the Keystone State, but when Mr. Yoder refers to us'ens as the Keystone Kops, I think he's like making an illusion to something else."

"Quite possibly so. Well, this would be the time, just a few months ago, when three Amish robbed it, and this pretty cashier here had a bullet graze her arm."

"Oh, yeah, and there was an old lady and her grandson in here, and she like tripped and fell and nearly got them both killed on that account."

"Listen, buster, in the first place she wasn't *old*—" Oops, I had better watch my nonangelic mouth. "She was *ancient*, older than Methuselah. Oy, and such a klutz you never saw. Anyway, I'd like that tape, please."

"Uh—I'm sorry, Your Royal Flyness. I know I promised Ma, and you oughtn't to go back on your promises to the dead, but if I give you that tape, Mr. Yoder will kill me, and I'm not so sure I'm going to Heaven."

"But that's the easy part of being a Christian! We can all be assured of our salvation; all we need to do is to confess our sins and believe that Jesus is our Lord."

"No offense, ma'am, but you ain't seen my lists of sins. Besides, what you just said don't seem very fair to me. Ain't that an invitation for someone like me to go out and do all manner of sinning, and when they figure they've had enough under their belt, *then* come to Jesus? Meanwhile the poor fool who turns to Jesus right away has to miss out on all the fun."

"Yes, but what if you got hit by a truck in the first five minutes of living your sinful life?"

"I'll take my chances." He gave me a manure-shoveling grin. "You know, you're kind of pretty for an angel. You allowed going out on dates?"

"Verily methinks I desire naught but to retch."

"Ma'am, I don't speak that Bible talk, so you're going to have to give it to me straight."

"Give me the robbery tape and we'll see."

"I can't."

"Johnny, I didn't want it to have to come to this, but it looks like I'm going to have to tell Ma."

"I'm sorry, pretty angel, but I'm a man of my word, and you see this really big guy came in and made me and Mr. Yoder swear that we wouldn't show nobody nothing, and besides, I ain't in charge of the tapes."

"Who changes them out?"

"I do, but I hand them all over to Mr. Yoder."

"What's this really big guy's name?"

"I can't tell you."

"In that case I'm calling your ma right now." I inhaled deeply, to get a lot of calling power, but unfortunately inhaled a lot of dust as well. "Mrs. Ash-choo! Achoo! Achoo!"

My sneezes always come in threes, but the third one in this case was particularly hard—hard enough to knock me out of the bush and onto the cold marble floor. I wasn't seriously hurt, but my jig was up.

"You ain't no angel," Johnny roared.

"Johnny, angel," I said repeatedly as I scrambled to my feet. Perhaps if I set the words to music I'd have the beginning of a hit rock-and-roll song.

"Get out now, before I call the police!"

I got. In more ways than one. As I hobbled through the rest of the lobby and out the foyer, I stuffed my purse with all manner of free brochures. I know, that was childish of me, and it was a very nongreen way of getting back at Mr. Yoder, and it certainly did nothing to retaliate against Johnny Ashton or the "really big guy," but it obviously served a need in me at the time.

What's more, after my fiasco of a visit to the bank, I began to truly let go and heal. Oh, what a blessing that was. Every morning I woke up with a smile on my face, and if there wasn't already one on it, in fifteen minutes or less, the Babester could put one on that would last all day. Folks actually began to call me *cheerful*—and mean it!

But all that began to change the week that the three couples from New Jersey came to stay as guests of the inn. Need I say more?

5

———◆◆◆———

Sea Turtles

Ingredients

12 ounces dry-roasted and salted macadamia nuts
1 cup flaked sweetened coconut
½ cup (1 stick) butter
1 cup brown sugar, packed
½ cup light corn syrup
1 cup sweetened condensed milk
1 teaspoon pure vanilla extract
12 ounces bittersweet chocolate, coarsely chopped
sea salt, to taste

Cooking Directions

Preheat oven to 400°F. Line 2 baking sheets with parchment

paper. Place macadamia nuts in 36 clusters of 4 to 7 nuts each, 2 inches apart; set aside.

Toast coconut in oven for about 5 minutes or until lightly browned. Pulse in food processor or chop into shorter strands.

Butter the inside of a heavy 3-quart saucepan. Melt ½ cup butter over low heat. Add sugar, corn syrup, and sweetened condensed milk; mix well. Increase heat to medium-high and bring mixture to a boil, stirring frequently. Reduce heat to medium and continue to boil, stirring frequently until mixture reaches 244°F on a candy thermometer.

Remove saucepan from heat, stir in vanilla and coconut. Cool slightly; spoon a tablespoon of coconut caramel over each nut cluster; cool completely.

Place chocolate in a microwave-safe dish. Microwave 30 seconds on high, stir and continue to microwave in 10- to 20-second intervals, stirring after each. Chocolate should be smooth, but not warm. Dip tops of caramel-nut clusters in chocolate and sprinkle with sea salt. Place in refrigerator to set chocolate. Store in an airtight container at room temperature, separating layers with wax paper for up to 1 week.

> Tip: To prevent the formation of sugar crystals in the caramel, wash down the sides of the pan using a pastry brush dipped in water.

Courtesy http://www.eatwisconsincheese.com/

6

The three couples from the Garden State arrived together, but in separate cars, driving caravan style. I happened to be in the dining room at the time, which has a good view of the driveway, but I didn't hear them until several of the doors slammed and the last of the folks had already piled out. By then it was already too late to see who had traveled in which car.

They say that couples grow to resemble each other over the years. I don't know if that's true or not, but for what it's worth, Gabe still had his hair, teeth, and just one chin, and folks often said that we made a good couple. But the couples that spilled out of the expensive Jersey vehicles were an odd mix of shapes, sizes and ages, none of which seemed to go together.

Nonetheless, a hostess has to do what a hostess has to do. I snatched a starched white apron from a hook behind the check-in desk on my way to greet them, tied it on with practiced hands, and arranged my lips in a fair approximation of a warm, inviting smile.

"*Gut Marriye,*" I said in honest-to-goodness Pennsylvania Dutch, but from then on, I faked it with a made-up accent.

"Velcommen to zee PennDeutsch Inn. Deed yousen pipple hobben a gut treep?"

"Yah, yah, eet vas yoost vonderful! Zee cat's payamas, yah?" A woman who looked very much like Barbara Bush during her White House years stepped regally toward me. She could easily have been the mother—or grandmother—of anyone there.

I gulped. "Uh, ma'am," I whispered, "I don't really speak Pennsylvania Dutch."

"Neither do I. But listen, you twit. If this bunch catches on that you're a fake, they'll take their money elsewhere. We may look like a motley crew, but we came here for a genuine slice of Americana—just like it said in your brochure." She pulled one of my brochures from her Hermès bag.

There are times when one is taken aback, and there are times that one wishes to take back, but I had been in the biz too long for either of those scenarios to come into play that day. I straightened my apron, felt to see if my prayer cap was still securely in place, and then licked my pale, unadorned lips.

"Ladies and gentlemen," I said loudly and clearly in my plain old American accent, "welcome to the PennDutch Inn. I am Magdalena Yoder, the proprietress, and I am a genuine Mennonite whose grandparents were Amish, as were their ancestors before them. I will let you shake my hand for a dollar."

There were no takers.

I plunged on. "The inn in which you will be staying for the coming week is an exact reproduction of the Mennonite farmhouse in which I was born." I raised my hand to silence some murmurs. "The original was destroyed by a tornado eight years ago. And before you get your bloomers in a bunch, I assure you that when I say 'exact,' that's what I mean. The current inn was built on the original foundation and everything was faithfully reproduced, including the urine stains in Great Uncle Leonard's bedroom—may he rest in peace.

"How many of you wish to experience the Amish Lifestyle Plan Option—or ALPO, as I affectionately call it? For a measly one hundred bucks more a day you get to make your own beds, clean your own rooms, *and* the pièce de résistance—muck out the barn."

"Hey," a carrot-topped man hollered, and practically in my face, "I thought it was only sixty-five dollars extra."

"It was, dear, but then I got to thinking: the more that one pays for something, the more it is that one is likely to appreciate it. It is my heartfelt desire that you treasure your stay here."

"Bull droppings," the white-haired woman in pearls growled.

I smiled beatifically. "Any takers for that?"

"I'm in," said a perky young blonde in a tight sweater and a ponytail. She was a wee little thing, whose head barely breached my bosom.

But thanks to example, one by one they all agreed to ALPO—all except the redhead and his wife. He soon identified himself as Carl Zambezi from Rockaway, New Jersey. His wife, by the way, was the Barbara Bush look-alike, and her name was Olivia.

"Carl dyes his hair and uses Botox," she said right in front of him, "but still, look at his profile, doesn't that face deserve to be on Mount Rushmore?"

"Well, I—"

"So, where's the bellhop? You don't expect Carl to fetch the bags from our car, do you? He has a bad back. Carl, go ahead and tell this woman how you hurt your back. Yeah, I know she's one of them Amish"—she pronounced it "aye-mish"—"but she's no spring chicken either, I can tell, so I know she can take it."

"Let me guess," I said, "he had to pick you up." Although she had broad shoulders and an uncommonly large head, she wasn't substantially overweight, so my gentle ribbing was not untoward.

Olivia stared at me with eyes as dark as cinders. Her lips

quivered. Meanwhile Carl's pale blue eyes focused on the ceiling. Suddenly they both exploded into gales of laughter.

It was laughter every bit as infectious as the bubonic plague. Soon I was laughing too, and slapping my knees like it was mosquito season. Before I knew it, the other guests, who had hung back a bit while their elders checked in, were laughing and carrying on as well.

Finally Olivia wiped the tears from her swollen eyes. "I'll give you that one," she said. She glanced at my impossibly steep stairs.

"Is that the only way up?"

"Indeed."

"And you don't have an elevator because . . ." She let her voice trail off as her expression took over.

"Oh, we have one, all right. But it's a teensy-weensy one and it's stuck between floors, and it may, or may not, contain the body of a dead Japanese tourist."

"You're serious?"

"Never more so. Now, mind you, I don't often lose tourists, but this particular one was extremely hard to keep track of, and had she not been quite so unpleasant, I might have made more of an effort to get an elevator repairman out here."

"What about the police?"

"What about them? For all intents and purposes, I am she. So say hello to me, if that is she with whom you wish to speak; otherwise kindly proceed to collect your luggage and make your way to your room so that I may wait on these other kind folks."

Olivia stalked out of the inn, staring at me the entire time. That meant she had to swivel her head as if it were atop a lazy Susan. Her husband, Carl, who was all of two inches taller than she was, followed behind her like a faithful puppy dog.

*   *   *

"It takes all kinds," Mama used to say. I can't remember if she was referring to me, or some of the strange people in our church community. Anyway, she was absolutely right. The next couple to check in was the Nyles—George and Barbie. George was a tall, deeply tanned man with a strong nose, a drooping mustache, and a wild thatch of curly brown hair. A woodsman, perhaps—although the rimless glasses he wore spoke to another side of his character. Barbie was a classic beauty with enormous green eyes and a heart-shaped face. Since she wore her long dark hair pulled back in a modest French twist, I took an immediate liking to this young gal in her early thirties.

I had to call deeply upon my reserve of Christian charity, however, when checking in Peewee and Tiny Timms. For one thing, Peewee—whose real name was Reginald—was no peewee. I've owned cows that weighed less than he did—okay, maybe not many, and they were on the sickly side—but you get the picture. He was *huge*. He also wore a very curious bowl-shaped black wig that came down almost to his bristling black eyebrows. With all that excess body fat, plus the synthetic hair, Peewee sweated copiously. To say that the sweat streamed down his face is no exaggeration. Wherever the poor man stood for even a few seconds, a puddle formed.

Tiny, his wife, would have qualified for petite, had it not been for the enormous pair of man-made brassiere fillers that jutted out from an otherwise flat chest. Believe you me: the transformation in topography was plumb amazing; I was reminded of Squaw Peak rising above Sun Valley in the greater Phoenix area. But as sweaty and uncomfortable-looking as Peewee Timms was, Tiny, on the other hand, presented herself as the epitome of good-natured cheer.

"Ooh, I just love how you've decorated this place. It's so—so—well, so authentic-looking. Isn't it, Pee? Take that spinning wheel over there. I know It's not for real and all, but—"

"But it is."

"No way!"

"Way."

"Isn't she just too much?" Tiny said. She grinned happily.

"She certainly is," Peewee said. The mere effort of speaking precipitated streams of perspiration that coursed down his jowls.

"You'll be staying in room four. Room five hasn't been cleaned by its last occupant, and room six— Well, I have a strict 'no pets rule,' and yet that so-called rock star managed to sneak a llama up to his room. I'm afraid I'm going to have to replace the carpets. At his expense, of course."

Peewee chuckled and brushed away a tsunami of sweat from his lower brow. "We'll try to obey the rules, Miss Yoder. We're just here to chill out, relax, and soak in the ambience of Aye-mish country."

"It's pronounced *ayem*-bience."

"What?"

"Oh, nothing; I happen to suffer from a rare medical condition known as *Magdalenus horribilis*. But don't worry. It's a non-communicable disease—that means you can't catch it."

Just then Little Jacob and his father pulled up in the driveway, having returned from a weekly grocery run in to Bedford. Upon seeing the three new cars, my son practically flew inside on the wings of excitement.

"Mama, Mama! Who's here? Where're ya at?"

"We're in the office, dear."

A second later his head was buried in my apron and his little arms encircled my legs. "Papa said to tell you that we had 'ventures in town.' "

"You did? Now, Jacob, be a polite young man and turn around and say hello to Mr. and Mrs. Timms."

He turned just enough to get a peek. "Do I hafta?"

"Yes, you have to. Wherever did you leave your manners, young man? At Pat's IGA?"

"At the pet store, Ma," he retorted, not wasting a second. "Papa stopped so I could see the puppies and one of them licked me all over my face and arms and Papa said maybe I could get it."

"He did?"

"Can I?"

There are times, especially early in my relationship with Gabe, that I wanted to lick him all over the face and arms, but now I just wanted to wring his neck.

"We'll see, dear," I said.

"No, I want a puppy." My dear little monster punctuated each word with a well-placed kick to my shins. *"Now!"*

"What you're going to get now, sweetie, is a nap." It was, after all, late afternoon, and even though he was four, I could tell that the excitement of a trip into town had taken its toll.

"I'm too big for a nap." This time the cute little hands had closed into fists and he was pummeling my midriff.

I pulled him off me like he was a spitting kitten. "You're not too big to mind your mama. Little boys who hit and kick do not deserve puppies. Now go straight to your room and lie quietly on your bed."

Off he went, stomping up a storm to show me that I was the meanest mama in the whole wide world—which I'm sure I was. I didn't spank him, mind you, because I don't countenance hitting; by the way, that rule applied to everyone in the family.

"I'm sorry you had to see that," I said to the Timmses, who had been watching, wide-eyed.

"Not at all," Peewee said. "If it had been me, I would have walloped the kid."

"Well, I still think you were mean," Tiny said. Her eyes filled with tears and she ran up the stairs, following closely behind Little Jacob.

7

If Tiny thought I was mean, she should have followed me out to the car and watched how I laid into my husband, the Puppy Promiser. A puppy was a daily responsibility that lasted for many years. How could he make a decision like that and not have me be a part of it?

"But, Mags," he said, "you should have seen his little face light up."

"I've seen his little face light up when he sees the Santa impostors outside the stores at Christmastime. But I don't promise him a fat elf of his very own to feed and clean up after for the rest of that old man's lifetime."

"Now you're just being ridiculous. Look, every boy needs a dog; any good psychiatrist will tell you that."

"*What?* Is that what you were told?"

"Well, maybe not in so many words, but I bet I would have had a happier childhood if I'd have had an impartial buddy like a dog to talk to. Mags, they're therapeutic. There's no denying that."

"Are you saying that our son needs a therapy dog?"

"You just said he threw a tantrum."

"Because he was tired."

"I get tired and I don't whale on my mother."

"Now you're just being ridiculous."

"So I am, am I?"

"You bet your bippy." With that, I stomped back into the house and into the kitchen, where dear old Freni was minding a pot of stew. I suppose it is possible that she didn't hear my stomping or the door slamming—she is well into her golden years, after all.

"Men!" I exclaimed in a voice loud enough for the dead to hear up in Settler's Cemetery.

"Yah," Freni said, without bothering to turn, "you cannot live with them, and they cannot live with you."

I mustered up a chuckle. "Good one, although surely not intended."

"No, this I mean. Magdalena, you are too smart for this war with the sexes, yah?"

"That's 'battle of the sexes,' and this is barely a skirmish."

"Hmm—for you English, maybe so. But didn't your mama tell you that there are more flies to be caught with honey than with vinegar?"

"Let's pretend that she did, Freni; what do I want with a bunch of sticky flies?"

Freni shook her head, which meant that her entire stout body shook, from her shoulders down. "It is not to be taken liberally," she said. "It means that—"

"I know what it means, Freni."

She turned then and waved a dripping wooden spoon in my direction. "You will listen to me, Magdalena Portulacca, or you too will take a nap."

Suddenly I was a ten-year-old girl again, and Freni was a much younger woman cooking at the very same stove. Upstairs Mama lay in bed, having recently given birth to Susannah. Yes, I'd been totally ignored by both overjoyed parents for the last week or so, but that was no excuse for what I'd done. How dared I have cut up one of the parlor curtains to sew clothes for my favorite doll, Melissa?

But it was just one panel, I tried to argue, and besides, no one ever used the parlor. Of course they wouldn't see things my way. Wasn't I too old to play with dolls? It was time I put away such foolish things and helped out with the housework. Cousin Freni was there only to wait on Mama (she had a bad case of the "nerves"), so of course there were a lot of other important things I could be doing—like washing out Susannah's poopy diapers or scrubbing pots and pans.

"Okay, already, I'll listen."

The dripping spoon froze just inches from my nose. "I have been thinking, Magdalena, not just about you and Dr. Rosen, but about me and Barbara as well." She actually winced when speaking her only daughter-in-law's name. "We are not seeing the forest before the trees."

"Come again?"

"Take this daughter-in-law, for example; she has many faults, yah?"

"Oh, yes, indeed! She's too tall and she's from Iowa."

"Is this sarcasm, Magdalena?"

"Absolutely not, dear. Any woman over five feet eleven should be shipped off to New Zealand, and the government should do a better job of stopping illegal immigration from the State of Iowa."

Freni's normally beady eyes shone brightly. "Ach, do you mean this, or do you just pull on my legs?"

"Sorry, dear, but I just pull on your legs—well, one of them, at any rate. But your point is what, dear? Are my Gabe and your Barbara the trees, or the forest, in your mangled metaphor?"

Freni threw her stubby arms up, hands open, in a gesture of extreme frustration. The wooden spoon sailed completely across the kitchen, where it smacked against the calendar that hung on the opposing wall beside the refrigerator. Believe me, I am *not* a superstitious woman, but there was now a meat broth stain on the Ides of March.

"*Gut im Himmel!* You want that I should call you a *dummkopf*? I am saying that we have much to be thankful for. Especially you. Your Dr. Rosen is tall—but not too tall—and he is not from Iowa. He is also handsome, as well as rich, and he loves you very, very much; this thing I know. Yah, he is not of the faith, and is a mama's boy, but no one is perfect and the final chapter for him is not yet written."

I felt strangely let down. "That's it? That's your big advice? Count my blessings?"

She nodded. "Yah, and I will count mine: *eins, zwei, drei, vier, fimf.*"

I knew without a doubt that her five enumerated blessings alluded to her beloved husband, Mose; her precious son, Jonathan; and her three adorable grandchildren. Alas, I am not one to let a bone go ungnawed.

"*Sex,*" I said.

"Ach!"

"Well, doesn't that mean six in Pennsylvania Dutch? You better count Barbara too, because it is thanks to her that numbers *drei, vier,* and *fimf* came along. But, come to think of it, a little sex was probably involved as well."

"Ach!" Freni clapped her hands tightly over her ears and fled to the pantry.

Feeling strangely better about the puppy situation, I headed out through the dining room and back to the office/foyer. I had a lot of work to do, if indeed the horde from Hoboken was going to experience an authentic Amish supper. The first thing on my agenda was getting these folks to work up an honest country-style appetite.

"Come on, people," I barked (gently, of course) to the stragglers who were still struggling to get their bulging valises up my impossibly steep stairs. "Tote that bag, and lift that tote, but if you gets a little drunk, then no fruit compote."

"That woman is certifiably nuts," I heard somebody grumble from the dark privacy of the stairwell.

"Indeed, I am," I said with satisfaction. Yes, sir, it had all the makings of a blessed week.

I didn't even have a clue that something had gone terribly wrong with my game plan until the sheriff's car pulled up my long gravel driveway. It happened just as I had begun to say grace. I feel compelled to explain here that the enormity of such an interruption cannot be overemphasized. My guests, as it turns out, were all papists, given to a brief prayer accompanied by a hand gesture known as the sign of the cross.

But since they had all signed up for the full Mennonite experience, I was determined to give them just that. A proper grace—that is, a Protestant grace—should be long enough to wilt a crisp tossed salad and turn mashed potatoes into concrete. If at least one person in attendance does not come close to fainting, it fails the test. For one must not only ask the Lord to bless the food, but to calm Aunt Wendy's eczema, cure Uncle Walter's halitosis, and find some way to talk some sense into Cousin Leona, to stop her from marrying that gold digger from Chile with the red toupee and the extra pinkie on his left hand.

Finally, when the time comes to wrap it up and say amen, the attendees are so famished that they will eat *anything*—perhaps even one another, like the survivors of an Andean plane crash—and they are grateful putty in your hand. Oh, what delicious power! Like a skilled conductor with an orchestra, one can prolong that moment of intense anticipation until it bursts into a collective gasp, quite like that moment of marital bliss that one experiences when—

"Magdalena!"

"Shhh, I'm praying."

"Sorry, hon," my Beloved whispered, "but the sheriff said he's not falling for that ruse this time."

I opened one eye and looked down the long table that my ancestor Jacob the Strong had built in the nineteenth century. The papists along its length, like their distant cousins, the Episcopalians, were not keeping their eyes closed. Believe me, a Baptist, or a Methodist, would have to have his or her eyes pried open during a prayer, lest the Devil somehow distract him or her. If, however, they prayed that the English would adopt some gender-neutral pronouns—

"Mags, hon, this is serious."

I closed my wandering eye; I never should have opened it. I was still returning thanks for the Good Lord's bountiful goodness, by whose hand we all were fed, and had yet to even touch on familial maladies.

"—and bless the plump little hands that kneaded this bread," I intoned. "It is, by the way, *excellent* bread, even if Freni did get the loaves a wee too brown on the bottom this time around, so I fully expect that we, your grateful servants gathered here, will partake thereof. And with *gusto*. But as for the beef stew— Mmm, mmm, mmm, does that smell good! No need for divinely inspired gusto there, Lord."

"Miss Yoder?"

"Yes, Lord?"

At least five out of six of my guests were rude enough to laugh at that point. One can be quite sure that both my eyes flew open in righteous annoyance.

"Over here, Miss Yoder," said the sheriff. He was standing in the doorway of my dining room, and in so doing re-created a scene from my worst nightmare. That nightmare, of course, had to do with the day Mama and Papa died, squished to death as they were between a milk tanker and a semi-trailer truck loaded to the gills with state-of-the-art running shoes. That evening as well a sheriff had stood in the dining room of the PennDutch Inn, twisting his cap in his hands.

"I can see you," I said as an aside to shush the lawman up. "Now, Lord, about the mashed potatoes: it really is a shame you didn't have potatoes in ancient Palestine. You would have loved these. They are smooth—"

"Mags, hon," Gabe hissed from eight feet away, "I don't see any potatoes on the table."

The sheriff cleared his throat. "Tell Miss Yoder," he said, "that if she doesn't join me in her parlor, I am going to arrest her for obstruction of justice."

That was when the assemblage released their collective gasp.

"*Arrest* me? You can't barge into my home and arrest me during prayer. That's un-American! Even a Democrat wouldn't do that."

"Do you have a warrant?" the Babester asked calmly.

The sheriff is not an unreasonable man. "Look," he said, "all I want you to do is to stop harassing your cousin Pernicious Yoder III, over at the bank, so that I can get some peace and quiet."

I, however, was still quite vexed that he had barged into my home. "He's *not* my cousin, and peace and quiet are redundant."

"What?"

Gabe put a steadying hand on my shoulder. "She means that Pernicious is not her *first* cousin, but as to you being redundant— Well, you know, Magdalena; she can split hairs with the broad side of an ax."

"Thanks, dear," I said. "Uh—I think."

"But, hon," Gabe said, "what's this about you pestering Pernicious? He's not still trying to get you to donate to the Giant Ball of String Society, is he?"

"Like I would!" That society, by the way, is about as nutty as a stroll down Hollywood Boulevard, or a jog through Clearwater, Florida—take your pick. The members are collecting bits of string from all over the world, which one unidentified woman in Charlotte, North Carolina, is supposedly tying together to form one very long string, which she keeps rolled in an ever-expanding ball. On June 17, 2019, the ball will be unrolled so that the string stretches around the world, thereby uniting all mankind in everlasting peace. Yeah, right; what a Crock-Pot full of *Huafa mischt* that is.

"No," I said quickly, "this has nothing to do with string. But speaking of which, be a dear, will you? And run back into the dining room and see how our guests are faring."

"Of course, dear. But what's that got to do with string?"

I smiled weakly. "You know, tie up loose ends—that sort of thing."

"I will not; I'm staying right here. Go on," Gabe said to the sheriff. "Fill me in."

It isn't pretty to see a man in a uniform flinch. "It's not just Pernicious who's complaining. Your wife has apparently made herself such a fixture around police headquarters that they even have a nickname reserved just for her."

I patted the white organza prayer cap atop my bun. This gesture is admittedly an affectation of mine that I engage in whenever I've been unduly flattered.

"They *do*?" I said in mock surprise. "What?"

"Rasputin."

I recoiled in horror. "Oh, what vile things I've read about that man!"

The sheriff offered me a crooked grin in consolation. "I'm

sure the guys at headquarters mean it kindly: that you have an indomitable spirit."

"That you do," the Babester said proudly. "Trust me, Sheriff, it takes a hard man to dominate her."

"And my husband is anything but a softie," I said just as proudly.

"Enough with the mutual-adulation society," the sheriff growled. "You should know, Mr. Yoder, that your wife has been running a full-scale investigation of the bank robbery on her own for some time now."

"Two corrections are in order," I said, stabbing the air with a shapely index finger. "First of all, my husband is *Dr.* Gabriel *Rosen*, not Mr. Yoder—that was my father. And secondly, it was a *failed* bank robbery."

The sheriff glared at me. "Which is neither here nor there as far as you're concerned. This matter is only of concern to the FBI and local law enforcement authorities."

"So then what am I, chopped liver?"

"Huh?"

"It's a Jewish expression," Gabe said. "What she means is—"

"My child and I were there. My son could have gotten killed. *My* son—not *your* son, not the *FBI's* son."

"My son too," Gabe said plaintively.

The sheriff took time out long enough to blow his nose on a plain white handkerchief the size of a picnic cloth. Having relieved his not inconsiderable proboscis of its contents, he rubbed it brusquely from side to side.

"I'll take it then that you intend to interfere at every opportunity and that I should expect to continue to find you underfoot, as I have been for the last three weeks?"

"Three weeks?" gasped Gabe. "You told me you were taking a drawing class in Bedford."

I focused my gaze adoringly on the love of my life. "Darling,"

I said, "I was in Bedford *drawing* on my life experience. You know that I have a tendency to swallow the end of my sentences." I turned my watery blue eyes to the sheriff. "It's a habit I've developed from having to eat so much crow."

"I would have thought you'd have some mighty tasty recipes by now, Miss Yoder."

"Touché."

"Oy veys meer," Gabe moaned.

The sheriff jerked his attention back to Gabe. "What was that?"

"Nothing, Sheriff. Really. I'm just admiring the repartee you're have with my wife."

"The *what*?"

"Our jolly banter, dear," I said, as I gently pushed the much larger man toward the parlor door and the outer vestibule beyond.

"Uh-huh. Well, I've known her since she was knee-high to a grasshopper," he said without a trace of shame.

After all, I'm ten years older than the sheriff and I used to babysit *him*. He was an ornery little thing too; once he put a banana up the exhaust pipe of my papa's car, and another time he took a bite out of more than a dozen freshly baked cookies that Mama had made for the church bake sale to raise money to buy layettes for newborns in the Congo.

I pushed harder. The sheriff stumbled backward, but he was never in any danger of actually falling on his well-upholstered hinnie. Hitherto unnoticed by me, all of my guests had gathered in the aforementioned vestibule—the better to hear our conversation.

8

"Well, if that doesn't beat all," Agnes said, as she mashed her fork tines down on the remaining crumbs of the carrot cake I'd brought. "The very fact that the sheriff came out to your place to warn you off the case is a clear sign that where there's smoke, there's fire."

"Sometimes there's just a good fire sale. Agnes, dear, you do realize that you just ate an entire cake, don't you?"

"It's carrot cake; it's good for you. Think of it as another way of me getting my vegetables."

"And the cream cheese icing?"

"Is really none of your business, is it, Magdalena? You brought me the cake as a gift. You said you didn't want any. So what I did with it was my business."

I sighed. She was right, of course.

"Sorry," I said. "I guess it's hard for me to switch gears from being a mommy."

"Oh, come off it, Magdalena; you've always been bossy. And that's not necessarily a bad thing. In fact, when used against others, being bossy can even be an amusing trait. Just don't pull that stuff on me."

I stared at my friend. Agnes stared back through round rim-less glasses. No, ding dang it, she didn't even have the courtesy to look me in the eye, but instead appeared to be focused outside, possibly on the hillside behind me.

"Say something erudite, Agnes," I said. "I'm sure it will go right over my head."

"You were followed, Magdalena."

"Oh yeah, the KGB has been hot on my trail all morning."

"Joke if you want, my friend, but when you pulled into my driveway this morning a car passed exactly five seconds behind you, turned around, and drove by nine seconds later. Then, as I was setting out the plates for our cake, I saw this woman hiking up over the crest of that hill, and there she is right now, staring at you through a pair of binoculars."

I spun so fast in my seat that I came dangerously close to tip-ping my chair all the way over. Since Agnes is not the world's most conscientious housekeeper, I might well have put my ex-posed body parts in contact with varieties of mold as yet unclas-sified by science. Still, it was worth the risk; sure enough there was a woman looking right at us.

"Why, I'll be a monkey's uncle!"

"You don't believe in evolution, Magdalena. And you're far too curvaceous to be an uncle. What say you we go out and con-front this interloper?"

"Let us lope away!" I cried, as I whipped my coat off the back of my chair.

Agnes was more of a huffer and a puffer than a loper, and not wanting to confront the strange woman by myself, I pretended to twist my ankle whilst going down the steps. Now please allow me to make perfectly clear that feigning an injury to one's own person under such circumstances is a deception of the smallest magnitude—surely, no more serious a transgression than, say, acting out a part in a school play.

"You won't sue me, Magdalena, will you?" Agnes had stopped moving altogether.

"Of course not, dear; we're bosom buddies—well, our bosoms aren't buddies—not that there's anything wrong with it—but your bosom, by the way, just don't float my hovercraft."

"I get it, Magdalena. But you do agree that you should have watched your step, right?"

"How can I argue with that?" I tried peering around my friend, but to no avail.

"So you'll promise you'll be good and not sue?"

"Sue, *shmoo*! How well do you know me? Uh—never mind, dear."

I tried matching my pace to that of Agnes, but even though I did my darnedest to hobble, I kept getting way ahead. Finally, I had no choice but to resort to desperate measures.

"Yoo-hoo, up there on the hill," I hollered. "Come on down and show yourself."

"And just so you know," Agnes rasped, "we're harmed."

"She means 'armed,'" I said, "although personally, being the traditional Mennonite that I am, I am totally committed to a nonviolent existence."

"Except for her tongue," Agnes panted. "It's as sharp as a board."

"She means 'sword,'" I clarified through cupped hands. "It goes along with my rapier-sharp wit."

"You're such a faker," Agnes groaned. She was clutching her side by then.

"What?"

"You're not even limping now."

"Oh that— Well, perhaps it's the adrenaline." I fell back, taking what for me were baby steps so that Agnes wouldn't have a heart attack. After all, I had never gotten around to taking a CPR class, and wouldn't have the foggiest idea of what to do if she

did have a heart attack—except to scream and pray. I *am*, however, pretty good at both of those.

On closer inspection, it was as if the woman on the hill had
stepped out of the pages of a storybook. Never had I seen someone so splendiferously attired, nor so regal of bearing. She wasn't
tall, perhaps all of five and a half feet, but she was clad in a full-
length white velvet coat, trimmed generously with white fur, and
with an enormous white fur collar and matching cuffs. Through
the break in her coat front, I could see that she wore white leather
boots that laced up to the knees and sported gold eyelets. Her
headpiece, which was half gold crown and half fur hat, set off
her blue-black hair to perfection.

"It's the S-S-Snow Queen," wheezed Agnes. "I knew I
shouldn't have inhaled that time I smoked pot in college."

"*You* smoked marijuana?"

I was aghast and agog, but mostly just gaping in wonder-
ment. Who knew that Agnes, a somewhat reclusive maiden lady,
had been such a wild woman in her coed days?

"Okay, so it was more than once. Will you get off my case already? It just goes to prove that college campuses these days are
nothing more than replicas of Sodom and Gomorrah.

"Sure," I said, "I'll get off your case—*and* not tell anyone
else—if you share with me what it was like."

"What do you mean by that? Do you want me to find you a
joint?"

"A *what*?"

"A marijuana cigarette—at least that's what they used to call
them. It's been so long, I don't know what they're called anymore. But if you're going to rat me out to the community, then
by all means, I'll drive into Pittsburgh and try to score one for
you. Of course I'll probably end up getting arrested and spend

the next thirty years in prison with a 'boyfriend' named Betty—but don't worry, Magdalena. I'm sure Betty will be very kind to me. Who knows? Maybe she'll even let me write to you."

My eyes welled with tears. "You'd do that for me?"

"Double space, of course; Betty won't want me to spend that much time away from her."

"No, I mean that part about buying me marijuana?"

"If it will shut you up."

Now *that* was a friend. Agnes always knew when to coddle me and when to take off the gloves and give me a gentle tap on the noggin. If we had been best buddies in college, I have no doubt neither of us would have gotten much studying done; we'd have partied hardy like there was no tomorrow, and I might have well ended up a Presbyterian like Susannah.

A soft cough ahead got my attention. The stranger was no longer peering at us through her binoculars, as we were but a scant thirty feet away. There was in her face the suggestion of Asiatic forebears—or not—but no matter, she was most definitely not the creation of some writer's imagination, but a flesh-and-blood human being.

"She's definitely not the Snow Queen," I said.

"Maybe not, but she *is* a foreigner," Agnes said.

"Of pleasing but ambiguous ethnicity," I said.

As we made our final panting approach, I bobbed slightly. "Greetings, and welcome to Hernia, O strange one," I said. "From whence didst thou hail?"

"Cincinnati, Ohio."

"Well, that certainly explains the accent," Agnes said.

I punched her fleshy biceps with an elbow even sharper than my tongue. "You can't get that from just two words," I said.

The elegant, beautiful stranger appeared to suppress a smile. "Are you the famous Magdalena Yoder?"

"Indeed, I am." It was only then, after having admitted who I was, that I began to fear for my safety. "I mean, let's just say that there are those who *think* I am Magdalena Yoder."

She cocked her head.

"Don't worry," Agnes said. "She's utterly harmless—although she did bring a giantess to her knees with a bra-cum-slingshot, and although she espouses nonviolence as her official creed, she's not above whacking the odd villain over the head."

A wary glance was now cast in Agnes's direction. "Surely, you're joking."

"Oh, but I'm not. Our Magdalena is quite the heroine. Why, once she even *rescued* a villainess by dangling her nemesis by her hair into a sinkhole. Of course yours truly was pressed into service on that one. I am, you see, her unofficial sidekick: the Tonto to her Lone Ranger, the Robin to her Batman. My point is—were I to be making one—that if you have come to request the famous Magdalena Yoder's services, be apprised of the fact that sooner or later I will be assisting her." Agnes crossed her arms over her breathless, heaving bosom.

"I am a guest at her inn," the stranger said.

I stepped forward. "*Excuse* me?"

"My name is Surimanda Baikal. I am coming from Russia. Then New York, then Cincinnati. Then I am drives here. But you are hard woman to find, Magdalena Yoder."

"But you don't have a reservation," I wailed.

She shrugged, almost burying her face in the white fur collar. "So? My plans, she has—how you say?—they change from day to day."

"*Your* plans?"

"Oh, come on," Agnes said, much to my annoyance. "You have enough room. The more the merrier. Right?"

"Stifle it," I hissed. "She doesn't fit in with this bunch."

"Maybe, but from what you've described to me, this bunch belongs in a loony bin. At least she'll add some class."

"Da, I vill add some class," the elegant woman said.

Decked out in her fur and velvet, with the crown piece on her head, Miss Surimanda Baikal *was* my image of an empress. When compared to the Zambezis, the Nyles, and the Timmses— Well, one could hardly compare a swan to six moorhen, could one?

"Velcommen to zee PennDutch Inn," I cried, my arms extended in an only slightly overly exuberant greeting (after all, someone as handsomely dressed as this woman would be able to afford a lot of ALPO). "Who cares if your untimely arrival is, at the very least, extremely inconsiderate? Of course you'll just have to make do with PUS tonight—that's previously used sheets—because laundry day is not until tomorrow. But look on the bright side: for the distinct pleasure of going beddy-bye whilst wrapped in the scent of a previous guest, I shall levy a surcharge of only fifty percent."

"That's ridiculous," Agnes muttered.

I gave my friend the Mennonite version of the Evil Eye, which amounts to a twitch followed by a glassy stare. "I couldn't agree more," I said. "There are those who would kill to get their hands on that most exclusive, that most prized, of all DNA, which must surely be lurking in those sheets; I should be charging one hundred percent over the nightly rate, not fifty."

The foreigner's green almond-shaped eyes grew as round and large as gingersnaps. "*Borat* slept at your inn? I take!"

"Why, Magdalena, you dirty dog, you," Agnes said, but I could hear the admiration in my friend's voice.

As the old saw goes, those who assume, make a donkey out of everyone—or something like that. Believe me, I have long since made peace with being an equid, or some part thereof.

"Do we have a deal?" I said.

"Dah!"

"Then let's get this show on the road; time's a-wasting."

The regal stranger seemed to withdraw, not unlike a turtle, into the safety of her velvet and furs. "What *show*?"

"It's just an expression, dear, an Americanism."

"And if you stay very long," Agnes said. "I'm afraid you'll be treated to a great many original Magdalenaisms."

"Thanks a lot, friend."

Miss Surimanda Baikal emerged, smiling. "Ah, you are the Golden Girls, no?"

"Excuse me?"

"Like the TV show. Only this one"—she pointed to Agnes— "is more healthy, like a good Russian babushka, and you are like the crabby one, Dorothy."

Agnes twittered behind a plump, healthy hand.

"I don't watch television," I said archly. "And be forewarned, my dear, although I have the patience of Job, I have the memory of Methuselah—well, at least I hope he kept his wits about him all those years. My point is that although I am a good Christian woman, and was born and bred amongst the gentle folk known as Mennonites, hereabouts it is said that I possess a tongue that can slice through a stick of butter left outside on a tree stump overnight in the dead of winter. Alas, this is no mere metaphor." I paused to catch my breath and lean forward for emphasis. "Furthermore, there is room for only one of me at the PennDutch Inn—perhaps even in all of Hernia—if you get my drift."

Miss Baikal hadn't stopped smiling. "This is threat?"

"Oh no, dear, just a statement of fact."

Agnes suddenly inserted a great deal of herself between me and the exotic stranger. "Magdalena, why would anyone leave a stick of butter out on a tree stump overnight?"

"*What?*"

"You just said—"

I stepped around her. "You will follow my rules, Miss Surimanda Baikal?"

The beautiful visitor grinned broadly. "Dah, I like rules. Is very Russian!"

9

"If that woman is Russian," Peewee Timms said, "I'll eat my hat."

It was all I could do to keep from revealing to Peewee that the thick black man-made thatch atop his head looked very much like a hat: a scaled-down version of the bearskin hats the Beef-eaters wear when they guard Buckingham Palace. Peewee had signed up for general barn chores, but had expressed a special interest in working with my two cows.

Matilda Holsteincoo III and Miss Cowabunga (my newest ac-quisition), like females everywhere, are quite discerning when it comes to who gets to squeeze their teats and when. As Mose had taken the day off, and Peewee wanted the "hands-on" milking experience, rather than use the electric machines, it fell to me to be his instructor (Freni was chained to the stove, and the only contact Gabe wants with a cow is on his plate).

"Put your head right up against her stomach; she likes know-ing that you're there. Gently caress her udder before sliding your fingers down her teats," I said. "Now start squeezing with your thumbs, then your index fingers, middle fingers, ring fingers, and so on. The point is that you are gently pushing the milk down—

away from her. Concentrate so that you don't accidentally start squeezing the other way. Get a rhythm going."

"Does it hurt?"

"It hurts her to have a full bag. It's like you and a full bladder."

"Yes, but—"

"She's a cow, for goodness' sake; modesty doesn't play into this."

The first squirt that hit the pail startled Peewee into letting go so that his rhythm was broken, but soon he and Cowabunga were working in tandem, and it was a beautiful sight to behold.

"You're a natural," I said. "It's like you've done this before."

"Maybe I have—in another life."

"Don't be silly, dear; there's only this life. Reincarnation is— Well, it's simply an impossibility."

While still maintaining contact with Cowabunga's stomach, he managed to turn and look at me. The strong flow of milk remained consistent.

"Yeah? How so?"

"Because of the gift of salvation, that's why."

"Come again?"

I sighed, despite my best effort to be patient. "Let's suppose that you were saved by faith in Jesus Christ in your past life, but that in this life you were a steadfast heathen who refused to believe. Worse yet, what if that in this life you believed in some other deity—like a Hindu god—when you died. What would happen to your soul? Would you go to Heaven or to Hell? Since the answer to the latter is impossible to sort out, it's quite clear to me that the Good Lord, whose foresight far exceeds mine, would have avoided this conundrum altogether by giving us only one life."

Peewee had the temerity to burst out laughing, although the flow from Cowabunga did not let up even then. "But that presupposes that all Hindus are headed for Hell! Isn't that being a tad judgmental of you, Miss Yoder?"

"Indeed, it is not! It isn't me who makes the rules; they're in the Book."

"Ah, but not everyone goes by your book. Take that so-called Russian woman—or the aforementioned Hindus, for that matter—what if they never had the chance to read your book?"

"That is a problem," I conceded, "which is why I give generously to the church mission fund. I once briefly considered becoming a missionary myself, but they wanted to send me to the Congo. The *Congo*! Can you imagine that?"

He smiled but said nothing.

"It's not that I couldn't have survived," I said defensively.

Still nothing.

"So what makes you think she's a fake Russian?" I asked.

"She doesn't speak Russian, that's why."

I stared at him. "How do you know?"

"I was a Russian major in college. Russia was still the big bugaboo then—communism was going to take over half of the world, and we needed to be prepared. Nobody anticipated China. Anyway, I went into advertising and never used my Russian except to eavesdrop on the odd conversation, and the one trip we took to St. Petersburg, but I still remember enough to make myself understood." He snorted with laughter. "So I used the basic introduction stuff on Her Imperial Highness, but I may as well have been speaking Swahili. She made some excuse in English about not feeling well and then hightailed it out of there like a deer coming face-to-face with a wolf."

"You don't say! When was this?"

"This morning, just after she checked in. Wherever she's from, don't you think that get-up of hers is a little over the top? By the way, I can tell you right now that the ladies don't much like her."

"Oh?" After returning to the inn to check in Surimanda Baikal, I'd hurried straight over to Yoder's Corner Market to engage in a little of what I call "good gossip," and so had missed out on whatever might have gone on back here at the PennDutch.

I know, there are those who probably frown on "good gossip," but frankly, I see the dissemination of good gossip as my civic duty. After all, a timely and accurate dispersal of facts may well prevent the spread of erroneous commentary that could hurt both the feelings and reputation of the subject. Better to defuse the malicious gossip vendors with the truth, I always say.

Peewee laughed happily. It was Cowabunga who snorted now.

"Yeah," Peewee said, "at least I can speak for Tiny. I tell you, Miss Yoder, she got her nose out of joint the second she laid eyes on that woman. 'A phony,' that's what she called her."

"A phony what?"

"A phony Russian, of course."

"But you hadn't spoken to her yet, had you?"

His head swiveled enough to show me his scowl. "Well, anyone could see that she was dressed up to look like she'd stepped out of the pages of *Dr. Zhivago*. Besides, my Tiny is an excellent judge of character; she certainly had you pegged."

I stiffened. "Excuse me?"

"Yeah, she said that she could see right off that you were tough on the outside—which made you a brilliant businesswoman—but inside you were one fabulous human being. Her words exactly."

My fabulous insides were suddenly glowing like the interior of a coke furnace. "You don't say?"

"Yeah," he said, "you're a big hit. From what I gather, the others seem to feel that way as well."

Moi, a big hit! Finally, a group of guests who appreciated me for who I was and the inn for what it was supposed to be. It was a moment I sinfully wished to savor—I'd even laminate it if I could—but then, thankfully, I remembered that Proverbs 16:18 warns us that pride goeth before destruction. The ten-gallon pail that Peewee was attempting to fill was now two-thirds full, which meant that Cowabunga was almost dry. A dry Cowabunga wouldn't take kindly to some stranger tugging on her teats, and unless I intervened on her behalf, Peewee Timms could possibly be kicked as far as the Maryland border—and him without provisions!

"Time to let up on the big gal," I cried.

As he stood, he flexed his fingers and craned his neck. "I can't remember when I've had so much fun."

"You really enjoyed that?"

"Oh yeah!"

"Then how about a repeat performance tomorrow morning—at, say, six o'clock?"

"You got yourself a deal, Miss Yoder."

Knowing that I was a big hit with everyone did not prevent me from saying grace at the dinner table. The Good Lord should be properly thanked, and if perchance we should lose some of our admirers by doing so—well, so be it.

"Bow your heads and close your eyes, please," I said. "I am about to subject you folks to a full-length Protestant grace."

"What does that mean?" Carl Zambezi said. "Olivia and I are Catholic."

"It means that her prayer will be much longer than anything you're used to," my Jewish husband said.

"It means that the food will get cold," my little munchkin said. "Won't it, Papa?"

"Shhh."

"But last time you said the mashed potatoes was like stones they was so cold."

"Well, there was that—and the gravy was more like a ball of Silly Putty by then."

Little Jacob giggled. "And tell them what you said about the peas, Papa."

"You mean that they were so cold and hard, I could have shot them out of your pellet gun—if your mother hadn't taken it away from you."

I stood up, inadvertently dragging a good third of the tablecloth with me. Thank heavens I don't serve my guests anything other than water with which to wet their whistles before dessert is served, because I hear that red wine can be difficult to remove from fine polyester blends. As for the Silly Putty gravy that spilled hither, thither, and yon, in a day or two it would harden enough for me to take hammer and chisel to.

"A pellet gun is not an appropriate gift for a four-year-old! Or for anyone, for that matter!"

"You see what I have to put up with?" the Babester said, but he winked.

Little Jacob, who was sitting at the far end of the table, next to his father, tugged on his arm. "Papa, tell 'em what you said about the wice pudding."

I stamped a slender but exceptionally long foot. "Stop it! Gabriel, just because you mother doesn't cook for you anymore is no reason to say vicious things about Freni's food."

"It's not Freni's cooking, dear; it's your interminable prayers."

"Papa, what does 'termin'ble' mean?"

"Oy vey!" I said, clapping my hands to my cheeks.

Olivia Zambezi was seated to my immediate left. Perhaps because she was the oldest female present, she felt she had the right to lean toward me and whisper behind the back of her hand. It was, however, a stage whisper that could have been heard in a back bleacher—with a military jet flying maneuvers overhead.

"Really, Miss Yoder, your behavior at the moment is a bit over-the-top."

"Uh-oh," the Babester said.

"Uh-oh," my little man said.

Nobody likes to be chided, much less in front of others, and least of all by a complete stranger. Okay, so maybe *some* folks go in for public scoldings, but certainly not *this* mild-mannered Mennonite woman. At the moment my hackles were hiked so high, they scratched my armpits.

"You are absolutely right," I said to Olivia Zambezi, as I settled back into my seat. "Gabe, darling, pull the cloth down at your end."

"Sure thing, hon."

"And you, dear," I said to Olivia Zambezi, whilst smiling broadly, "are a lovely bunch of *Huafa mischt*."

"Why, thank you."

"Think nothing of it," I said brightly.

"What's *Huafa mischt*?" Barbie Nyle just had to chirp.

"It must be flowers," George Nyle said. "Probably roses."

"Papa," my littlest troublemaker said, "why did Mama call the old lady a bunch of horse poop?"

It was one thing for the New Jersey gang of six to suddenly decide that they preferred to drive all the way back into Bedford for pizza, but they didn't have to invite Surimanda Baikal to go with them. Although what really took the cake was when the Babester asked if he and Little Jacob could tag along. Permission was granted as long as he brought dessert home with him, which he was more than happy to do.

So there I was, alone and abandoned, a hapless orphan waif (indeed, my adoptive parents are dead, squished as they were in that horrible tunnel accident). All this pain and sorrow, this *tsuris*, just because I wanted to say a proper grace before eating. Was that really too much to ask? Okay, so perhaps I'd been out of line with the *Huafa mischt* comment, but I'd had a hard life; and Gabe should have stuck by me—no matter what. Isn't that what marriage was all about?

Yes, I know, life is hard for all of us, but for me it has been particularly hard. Who but me could understand the trauma of being just shy of twenty-seven and having to shop for a pair of coffins, each over four feet wide, but only two inches high? Even just recalling that horrible day caused me to throw back my head and commence howling.

"Nobody knows the trouble I've seen. Nobody knows but Jesus."

Someone tapped me on the shoulder.

10

Rosemary Blue Cheese Ice Box Cookies

Ingredients

2½ cups all-purpose flour
1 cup cornstarch
½ teaspoon salt
12 ounces blue cheese,* softened
1 cup (2 sticks) butter, softened
½ cup granulated sugar
1 cup dried cranberries, finely chopped
1½ cups nuts (pecans or walnuts), chopped
1 to 2 tablespoons fresh rosemary, leaves only
white or natural sanding (coarse) sugar

*Domestic Blue cheese gives cookies a clean flavor, color, and texture. Use less flour
with a Stilton-style cheese and more flour with a French-style Roquefort.

Cooking Directions

Whisk together flour, cornstarch, and salt in a bowl; set aside. Cream together blue cheese and butter with an electric mixer. Add sugar and beat until light and fluffy. Slowly add flour mixture to butter and cheese mixture; beat to combine. Add cranberries and mix on low just until evenly dispersed.

Divide the dough into two pieces and use parchment paper or plastic wrap to form the dough into two 1½-inch-diameter round or square logs. Set out two fresh pieces of plastic wrap and sprinkle the chopped nuts evenly over both. Roll the logs of dough in nuts until covered. Tightly wrap and seal the logs; refrigerate until firm (at least 2 hours). Preheat oven to 325°F. Working with one log at a time, unwrap and slice logs into ¼-inch discs. Place 1 inch apart on parchment-lined baking sheets. Gently press about 3 small rosemary leaves on each cookie. Sprinkle each cookie with sanding sugar.

Bake on a middle rack until bottoms begin to brown and tops just begin to turn from pale to golden; 12 to 18 minutes. Cool on sheets 1 to 2 minutes before removing cookies to a cooling rack to cool completely. Store cookies in an airtight container for up to 1 week.

Courtesy http://www.eatwisconsincheese.com/

11

I shrieked, and because I was in the parlor at that point, I jumped on the nearest chair—*sideways*.

"Oh, calm down, Magdalena; you always were such a drama queen."

I whirled, which meant that I toppled off the chair. But although I flailed like a downed helicopter, still I managed to somehow land on my feet, and facing the opposite direction to boot.

"Grandma!"

"As big as life and twice as ugly."

It was a true statement. Indeed, there she was, Grandma Yoder, in all her fierceness, complete with bristling bun and bristling mole. The only problem was that Grandma Yoder had been dead for thirty years—no, it was closer to forty by now. How time flies, even when you're not having fun.

"Don't look so surprised, Magdalena Portulacca; you've seen me before. The fact is, you see me just about every time you manage to—uh—you know."

"You mean 'screw up'?"

Apparently Apparition Americans can be just as sensitive as their real-life counterparts were. Grandma Yoder's face turned six shades of white as she raised a knobby finger, which she pointed just inches from my face.

"I have half a mind to wash your mouth out with soap, little girl."

"I'm not a little girl, Grandma; I'm fifty-two years old."

She stepped back and gave me the once-over, as if really seeing me for the first time that evening. "Hmm, so you are; but this is still my house, and I won't be having you using that kind of language."

I pushed the chair aside and took a step forward. "No, it's not your house anymore, Grandma; you died. And Mama and Papa died. This house is mine now—in fact, this isn't even the same house; the original blew down in a freak tornado."

"Ha, but can you blame it? Look at the way you've been treating this one? There's a scuff mark on the wall over by the door, and that left lower screw on the hinge should be tightened by a quarter turn."

"Still a stickler for minutiae, I see."

"It's won or lost in the details, Magdalena; that's what you still don't seem to understand."

"*What* is? What's lost in the details?"

"*It.*"

I wanted to grab her by her bony shoulders and shake her. In fact, I tried to, but there is no grasping an Apparition American; they are as ethereal as a Middle East peace plan. Anyway, she'd never get me to agree with her—even if just out of spite—although I really did believe that "broad strokes" approach was the only way to accomplish anything in the rat race this world had become.

"Your way might have worked for you, Grandma—although from what I've heard, you were about as happy as a petunia in an onion patch—but I think I'm finally old enough to make my own mistakes—uh, decisions—thank you very much."

Grandma sighed, an action that has been known to keep dust motes afloat for half an hour. "Fine, have it your way—as *always*. But see where it gets you. You keep this up and you're going to lose that hunka hunka burning love, not to mention that adorable great-grandson of mine. What's his name? Little Samuel?"

"No, Grandma. Samuel was Grandpa's name."

"Well, there's no need to get huffy!"

"I didn't. But since you've obviously been hanging around for some time, you should have been paying better attention to your great-grandson's name. And what kind of Mennonite grandma says 'hunka hunka burning love'? You didn't listen to the radio when you were alive; you said the Devil lived in there, and inside every TV set in America."

"And I was right! But I was wrong about Elvis. He's da bomb. We listen to him all the time over here—but in person. In fact, your grandpa and I are going to a concert tonight."

At that point I knew that either I was doing some serious hallucinating, or else I had somehow managed to fall asleep and was having one heck of a nightmare. Grandpa Yoder watching Elvis Presley shimmy those hips was as close to being sacrilegious as saying that Noah's ark was just a story, because there are at least five million insect species in the world, and they would have had to enter in pairs, and just the weight of them alone would have sunk that wooden tub (of course, *I* don't believe this sacrilege).

"Magdalena, get ahold of yourself," I said. At least I thought I said that, but my teeth seemed to be stuck together with taffy, and although I could move my lips, no sound was coming out of my throat.

I tried again. And again. Then again. Finally I could hear a muffled sound, like a voice underwater. I started struggling physically, making swimming motions, even though I was standing in the middle of the parlor—except that I wasn't.

"Well, ding dang dong dang it!" I swore, when I woke up on the settee, having whacked the back of my hand on some carved wooden roses along the back. "I must have fallen asleep on this genuine reproduction Victorian love seat."

There was no response—from anyone. No withering, critical grandmother to tell me that I'd paid far too much for a fake that was probably carved in a sweatshop somewhere in China from wood that had been stripped from the last of patch of rain forest on the island of Borneo. I was alone in my inn, alone with my mouth and my thoughts, and the realization that it was really all my doing.

However, since there is nothing to gain by dwelling on the past—at least, not without an audience—I quickly decided to concentrate on the future. The *near* future. After all, the evening was yet young, and I had miles to go before I'd peep.

"You want to do *what*?" Agnes barked into the phone.

"You heard me: I want to play Peeping Magdalena."

"You're my best friend, and I thought I knew all your tricks, but this is a new one."

"Well, I'm all alone—and don't ask why—so I thought this might be the perfect time to fit in some sleuthing."

"The Russian!" I felt a mild shock, as a surge of electrical impulses flowed from Agnes over the wires and to my ear. The woman was besotted with Surimanda Baikal. Frankly, it was unseemly—it was probably even forbidden somewhere in the Book of Leviticus.

"No, dear, not her—although come to think of it, I should take this opportunity to hoof it up my impossibly steep stairs and riffle through her belongings."

"You wouldn't!" Agnes sounded positively gleeful. "Magdalena, what if you get caught? What if it's a trap of some kind?"

"Riffle first, rue later," I said blithely.

"Ooh, you're bad," she said. "In a fun sort of way. Me? I'm just plain old boring Agnes. Boring, fat Agnes. Do you know I haven't had a single date since that jerk dumped me?"

She was referring to a visitor from one of the square states who swept round Agnes off her feet, proposed marriage, but then left her standing at the altar. If you ask me, she hasn't quite found her footing since then.

"Well, tonight's your chance to shake it up a bit, because I'm inviting you to come along peeping with me—nay, I insist that you accompany me."

"Really?"

"Forsooth. I'll be there in twenty. We'll split the difference and meet in ten in front of the police station. I'll drive from there."

"Uh—hey, you know I'd really love to do that; in fact, you don't know how much I'd love to, but tonight's really not good for me."

It was then that I first heard a voice in the background. A woman's voice, perhaps.

"Oh," I said. "Do you, perchance, have company?"

"Don't be absurd, Magdalena. You know I never have company—well, sometimes I still get my monthly visitor, but the doctor says even he won't be stopping in much longer."

I jiggled a pinkie in my ear to make sure it wasn't clogged. "You're monthly visitor is a *he*?"

"Well, I guess I never thought about that until now. But he's silent, messy, and a pain in the—"

"There! I heard it again. Whose voice is that?"

"No one's."

"No one doesn't have a voice, so I'm not buying it. Are the

uncles over? Did they bring women? Because I thought they were gay."

"Only one is gay," Agnes whispered, "and for the millionth time, I'm not telling you which one. But no, it's not them. It's the strumpet."

"Who?"

"Dorothy Yoder."

"*Oh*. What's she doing there?"

"She says she's lonely. She's tired of her life of debauchery and wants to walk the straight-and-narrow path again, but none of her old friends will take her back."

"I didn't know she had any."

"Did you know she played the trumpet?"

"You're kidding."

"I wish I was. Now that she has the breath to blow it, she practices almost nonstop. She says it brings her peace, but it's driving me crazy."

"Hmm. Well, I don't hear it now."

"That's because I'm trying to keep her mouth full of food. Right now she's eating a crumpet."

"Somehow I don't think that's such a smart plan. If she balloons back up again, it's going to be all your fault. She'll hate you for it."

"I'll just have to lump it."

I'm not normally a jealous person, and my pendulum does not swing the other way—not that I judge, mind you—but Agnes was my best friend, and it was my duty to make sure she stayed that way. This was for her sake, as well as mine.

"How long is she staying?"

"Well, that's the thing: she and Sam got into a slight misunderstanding—"

"You mean a big fight?"

"And how. At one point she climbed out of a second-story

window and threatened to jump. It was horrible; Sam just egged her on. 'Go ahead and jump,' he said. 'You don't weigh as much anymore; it won't harm the sidewalk.'"

"That's awful! So what did she do? I mean, obviously, she didn't—right?"

"Right. But when she backed down and wanted to just get away, she couldn't because he'd hidden the car keys. He did it to be mean, of course."

"What a grump."

"It was awful being around him, to hear her tell it. Anyway, she had to ride his bicycle all the way over here, but first she had to fix a flat—pump it up and all that. But since it's almost eight miles out here she decided to take a short cut across the Neiderlanders' pasture, which at night, as you know, is as dark as the ace of spades."

"You know I don't play with face cards, dear, as they are used for gambling; I only play Rook."

"Yes, well, she hit a stump—it was only a little one, but enough to cause her to fall on her rump. Somehow she ended up in the old village dump. It was the funniest thing—well, to hear her tell it at any rate."

I sighed. "Well played, Agnes. Now, can we finally get back to business?"

"Business?"

"Peering into windows in the dead of night. Are you in, or are you out?"

"But I can't," she wailed. "What am I supposed to do, kick her out?"

Frankly, I was so grateful that it was someone else wailing for a change, instead of me, that I lowered my guard and let bad judgment prevail. "Bring her along, dear."

"What?"

"Please, don't make me say it again. Fill a Ziploc bag with crumpets and meet me at the police station in ten minutes."

"You got it," Agnes practically shouted in my ear.

"Oh, and one more thing: tell her to bring the trumpet with her. Who knows, but it might come in handy?"

12

I'd never spent much time around the harlot Dorothy Yoder. And although I probably shouldn't admit this, she was actually a whole lot of fun. Once on the road to Bedford she put away her bag of crumpets and joined right in with our game of I Spy with My Little Eye. But since just about everything Dorothy picked was sexually suggestive, poor Agnes, who had never known a man in the biblical sense, was at a distinct disadvantage.

Strung along the Pennsylvania Turnpike like a strip of discarded Christmas tree garland, Bedford is a bustling city of four thousand or more. The downtown area, which snakes through the valley, is fairly cohesive, but the residential neighborhoods cling to the hills in disjointed patches. Actually, we call these hills "mountains" hereabouts, a fact that elicits hoots of derision from West Coast visitors (who have apparently left their manners behind).

At any rate, Pernicious Yoder III, being a wealthy bank manager, lived east of town high atop Evitts Mountain, in what I've heard described as a pseudo-Tudor mansion. Stone columns flanked the quarter-circle drive, and flickering gas lanterns illuminated a massive front door beneath the portico. It was an imposing residence, but a trifle cliché if you ask me. Now, a replica of the Taj Mahal, or a mini-Versailles, *that* would have been interesting.

"Wow," Agnes said in a hushed tone. One would have thought she'd never been anywhere—which she hadn't.

"Good grief," Dorothy said, "we're not stopping here, are we?"

"Not exactly," I said. "I'm going to pull over next to the woods up there, and we'll walk back."

"But we can't!"

"Yes, we can. Your legs work perfectly well now, and I know for a fact that Agnes is as healthy as a horse—no offense, Agnes, dear."

"Neeeiiigh."

"You see? She even has a sense of humor about it. So come, ladies, times a-wasting."

Dorothy's fingers dug into my shoulder like the claws of a giant prehistoric elephant eagle—had such a thing really existed, which, of course, it didn't. "You're not hearing me, Yoder. I can't be seen near that house."

Since she'd spit her words out like nails from a gun, I spit some back to her. "Pray tell, why not?"

"Because Perni and I—uh—well, were intimate for a while and we sort of used his house as a rendezvous place while his wife was out of town visiting her sister. Even if he doesn't see me, his neighbors might."

One woman gasping for breath in a closed automobile can use up a significant amount of oxygen, but two of them—gaping and rasping like a pair of giant banked fish—present a life-threatening situation. Heroically, I managed to lower three of the four automatic windows. Even then I had to wait until the initial shock wave passed before I could speak.

"You *what*?"

"Oh, get over it, Magdalena. You know I had a difficult period of adjustment, and you better than anyone should know that the Bible commands us not to judge, unless we ourselves be judged."

"But I was an *inadvertent* adulteress. I didn't have a clue that Aaron Miller was married."

"Did you ever ask him?"

"What? Of course not! Why would I have done that? He moved back to the family farm across from me, he was obviously single, he— Well, I certainly didn't know he had a wife who was out of town."

"I didn't know Pernicious did either," Dorothy hissed, "until after the fact."

"That may be so," Agnes said, "but you knew that you were married, and to his cousin to boot."

"Fourth cousin, twice removed, and only on his father's side," Dorothy said, but she'd suddenly lost some of her steam.

Good old Agnes. I could always count on her loyalty, and she on mine. We were sisters joined at the hip—metaphorically, at least. Yes, I had a real flesh-and-blood sister, but she languished in the state penitentiary, having been convicted of aiding and abetting the escape of an accused murderer, the diabolical Melvin Stoltzfus (who, I'd just learned, was my biological brother).

"Whatever the case may be," I said in my best conciliatory tone, "you can put your time as a two-timing trollop to good use and tell us the layout of the house. It will make our reconnaissance mission so much easier."

"Reconnaissance?" Agnes squawked.

"Perhaps that was an echo I just heard," I said, not unpleasantly. "But if not, you might want to speak up, Agnes; there's a woman in Altoona who couldn't make out what you said."

Agnes put her right index finger to her lips. "Shhh. But I just want to go on record, Magdalena, as saying this might be the dumbest idea you've ever had, and you've had some doozies."

I smiled happily. "I have, haven't I?" I turned to the floozy in the backseat. "You're our lookout. My cell number is 555-3289. I've got it on buzzer. Now come on, ladies, let's rock and roll."

"Magdalena, you've never rocked and rolled in your life."

We were crouched on all fours in the shadow of a large rhododendron, but still only inches from the house and a large picture window. This was no time to be having a conversation, much less a highly charged, emotional one like this.

"I have so," I hissed.

"Oh, yeah? A good Mennonite girl like you? You once told me that premarital sex was wrong because it might lead to dancing."

"I did not! I said that having sex while standing up could lead to dancing."

There followed a minute of blessed silence—well, relatively speaking. Agnes is a heavy breather under the best of circumstances, and we'd had to make a mad dash across a patch of well-lit yard to get to our current position. But, like I said, it was only a minute.

"Do you mean," she said "that it *is* possible to have sex while standing up? I thought that was only a myth."

"A *myth*? Where does one hear such myths?"

"Well, if you must know, at my VALID meetings."

Agnes belongs to a support group of like-minded spinsters who call themselves the Virgin Awesome Ladies of Impeccable Demeanor. However, since I am her very best friend in the entire world, I have been known to tease her, and may have even hinted that the acronym stood for Vapid Avaricious Lounge-lizards of Intense Desire.

I sighed. "Yes—theoretically it is possible to have sex in a standing position, not that I'm speaking from personal experience, you understand. But trust me, don't believe those stories about honeymooners swinging from chandeliers. A moving target is indeed hard to hit, and when the bough breaks—well, in this case, the chandelier chain—down will come Magda—I mean baby, crystals and all."

"You didn't!"

It was time to change subjects. "Do you want to hear about my dancing or not?"

"Yeah, sure."

I knew she didn't believe me, but it was true. And although it may seem very strange to some people that I should take the time to share such a shocking, and personal, experience whilst sniffing around in another Yoder's bush, this was one sin I had yet to come to grips with, and I needed to get it off my bony chest.

"Remember Alice Gillespie's sweet sixteen party?"

"Of course, I do. Even we liberal Mennonites didn't have those back then, but Alice was a Methodist; they got to do everything."

"Did you go?"

"You bet. The Gillespies rented the Holderman barn and fixed it up to look like the high school gym. Then they brought in this rock band from Pittsburgh, and— Oh, wait a minute. You being an Old Order Mennonite—you didn't go, did you?"

I let the Devil take over and gave her a wicked grin as I recalled my shameful behavior that night. "That's what you think. I told my parents I was going to an all-night Bible study over in Summerville with Judy Bontrager, except that I didn't. You see, Judy had just gotten her license. Anyway, we went to the party as well, only we hung out by the henhouse with the rest of the kids who wanted to come, but who weren't supposed to be there."

"You didn't!" I heard admiration in Agnes's voice like I'd never heard before.

"There must have been fifteen or twenty of us by the henhouse—hiding in the shadows, like we are here. But we could still hear the music. Nice and loud too, because we were downwind from the barn. At any rate, at first we just stood around and mostly talked about how cool it was that we had all sneaked away from our parents, but then Marlene Jacobs began moving to the beat, and the next thing you knew we were all twisting the night away."

"You weren't!"

"But I was," I whispered. "I even shimmied and shook. My nimble young body did *gyre and gimble in the wabe.*"

"No way!"

"Way," I said, even now electrified by thought of all that pulsating energy flowing through and not going to waste. "And the momwraths outgabe," I added.

"Uh—I think now you've lost me."

"You may not be the only one. But do you at least believe me?"

"Yes, and I hate you."

"I beg your pardon?"

"Magdalena, you have everything. You have a handsome husband, you have a child, you know what it's like to swing from a chandelier, and now I find out that you've even danced. I don't know why you even bother to be friends with me. Face it: we have nothing in common."

"Don't be silly, dear, of course we do; we're both fond of *moi.*"

"I can't believe you said that."

"I was only trying to be fun—will you look at that!"

We'd been keeping watch on a living room, or perhaps a den, but it had suddenly sprung to life as Pernicious Yoder III entered, followed by a young woman. It took me a moment to recognize Amy, the young teller, because this evening she was dressed casually in jeans and an Obama '08 sweatshirt. Her hair was pulled back in a ponytail that rode much too high— Okay, I didn't recognize her at all until I heard her name spoken.

"Thanks for coming, Miss Neubrander," Pernicious said. "I know this is highly irregular, and just so you don't feel too uncomfortable, I want you to know that Mrs. Yoder is in her bedroom watching television."

"Yes, sir."

Pernicious gestured for her to sit, which she did, perching like a bird on the edge of a red-and-green-checked wingback chair. He, however, remained standing. He who looms has the most power, I mused.

"I suppose you're worried," he said, "that I might have some bad news for you. Especially given this economy—Fanny Mae, Freddy Mac—they sound like the Bobbsey Twins, heh, heh. Of course you're too young to remember those books—so am I, as a matter of fact, but I found a box of them in the attic at my grandparents' lake house when I was a boy. Forgive me. The older I get, the more I tend to ramble."

"That's ridiculous," I hissed under my breath. "That man's no older than I am."

"So old?" Agnes said, absolutely deadpan.

I elbowed her—gently, of course. "Shhh."

"The thing is," Pernicious continued to prattle, "I've come to regard you as a very valuable employee. Very valuable, indeed."

Amy smiled, but she didn't look happy. "Thank you, sir. I try my best."

"Yes, well, we at First Farmer's Bank like to reward our valuable employees, to let them know just how much we appreciate them. Therefore, it is my pleasure to inform you that you are being offered a promotion. Your new title will be Chief Assistant Clerk in Training and it comes with a salary increase of six percent."

Amy gasped softly, touching her bosom with her right hand.

"But, of course, Miss Neubrander, with a new pay grade come new responsibilities. You realize that, don't you?" Pernicious paused and peered at Amy like a heron about to pounce on a fish.

"Yes, sir. Uh—what sort of duties, sir? I am a Christian, you know."

Pernicious, who in my book is a wicked man, snickered. "It's not what you think, young lady. I told you that Mrs. Yoder is in the next room watching her favorite mind-numbing shows. *American Idol*—ha! What a load of crap. Those kids can't sing a note, if you ask me. Do you sing, Amy?"

"I'm in the church choir, sir—if that counts."

"Indeed, it does! Sing something for me, Amy."

"Here? Now?" The poor child looked like she was about to be executed, and had been asked to choose between hanging and lethal injection.

"No, a century from now on the moon. Of course here and now! Come on, let me hear something. Anything—one of your favorite hymns. Okay, I'll give you a minute to think about it. In the meantime, I have another favor to ask you."

Amy squirmed, pushing her way to the rear of the wingback. "Yes, sir."

"Don't look so scared, Amy. All I'm asking is that, from here on out, any comments you make—to *anyone*—concerning the— uh—unfortunate event be cleared by me first."

I couldn't believe my ears! The *unfortunate* event had almost gotten the poor girl killed. Why on earth would Pernicious put a gag order on something that was a matter of public record anyway?

The answer had to lie in inbreeding. When we become our

own cousins, there is a danger that our thinking will become muddled, especially as we age, which Pernicious, by his own admission, felt he was doing. Shortly after her fiftieth birthday Cousin Feodora Yoder became convinced she was married to her toaster oven. It was a harmless delusion until she took it to bed, where it shorted out, causing second-degree burns on parts of her body that even the Good Lord hadn't seen.

But Amy was nodding like one of those toy dogs folks used to put in the rear windows of their cars. "Yes, sir. I understand, sir."

"Good. Then we have a deal." Pernicious bent stiffly to give her a quick pat on the knee. "Now sing, Amy."

"Well—"

"Why don't you stand, first—like you're in choir practice?"

"All right." Amy appeared to struggle to her feet, but once up, she puffed out her diaphragm, threw back her head, and belted out the most awesome, spine-tingling version of "How Great Thou Art" that I have ever heard. I could tell that Pernicious was impressed, but I'm sure that angels in Heaven were as well; in fact, quite possibly they were a mite jealous.

Amy's voice was glorious. There is no other way to describe it—okay, maybe it was a bit like Streisand on steroids. So inspired was I, so uplifted spiritually, that I forgot who and where I was and gave myself over to the moment. That is to say, I stood up and sang along with her.

Unfortunately, it's been said that my voice is reminiscent of a female donkey in heat, and if it doesn't attract any handsome burros, it at least sets dogs to barking as far as a mile away. That night was no different than any other, which meant I may have hit a few sour notes. Perhaps I hit only sour notes and at an unearthly, earsplitting pitch—but just perhaps.

What matters is that when Pernicious Yoder III glanced out the picture window and saw yours truly violating his bush, he was not a happy man.

13

For a hoochie mama, Dorothy made a great getaway driver. Or maybe it was precisely because she had so much experience fleeing from irate wives. At any rate, when she spied the two of us running to beat the band, arms and legs flailing, and one of us puffing like the Little Engine That Could, our town's legendary harlot hopped into the driver's seat and revved up the engine. The second the door slammed shut on Agnes's prodigious posterior, Dorothy stomped on the accelerator and we shot down the face of Evitts Mountain like an out-of-control carnival ride. Although I've no way to prove it, if I was a wagering woman ('tis a sin to do so), I'd lay money on the fact that we skipped a few hairpin curves, traveling as we did in a more or less straight line.

Nevertheless, if Pernicious Yoder III was following us, with Dorothy at the wheel, he was plumb out of luck. Not only did she know her way around Bedford, but she knew every nook and cranny. In one particularly dark and ominous cranny, she finally stopped.

"Okay, now what?"

"I think I peed my pants," Agnes said.

"Oh Agnes, you didn't," I wailed, past caring what others thought of my distressed vocalizations.

"Was that fun, or what?" Dorothy said.

"You enjoyed that?" I said.

"Heck, yeah. I haven't had so much fun since Sam and I were kids, and I used to drive getaway for him when he'd paint the overpass."

"That was *Sam*? My cousin Sam of grocery-store infamy?"

"Why do you think the other kids called him 'Cop'? It stood for 'Champion Overpass Painter.'"

"But what he painted was mostly love messages to me!"

"Yeah, well, I couldn't control everything he did—although I did try my level best. That's why I had to finally marry him. But even *that* couldn't stop him from thinking of you; he'd call your name out at that critical moment."

"What moment would that be?" Agnes said.

"I think I'm going to be sick," I said.

"Oh shut up, Magdalena," Dorothy said. "It's *you* who makes me sick. As long as I've known you—which is my entire life—you've played the part of the hapless victim. First you thought you were too tall, too skinny, too ugly, yet all the while you really were the most beautiful girl this five-horse town—and I mean that literally—has ever seen. You could have gotten any boy you wanted, but oh no, you thought you were too good for any locals."

"*What*?"

"It's true, Magdalena," Agnes said. "In high school all the boys were throwing themselves at you just like the skinny girls threw their Twinkies and Hostess fruit pies at me."

"Well, I wasn't even allowed to group date until I was sixteen, so there."

"Then what did you do?" Dorothy said.

"Well, you have to admit, most of the Hernia boys were rather—"

"There you go," she snapped, "dismissing the locals as beneath you."

"Although she did end up marrying one," Agnes said. "I mean, Aaron Miller counts, because even though he moved away for a long time, he was born and raised here."

"Thanks," I said.

"For nothing," Dorothy said, "because he just proves my point. Aaron Miller just happens to be the most handsome man to walk the face of the earth. And *who* did he pick to commit adultery with?"

"*Whom!*" I screamed. "And that was only pseudo-adultery, given the fact that one party"—that would be I—"was as innocent as a wide-stanced senator."

Dorothy snorted. "If you say so. But, Magdalena, as you well know, Aaron Miller is a bit like a five-dollar present that's been wrapped in ten-dollar paper and topped with a twenty-dollar bow. To say that he's *short* on charm would be putting it kindly."

I may be as dense as balsa wood, but a lot more gets through than folks give me credit for. "Wait just one Mennonite minute. Are you saying that you and Aaron—well, you know? Now *that* would be adultery."

"Yes, that's what exactly what I'm saying. Last month when I flew to Minnesota to see my sister, I purposely looked up Aaron—just to see if he was still looking so hot—and you know what? He was an absolute stud muffin! Well, one thing led to another and we burned a hole in that mattress, I'm telling you."

"If you don't mind me saying so," Agnes said, "smoking in bed is very dangerous."

"We weren't smoking cigarettes," Dorothy said with a surprising amount of patience. "We were, however, extremely active. By the way, Magdalena, your ex-pseudo-husband and what's her name were already separated and headed for divorce court. I may be an out-of-control nymphomaniac, but I'm no home wrecker."

"And I'm still a virgin," Agnes sobbed.

"There, there," I said and, reaching into the backseat, patted one of her knees. "Maybe you and Dorothy can average your scores—help bring her down below a hundred."

"Very funny," Dorothy said, but she didn't deny it. "What do we do now?"

"We drive over to Amy's house and put the screws to her."

"The screws?"

"It's a slight exaggeration," Agnes said. "The screws Magdalena uses fit into table-mounted brackets so that method can only be done at her house. On the road—like this—she prefers to use flaming slivers of bamboo inserted under the fingernails."

"Oh cool," Dorothy said.

Amy lived in a third-floor walkup apartment in what might euphemistically be referred to as a working-class neighborhood. The stairwell smelled predominantly of cabbage, with just a trace of urine. It was a heady but familiar bouquet, for I had interviewed many suspects in her circumstances while working previous cases.

Apparently the girl had just beaten us home, because she was still wearing her coat when she answered the door. I saw the hesitation in her eyes before she tried to slam it shut. Not only was this an invitation for me to stay, but it gave me an opportunity to slip one of my slender size elevens in the open space, making it impossible for her to close the door all the way.

She sighed and rolled her robin's egg blue eyes. "You might as well come in, Magdalena. Lord only knows, if I don't let you,

you'd camp out there all night. You'd probably even light a fire and roast marshmallows."

"And weenies. I enjoy grilling weenies—just like I do grilling people. I grill them until they split open at the seams and threaten to fall into the flames."

"I didn't know weenies had seams."

"Hmm. Well, in any case, here I am as big as life and twice as ugly. Good call, though."

"Some choice. And you may as well let Agnes in, as well as the Whore of Hernia."

I put my hands on my hips. "Whore of Hernia? Now *that's* rude! I'll have you know she's our resident harlot, not whore. You don't take money for sexual favors, do you, Dorothy?"

The principal woman under discussion pushed me aside. "That all depends," she said in a disgustingly throaty voice. She looked Amy up and down. "What did you have in mind, sister?"

"Ooh," Agnes said, "I think I'm going to be sick."

"Cool it," I snapped to Dorothy. I gave Agnes the "settle down" sign with my hands. "Ladies, I'm here to discuss the day of the attempted bank robbery, not to pimp out my grocer's wife."

Amy laughed nervously. "Magdalena, no Mennonite I know would use such language—not even an ex-Mennonite. Are you sure you're not a fraud?"

I held out my wrist. "Prick me, if you will, and see my Mennonite blood. And just two generations ago it was Amish. But all that's beside the point. We're here because we saw you with Pernicious Yoder III. We heard you, in fact. The two of you were striking a deal."

Amy turned the color of congealed bacon fat. "You were spying on me!"

"Indeed, as is my duty."

"He's my boss. I work for him, remember? It's *my* duty to do what he says."

"Even if you know it's wrong?"

She peeled off her coat and threw it over the back of a sagging and somewhat hideous red-and-green-plaid armchair. Then she yanked off her shoes and tossed them toward an open doorway. The polite, neat, young cashier that I had been so fond of in the past was gone, replaced by a slovenly young thing who lacked principles.

"Look, Miss Yoder, I didn't invite you here, and I certainly don't want to hear you lecture. Either you leave on your own accord now, or I'm going to have to call the police."

"The police?" Agnes began wringing her hands like she was trying to extract water. "Magdalena, we have to go."

"Oh, give it a rest," Dorothy said impatiently. She unbuttoned the top button of her blouse and set to work on shortening her bra straps. "Up you go, girls—Nancy, Louise. If calling the police is what she wants, you two need to be ready to greet them."

Agnes was aghast. "They have names?"

"Don't yours?"

"Of course not! Magdalena, do your whatchamacallits have names?"

"They're called breasts," Dorothy hissed.

Although Agnes was my very best friend in the entire world, I wasn't about to squeal on Esmeralda and Hermione—and certainly not with Dorothy and Amy listening. Besides, an idea had been forming in my little pumpkin brain that could be beneficial to both Amy and me. To everyone in my family as a matter of fact. And not only that—and this is *not* a Christian attitude, and I have since repented of it—what I was about to propose would really stick it to Pernicious Yoder III.

"Ladies," I said, clapping my hands, "this is no time for girl talk." I turned to Amy with a smile that stretched painfully from ear to ear. "Whatever he's paying you, I'll double it."

The lass recoiled as if I were the Devil. "What did you say?"

"I said that I'll double your pay—whatever it is."

"Do you want me to work for you?"

"Yes, as a matter of fact, I do. Running an inn involves a great deal of bookkeeping and accounting, as well as greeting customers, and frankly, I don't have the time to do either anymore." I swallowed a tablespoon of annoyance before continuing. "With your bubbly personality and keen mind, I see you as a great fit."

"*Really?*" Amy said.

"I think I'm going to puke," Dorothy said.

"It couldn't have been the crumpets," Agnes said. "But just so you know, Dorothy, I have a good lawyer."

I ignored the ignoramus asides. "Really," I said. "You'll be making *twice* the money; think about it."

"Yes, but he offered me a promotion—with a new title: Chief Assistant Clerk in Training. Do you know how long I've been waiting for that title?"

"Far too long, I'm sure. I tell you what: I was originally going to hire you as Chief Front Desk Manager in Training, but I am going to give you an instant, on the spot, promotion to Front Desk *Supervisor*."

"But that's a shorter title."

"Exactly. The shorter the title, the higher the position. Think about it—*Vice* President Biden, but President Obama. In no time at all you'll be working your way up to plain old just supervisor."

"I'd take the deal if I were you," Dorothy said. "Magdalena's husband is a hunk—and then some. Maybe you'll get lucky."

"Ooh," Agnes squealed, "pop her one."

"Okay, I'll do it," Amy said. "But what exactly is it that you want from me?"

I took off my shoes as well as my coat. "Make me a cup of hot cocoa, dear. And don't forget to float lots of those miniature marshmallows on it—oh, and I'd like some ladyfingers to go with it. You know, for dunking."

"Some what?"

"Ladyfingers. They're a kind of cookie."

"I've never heard of them. But I have some windmill cookies with almond slivers in them. And I might still have some ginger-snaps."

"Bring them both, dear. After all, I'm one of those folks with a one-word title."

"Which is?"

"Boss."

" 'Bossy' is more like it," someone said, but I ignored whoever it was. With hot cocoa and two kinds of cookies in my near future, I could afford to be generous.

14

Amy was adamant about having never seen any of the bank robbers before. She said that about a quarter of her customers were Amish, most of them men. All told, she said, she knew the names and faces of at least eighty percent of the people she dealt with, because they were repeat customers. First Farmer's Bank was a workingman's institution, where laborers came to store their hard-earned money in lieu of tucking it in the mattress. It didn't offer fancy services, and it had no gimmicks.

When I grilled her about the way Pernicious reacted to the attempted robbery, Amy got green in the face, and for a moment, it looked like she was going to lose the two gingersnaps and one windmill cookie she'd eaten. Wisely, I held my plate well away and aloft.

"I can't ascribe motives to someone else's behavior," she snapped.

"Of course you can, dear. Why, just now I'd say you're trying to cover something up."

"I bet she's having an affair," Dorothy mumbled.

Agnes gasped. "Is that true? I swear, there's more hanky-panky going on in this world than I ever dreamed of."

"Why don't you two take a walk?" I said. "You know what they say about a watched pot and all that."

"She's not a pot," Agnes pouted.

"Of course not," I said, "but the same principle applies to weenies."

"Weenies?"

"*Grilled* weenies," I growled. "Now am-scray, the two of you!"

I could see the light click on in her head. "All right," she said, "but you don't have to be rude about it."

"Magdalena's nuts," Dorothy said, but I chose not to take offense. After all, it wasn't every day that a genuine harlot called me names.

"Now where were we?" I said when we were alone. "Oh, yes, did Pernicious threaten you in any way?"

"Miss Yoder, are you related to him? I mean, you know, yinz have the same last name."

"*Yinz?* Amy, you're originally from Pittsburgh?"

"Yeah, I moved to Bedford when I was twelve."

"I see. To answer your question, virtually all Yoders in North America are descended from a pair of brothers who emigrated from Switzerland almost three hundred years ago. But since both our forebears settled in Pennsylvania, we are more closely related to one another than to those Yoders living in other parts of the country."

"Uh-huh. Well, it wasn't Mr. Yoder who threatened me."

"Was it the clueless guard?"

When she shook her head, her mousy brown hair parted in greasy clumps. "No. It was some guy on the phone—a foreigner, I think."

"You mean like Al Qaeda?"

"No, more like Al Canadian."

It was then that I realized that Amy, as sweet as she was, did not genetically descend from Alfred Einstein. "What? You mean, French?"

"I don't know—it was different, that's all. Anyway, he wanted to speak to Mr. Yoder, so I put him through. He called three times after that, and each time he asked for Mr. Yoder's direct number, but I refused to give it out, on account of Mr. Yoder says I'm not supposed to. Even if God calls and asks for it, he says I'm supposed to make Him wait a few minutes and then put Him through. But never to give out that number. *Ever.*"

"Why, that's just plain sacrilegious, not to mention the fact that Mr. Yoder could well be imperiling your soul. I mean, what if the Lord did call, and you put Him on hold? Think what would happen if He turned the tables on you. Let's say that you're taking off from Pittsburgh airport, headed for Charlotte, when your plane gets hit by a flock of geese. So you pray for deliverance, but God says, 'Just a minute, Amy,' so when your plane goes down, it doesn't come in for a textbook landing on top of the mighty Ohio River. It plows up mud on the bottom, and all this because you put the Good Lord on hold."

"Holy crap, Miss Yoder, I hadn't thought of that!"

"That's no reason to swear, dear. It's just something to think about. Like wearing underwear at all times."

She chuckled knowingly. "Yeah, in case I get hit by a car."

"No, in case of the rapture. When you're floating up to Heaven, you don't want the people left behind getting some final thrills they don't deserve, do you? And of course this underwear rule applies doubly to men. I mean all that business swinging free in the breeze—what if they hit a tree branch? No, a rupture during the rapture must surely be avoided."

"Miss Yoder, you're awful!"

"Just practical, dear. Think how embarrassed that Spears woman would have been."

"Somehow I don't think so—I mean I think she intended for people to get a peek. Anyway, are you going to let me finish?"

"Go for it!" I cried.

"Miss Yoder, you're weird." The greasy locks got another workout. "As I was about to say, the fourth time that foreigner called—after he spoke to Mr. Yoder—he starts lecturing me, telling me my phone manners aren't what they should be. *Then* he tells me that it was my fault that I got shot in the robbery attempt. *My* fault! Can you imagine that?"

"I can, but only because I've met some folks in my time who are even weirder than I." Really, the nerve of that whippersnapper calling me weird, and here I always thought she was such a pleasant young woman.

"Hey, you're not the one who should be bent out of shape. I was just doing my job when those three men came in and pulled out their guns. But that's not the whole thing!" She paused to glance out the window. "You see, this guy on the phone said that I wasn't allowed to say one more word about what happened that day to anyone—or *else*."

"Or else what?"

"You know." She made a slicing motion across her soft white throat.

"He *said* that?"

"Well, maybe not in so many words, but isn't that what 'or else' means?"

I thought back to when Mama used to threaten me with those very same words. Would she have sliced my scrawny tanned throat for not picking up my woolen stockings, or for sticking the hanger through only one side of my dress, or for leaving a soap ring around the edge of the tub, or for answering her nervous calls as slow as a "drugged seven-year itch"? Somehow I don't think so. However, she would have—and did—warm my bottom with a willow switch or, if one of those wasn't handy, the palm of her hand.

"What did you say in response?" I asked.

"I hung up. Then I went to see Mr. Yoder, only he said I should stop making things up—if I wanted to keep my job."

"Now *that* sounds like an 'or else' to me."

"Huh?"

"Go on, dear."

"Well, there isn't much more to tell, because I kept my mouth shut. Even when the police came a third and a fourth time, I just kept giving them the same old answers, even if that did make them kind of pissed— Oops. Sorry, Miss Yoder."

I scowled obligingly. "Just don't let it happen again. Foul language is indicative of either a foul brain or poor dental hygiene. Either way, it is not to be tolerated."

"Forgive me, Miss Yoder, but you're such a prude."

"And you're such a disappointment, dear. You're not at all like the sweet young thing that used to work behind the counter at First Farmer's."

"I guess a bullet wound to the arm will do that—make one rough around the edges, I mean. Or maybe this is the real me. Anyway, you seem to be missing the point."

I sighed, before slapping my own mouth. I did it gently, of course. She was quite right on that score. It wasn't the first time that my priggish, obsessive-compulsive need for civilized discourse had led me down meandering paths of judgmental verbiage.

"Please elaborate, dear. Nary a word shall pass these shriveled lips till thou hast completed thy elucidation."

"Huh?"

"I'll keep my mouth shut and let you talk."

"Yeah, okay. Well, all I'm saying is that Mr. Yoder knows

something about the bank robbers that he's not saying, which is funny, on account of he didn't see them except for on the surveillance tape. And someone is threatening him if he goes to the police, and now I'm starting to feel the same kind of pressure. So you know what? I accept your offer, Miss Yoder—only you gotta give me medical insurance too."

"If you stop saying 'gotta.' I run a high-end business."

"Whatever. And I want a uniform."

Now that was a pleasant surprise. Who would have thought? I hadn't bothered to suggest it, being positive that she'd reject the whole idea as being too controlling.

"What a great idea, dear. Of course, we wouldn't want you to dress like a traditional Amish woman, but in something simple and modern—like a waitress uniform."

"Why not as an Amish woman?"

I smiled wickedly. "Well, our local Amish are amongst the most conservative in the world. Their clothes are all handmade and take hours upon hours to complete. Why, the bonnets are masterpieces, with hundreds of little pleats that require thousands of stitches. Of course, you'd be a huge hit with the guests in that getup, but I could never ask you to dress in something so quaint."

"I'll do it."

"Mmm—I don't know. I'd have to locate an Amish seamstress who would be willing to sew an outfit for the English—that's what they call us—and it won't be easy. And of course, you'll need two so that you can launder one and still wear the other. That could cost a pretty penny because some of these Amish have really wised up to the ways of the world when it comes to commerce."

"Please let me do it, Miss Yoder. You can take the uniforms out of my salary. *Please*."

"Oh, all right. Why not? But you have to wear the clunky

shoes too, and no complaining when the weather gets hot. A good Amish woman is all about yielding to authority. And that rule applies to fake Amish women as well."

"You've got yourself a deal!" Amy cried happily, and would have thrown herself into my arms, had I not even more quickly placed my arms across my bounteous bosom. Five hundred years of inbreeding has rendered me incapable of both giving and receiving hugs without putting a great deal of thought and effort into them. Above all, hugs must be accompanied by a good deal of backslapping, lest they degenerate into dancing.

"Yes, a deal," I said. I also had an idea. At that point it was just the kernel of a theory, a seed barely sprouted in the rich furrows of my brain. As there were numerous things germinating, and thriving, in there, including a number of weeds, I wasn't about to get too excited about this one, but still—a cotyledon was better than nothing. "I'll get started on finding a seamstress first thing tomorrow morning," I said.

Freni Hostetler, my dear friend and much convoluted (our family tree, not her) kinswoman, is not a morning person. Neither is she particularly an afternoon, evening, or night person. One can usually tell by the way she bangs my pots and pans around if she has had a good night, or perhaps rolled off the side of her bed.

That morning the din in the kitchen sounded like a pitched battle between the ancient Greeks and the Romans, both sides wearing full body armor. If we had been alone, I might have been tempted to ignore the clanking and clanging out of much-deserved spite—for a few minutes at least. After all, my husband, who hails from Manhattan, can sleep through anything, and I mean that literally. Last summer he slept through a thunderstorm so bodacious it woke the dead in three surrounding counties and rattled fillings loose in the teeth of dozens of Herniaites—as we refer to ourselves.

But guests who are paying through the nose expect the luxury of sleeping in a little bit, just as long as those same guests haven't signed up for milking duties. A full udder, just like a full bladder, can be a painful thing, and emptying it cannot be put off. Knowing, as I did, that not everyone had volunteered to rise with the cows, I scurried into the kitchen to try to calm the storm.

"Freni," I managed to hiss without a single "S," in the tradition of many established novelists. Of course, she didn't hear me, so I shouted through cupped hands, "Freni!"

Two pot lids froze in midair and the stout woman turned slowly. "So, finally, the beauty sleep is over?"

"Yes. At six thirty, I'm as beautiful as I'll ever need to be. How about you?"

"Ach, we Amish don't care about such things; you know that."

"That's true. But you obviously care a great deal about something else at the moment. What is it?"

Freni stared at me through lenses as thick as the bottoms of the old nickel Coke bottles. "That woman, she drives me up the walls, yah?"

"Several walls simultaneously?"

I could feel her stare intensify. "Always the riddles, Magdalena."

"That woman," I said, "is your dear, sweet daughter-in-law, Barbara. And the only reason you don't like her is that she's from Iowa—and she's married to your son, Jonathan."

"And she is too tall, yah?"

"Too tall for what? In September you had her picking apples from the top of your tree, and she didn't even have to use a ladder."

"Yah, and she cleans good the dust from the top of my cupboard."

"You see, she's indispensable. Not to mention that she gave birth to your three grandbabies, whom you absolutely adore, and two of whom take after their mother."

"Yah, maybe they will be too tall as well."

"Freni, count your blessings. You know how much Barbara misses her family in Iowa, and your precious Jonathan would do anything to please her. I think you're fortunate that she hasn't picked up stakes and heeded the words of Horace Greeley."

Despite the smudges of grease and flour on her lenses, I could tell that Freni was blinking. "What words?"

"Just silly unimportant words." It was time to change the subject. "Freni, do you know any Amish women who could sew a complete traditional outfit for me?"

She blinked again, but then like a faulty headlamp that had finally started to function, her face was transformed into a circle of beaming light. "You are the daughter I never had, yah? But still, you want to be Amish! For once I do not know what to say."

"Oh Freni, alas, 'tis true. I am not the lass of thy loins—would that I were—but thou must not misconstrue my motives for acquiring the aforementioned garment."

"And now more riddles."

"No riddles. I just want to know the name of a good seamstress. You see, I've hired a girl for the front desk, and I want to get her a nice authentic Amish outfit."

Poof! The glowing orb of light was extinguished, and it was all my fault—except that it wasn't; Freni should know that I will never become an Amish woman. Amish women don't shave their legs, or under their arms, or their mustaches—not that I need to do that quite yet. And they certainly don't drive cars, and they have to be subservient to their husbands, which, of course, any good Christian wife should be, just not to *that* degree, and they don't get to have air-conditioning, which surely ranks among one of God's greatest gifts—

"Magdalena! Are you out there?"

"*What?*"

"You are out in the spaces of your mind, yah?"

"I'm fine. Just prone to daydreaming—as is my wont."

Freni nodded, which is quite a feat, given that she has no neck. "You have always many such dreams. Now tell me about this girl. Is she a good Christian?"

I was taken aback. That was one thing I had failed to ask. Ding dang, where were my standards these days? On the other hand, ever since I'd said "I do" to an upstanding Jewish man, I felt uneasy about inquiring about other folks' religious affiliations before agreeing to do business with them. Such inquiries—very discreet, of course—were still common amongst my acquaintances. There was even a Christian business phone book of sorts that I had seen in circulation, although I personally refused to consult it.

After all, if given the choice—and this still a free country—who in Hernia wouldn't prefer to buy their shoes or plumbing supplies from a good Christian than from a nonbeliever? And just to set the record straight, our good folk were not just discriminating against Jews, Muslims, and Hindus, but anyone who was not "born again"—i.e., the Roman Catholics and Episcopalians.

I cringed dramatically. "Oops. I'm sorry, Freni, but Amy is a heathen."

"Ach!" She dropped both pot lids as she threw her pudgy hands up to shield her face from impending evil. Then on second thought, she abruptly dropped them. "You are joking. Yah?"

"Oh no, I'm quite serious. This woman's a card-carrying member of PAPA—Pagan American Princess Association."

Freni gasped. "Get behind me, Satan!"

"Speaking of whom," I said casually, "I was thinking of opening a snack bar in the lobby that Amy could run. We could stock it with Devil's food cupcakes, deviled eggs—"

Freni was beside herself, which made for a crowded space in front of the stove. "Then I quit!"

It was oops for real this time; I hadn't seen this one coming. Freni has quit a grand total of 187 times. Thank heavens the last time I hired her back, I made her sign a contract stating that she would give me two weeks' notice *and* put me in touch with at least three other Amish women who could benefit from earning a little extra pocket money. Since Freni—and she does so with the greatest of humility, not to mention justification—considers herself to be the best cook between the Allegheny and the Delaware rivers, it didn't seem likely that she would have ever been able to name a replacement.

"Then quit, dear," I said calmly. "I'll mark the date on the calendar."

She tore at her apron. "I quit now."

"You can't! Remember?"

"So I signed this paper—but this was *before* you invited this heathen woman."

"Besides, dear, I was indeed just joking; I have no idea what Amy believes. For all I know she's a Holy Roller or even a Southern Baptist who believes that you're not going to Heaven because you haven't been dunked."

"Ach! This is so?"

"Well, I don't know about Baptists for sure, but there are some denominations who do believe that. At any rate, you're not quitting, so don't get your bloomers in a bunch."

Freni looked like the proverbial sheep that had been asked an algebra question. "My bloomers?"

"Your panties—your underwear. Freni, you still wear them, don't you?" Freni's particular subset of Amish is amongst the most conservative there are, and they do not wear the type of undergarments that we are generally familiar with. Instead, the women wear a heavy muslin underslip and the men don loose-fitting muslin underpants that reach to the knees. It took me many moons to talk Freni into wearing a brassiere and white cotton briefs by Hanes Her Way.

"Ach, I cannot believe—Magdalena, you are so—ach!" Freni flushed as she furiously tried to flail past me. Forsooth, given her fervor, it appeared that I was finished. Fortunately for me alliteration was not her forte, so that finally when she ceased to flounder, her speech was neither flowery nor foul.

"You make me so mad sometimes, I must spit cotton! Always the jokes, Magdalena. Always the teasing. This time I have had enough; this time I will not recommend to you the name of Mary Berkey."

"But you just did," I said gently, before clapping a hand over my big mouth.

15

Lemongrass Snowballs

Ingredients

1 cup (2 sticks) butter, softened
½ cup confectioners' sugar
1 teaspoon lemon extract or lemon baking oil
2 cups all-purpose flour
⅔ cup unsweetened coconut, fine or medium shred
2½ tablespoons lemongrass puree or 1 tablespoon lemongrass powder*
2 cups (12-ounce package) white chocolate chips, chopped and divided
Additional coconut and lemongrass powder for decoration (optional)

*Either lemongrass puree or ground powder can be used. The puree can be found in squeeze tubes in most supermarket produce sections and dry powder can be found in either the spice section or in the Asian food section of the international area.

Cooking Directions

Preheat oven to 350°F. Beat butter and sugar with an electric mixer until creamy. Add lemon oil or extract. Gradually beat in flour, coconut and lemongrass. Stir in 1½ cups white chocolate chips. Shape dough into 1-inch balls and place ½ inch apart on parchment-lined baking sheets. Bake on middle rack until cookies are set and light golden brown on bottom, 10 to 12 minutes.

Cool on baking sheets 2 minutes; remove to cooling racks to cool completely. Microwave remaining white chocolate chips in heavy-duty plastic bag, kneading at 10- to 15-second intervals, until totally melted and smooth. Cut a tiny corner from bag; squeeze to drizzle over cookies. Sprinkle with additional coconut and lemongrass powder, if desired. Refrigerate cookies for about 5 minutes or until chocolate is set. Store cookies in an airtight container at room temperature for up to 1 week.

Courtesy http://www.eatwisconsincheese.com/

16

Was I ashamed of myself for having played a joke on a seventy-six-year-old woman? Maybe just a little. Was I sorry for lying? No, because I hadn't lied; telling a fib within the confines of a joke is not lying, and I should know, because I do it all the time. Now where was I? Oh yes, the breakfast Freni had been working on was utterly ruined by her sudden departure, and I was forced to feed seven hungry, and somewhat grouchy, guests cornflakes and home-canned peaches.

"What's this?" Carl demanded, his visage as stern as ever.

"A bowl of peaches, dear. Take a couple, put them on your cornflakes, and then pass them around."

"Why would I want to do that? They look like dog crap."

"I *beg* your pardon?"

"You heard me, Miss Yoder. The brochure said that we would get a full farmer's breakfast—eggs, meat, potatoes, pancakes, toast. These aren't even peaches; they're brown balls of crap."

"It was a bad year for canning, I'll admit, and they might have been cooked a trifle long. Still, they are quite edible, so you will take at least one and then hush up about it."

Everyone in the room froze in shocked silence, most especially my beloved husband, Gabe. No doubt he thought it was that time of the month for me: time to give me wide berth, most especially if he entertained any hope of bedding yours truly in the near, or even the distant, future. Of course that was a lot of bunk, given that I am really a pussycat and not given to holding grudges, no matter how well deserved.

Since the clanking of cheap stainless-steel spoons was the only sound to be heard for an unnervingly long period of time, it behooved me to otherwise finally break the silence.

"Tiny, be a dear and pass that plate of delightfully brown toast around."

I possess extraordinary peripheral vision, and I could see Surimanda Baikal's torso stiffen. "Forgive me, Miss Yoder, but this brown is the color of your hair, dah? This toast, she is the color of *my* hair—like coal."

George Nyle and Peewee Timms, cowards both, chortled under their respective breaths.

"How very rude," I huffed. "*You* try using an institutional-size toaster that's on its last legs. Even on the medium-high setting, nothing seems to happen, but then, when you slide the gizmo up just a hair, suddenly you've got hellfire and brimstone."

Surimanda Baikal looked like President Number 43 after he'd been asked an algebra question. "What is this gizmo and brimstone?"

I am better at complaining than explaining; besides I didn't have time for a language lesson just then. This, not impatience, is why I steered the conversation in an entirely new direction.

"One of my errands this morning takes me to visit a traditional Amish woman—one who has remained virtually untouched by tourism and the modern world. After all, we are a tiny, somewhat isolated community, not at all like Lancaster. Would any of you be interested in accompanying me?"

Surimanda Baikal immediately raised her petite aristocratic hand, but the other six guests traded looks as if their glances were hot potatoes and the guests were playing a party game. Frankly this really annoyed me. It hadn't been easy to make this offer. Mary Berkey was more than likely to be skittish if I brought any English with me, and besides, not a single one of these guests was likely to add joy to my day.

I decided to pare my offer down. It had been too generous to start with, and as we all know, universal availability breeds contempt. Diamonds are coveted because the diamond industry conspires to have us believe that they are rare; the truth is, however, that these stones, which are controlled by a cartel, fill up warehouse after warehouse, and are purposely released in a trickle to the retail market.

"I've changed my mind," I said. "I'm only going to take two of you. Miss Baikal, you get to come along. The rest of you nominate one person who you think is the most deserving of this honor, and he or she should meet me at the front desk in exactly one hour. Oh, by the way, has everybody met Amy, my new receptionist?"

The subsequent buzz sounded as if a hornet's nest had been knocked loose from my barn rafters and thrown in the middle of the dining room table. It was clear to me that no one gave a hoot about Amy; all the chatter had to do with the selection of the unlucky victim.

"I met Amy," Gabe offered gallantly. He was sitting at the other end of the table, spooning sugar on our son's cornflakes. "I think she'll work out nicely."

"Her mother's hideous," I lied. "Look at the mother to see how the daughter will age; isn't that what they say?"

"Hon, you know I only have eyes for you. Besides, she's far too young for me. I would only ever consider a mature woman who knows her own mind."

My extraordinary peripheral vision gave me a glimpse of Olivia Zambezi hiking her bosom heavenward with one hand, while patting some stray hairs back into her gray coiffure with the other. How does that old saying go: hope springs eternal in even the most sagging of breasts? Well, something like that.

"Here's to my mind, dear," I said, speaking to the coffeepot in front of me. But Olivia's unseemly, not to mention pathetic, attempt to appear comely in Gabe's eyes had reminded me of the puzzle involving the transport of a goat, a wolf, and a head of cabbage. The trick is to get them all across the river in a small boat, *one* at a time, before the wolf can eat the goat, and the goat can eat the cabbage. Using this paradigm the three wives present at the table all represented wolves, the tiny blond one with the not so tiny assets stood the best chance of being the most successful predator: Gabe had a "thing" for blondes, natural or bottle.

"Tiny, dear, I pick you to come along on this morning's exciting excursion."

"Oh, thank you, Miss Yoder," she trilled in her tiny voice.

"Meanwhile, what am I supposed to do?" Peewee whined.

"Why, read a book, dear. Take a long walk. There's a wooded trail through a boulder-studded glen just across the road. Or drive into town and check Yoder's Corner Market. In the so-called produce section, you'll find a head of lettuce that bears my initials. They were carved into the stem three years ago."

"Piffle," Peewee puffed dismissively.

"She isn't kidding," Gabe said. "But you'd have more fun at Miller's feed store or watching the blacksmith shoe the Amish horses."

"That really still goes on?" Barbie asked.

"Yes, ma'am," I said. "We permit only well-dressed horses in Hernia. In fact, the farrier's name is Jimmy, so the horses all wear Jimmy's shoes."

The women groaned in unison, whereas the men looked as

if they'd been asked to name the three countries which compose North America.

"Hey," Gabe said, "now that we have someone to watch the desk, why don't I take you on a tour of the area?"

"And what about our son?" I asked archly.

"What about him?" Gabe said. "What *were* you planning to do with him?"

Caught between a rock and a hard place, I chose to lean on the rock. After all, diamonds, sapphires, rubies—they're all rocks.

"Why, he's coming with me, of course. I was checking to see if you'd thought of him."

"I want to go with my papa," Little Jacob said.

"But your mama is so much fun," I cooed.

"Yes, but Papa lets me *do* things."

I gave everyone at the table a stern look; in other words, my glare informed them, unequivocally, that they were to stop listening to what was essentially family business. "What things?" I said.

"He buys me ice cream."

"What else?"

"And candy."

"Uh-huh. What else does he do?"

"He lets me put my arm out the window."

"*What?*"

"Just his hand," Gabe said. "Every little boy needs to feel the breeze on his hand."

"Tell that to Kurt Zimmerman—or One-Armed Kurt, as the kids used to call him at school."

Gabe recoiled. "Is *that* how he lost his arm?"

"Lost it to the side of a farm truck on Yutzy Road."

Our guests gasped.

"Well that settles it," I said. "This morning our son rides with me."

*   *   *

Mary Berkey has been a single mother for the past half dozen years, ever since the day her husband suddenly disappeared, leaving her with six children under seven. One minute Lantz was there, tending to their commercial chicken operation, and the next minute he was gone. It even occurred to Mary that the rapture had taken place, leaving her behind; although why her somewhat-innocent children hadn't been caught up to Glory was a bit puzzling to her.

I mention the rapture business because it proves that I am not a nutcase for having jumped to a similar conclusion from time to time; after all, this is the way Mary and I were both brought up to think. I must confess, however, that I am as curious as a stimulus package full of cats as to what it was that Mary had done to make her think that she was undeserving of Heaven, even after she had accepted Jesus as her savior. Oh well, you know what they say about the quiet ones.

At any rate, several weeks after her husband's disappearance, Mary Berkey noticed a foul odor emanating from the tall silo in which they stored the chicken feed. She had it emptied, and sure enough there was Lantz's badly decomposed body—still dressed in his outside work clothes. An autopsy showed that the poor man had fallen into the silo from the trapdoor in the roof, and had literally "drowned" in the sifting grain.

There were those in the community who chose to believe that Lantz had committed suicide. However, as far as anyone knew, there had been no suicide note, so most of us chose to believe otherwise. After all, there were well-documented cases of men having fallen into silos while inspecting their grain levels, and subsequently suffocating. But sadly, there were even a few folks—and I am not one of them—who went so far as to speculate that perhaps Mary Berkey, in a moment of passion, may have pushed her husband through the trapdoor and into the silo. Their flimsy theory rests solely on the fact that the Lantz and Mary Berkey union, six children aside, was clearly not a match made in Heaven. While most Amish couples strive to at least present a peaceful face to the world, the Berkeys were either incapable of doing so, or else their marriage had deteriorated to the point that neither of them cared anymore.

Whether it was the stigma of a possible suicide, or the rumor that she may have murdered her husband, the sad fact is Mary Berkey would always live under a cloud of suspicion. Although no formal shunning was ordered by her bishop, Mary's in-laws (Mary's own parents were no longer alive) refused to have anything to do with her after the funeral. This harsh treatment unfortunately set the tone for others, and soon Mary and her children found themselves living on the periphery of the Amish community.

No longer able to run the chicken farm by herself, she began taking in sewing and soon developed a reputation for excellence at it. Although her fine work did nothing to enhance her social standing, or improve her relationship with her suspicious in-laws, it did keep body and soul together for her and her six children. Every Amish woman knows how to sew, and while most sew their own dresses and intricately pleated bonnets, no one in a six-county radius could do so as expertly as Mary Berkey. Eventually overworked Amish women were thinking up reasons *not* to make their outfits. So popular did Mary's expertly sewn clothes become, that in one district the bishop saw reason to ban them, citing the sin of pride inherent in their ownership.

No sooner had I pulled into the long gravel drive than the front door to the white frame house opened and a passel of kids, ranging from ages seven to fourteen, piled out. Close on their heels came Mary, a tall, angular woman, with a pinched narrow face and cobalt blue eyes. When she saw that it was me, her thin lips parted, forming a sparse smile, and she waved.

"Don't the children have school?" Tiny asked. It *was* a reasonable question.

"They're homeschooled," I said. I saw no reason to tell Tiny that the children were homeschooled because their mother was an outcast—an unofficial outcast, of course.

When we got out of the car, Little Jacob was immediately mobbed with friends. He'd played with the younger Berkey children a number of times, and they were all very fond of him. But as the ladies and I made our way up to the house over an uneven stretch of yard, badly in need of reseeding, Rudolph, the youngest Berkey, ran over and grabbed my arm. His sister Veronica, who had been chasing him, nearly knocked me over. The poor girl is built like a panzer, but alas, possesses only half the grace of a German tank—or of a war machine of any nation for that matter.

"Miss Yoder," Rudy said—rather he shouted in the way some seven-year-olds do when they're highly agitated, "why does the little Englishwoman have such big udders?"

"Don't be rude, Rudy," I snapped.

"But why?"

"They're not called 'udders,'" Veronica said between gasps. "They're called 'bossoms.'" She pronounced the word to rhyme with possums.

"Oh."

"And that's the way God made her," Veronica said.

I must admit that Tiny had a pleasant laugh. "Actually, Dr. Sayeed was running a two-for-one special, and I thought to myself, why would anyone want just one? Of course I'd want two! But when you think about it, it really is like getting them for half price, right?"

I could almost hear the wheels turn in Veronica's head as she began to process this alien information. But after a few seconds her brain spit it all back out. This was too much too soon—perhaps more than she'd ever want to know.

"Come on, Rudy, let's go see if Little Jacob wants to play with your snake."

Now *that* set off an alarm bell in my head. "That better be a real snake," I hollered after them, "and it better not be poisonous." One can never be too careful with one's children if you ask me. If one must err, 'tis better to err on the side of over-protection, because one can always loosen up. Make your kids wear their helmets when they ride their bicycles, no matter how much they complain. So what if the other kids in the neighborhood don't wear theirs? So what if they don't like you for imposing this rule on them? Tough chocolate chip cookies, that's what I say. Not wearing a helmet can result in a dead, or brain-damaged, child.

The brood's mare—I mean, mama—stepped forward. "Magdalena," Mary said, reading my large-print mind, "still you overprotect him. But I tell you, it will make the boy rebel; it will not make him safer. Boys will be boys, yah?"

There is nothing in this world guaranteed to hike my hackles quite like criticism of my parenting skills. I have given this matter much thought and have concluded that the reason for this is that my child means more to me than anyone or anything else in the entire world, including myself, and ergo I must believe that I am doing my best by him. If not, then shame, shame on me, and there isn't a healthy soul alive who enjoys a plateful of scorn.

"You raise your"—I swallowed the word "brats"—"and I'll raise mine."

"What did you say?"

I smiled broadly. "This is Surimanda Baikal from Russia, and Tiny Timms from New Jersey. For some reason Tiny is interested in dressing like an Amish woman. Of course, you'd have to put a lot of darts in the bust area—maybe even some clever metal scaffolding—but if anyone can do it, you can."

"Yah, I can. Elma Gindlesperger—she had the glands too,

you know. I made for her also the dress of much support. And a swimming costume as well."

Elma was, of course, a Mennonite of the more liberal persuasion, and *not* of the Amish faith. "Poor, poor Elma," I said. "When her cruise ship sank, she managed to stay afloat for eight days before the sharks ate her—in sight of land!"

"This is very quaint," Tiny said, sounding a mite miffed, "but do you mind if we get started?"

17

Tiny survived her bust-measuring ordeal, and Rudy's snake turned out to be a baby garter snake, which is a completely harmless garden variety. Undoubtedly more dangerous than either of these two events was my visit to the state penitentiary.

The *urgent* call had come during my absence that morning. It was a matter of life and death, my sister said. If I didn't make the two thirty afternoon visiting session, it proved I didn't love her and she would never speak to me again. While there have been more than a few times when such a threat would have been greeted as a welcome challenge, I felt something quicken in the depths of me that stirred me to action.

Now, I do believe in women's intuition, plain and simple. I've always maintained that a hunch from a woman is worth two facts from a man. I also believe that a woman's voice should be heard, despite the admonishments of the otherwise brilliant, but undeniably misogynistic, apostle from Tarsus. That said, I followed my hunch, and was quite vocal until the warden relented and agreed to add me to the list of that day's visitors.

However, since this was a maximum-security facility, I still had to endure the most rigorous and humiliating search imaginable. My torturer was a Goliath of a woman with an unpronounceable name embossed in black letters on a pearl gray badge. As her hands, which were the size of Virginia hams, moved up and down my person in the most familiar way, I felt compelled to speak out.

"My dear," I said, "I haven't felt anything quite like this since my wedding night."

"Are you complaining, lady?"

"Au contraire, I'm trying very hard not to enjoy this."

"What's that supposed to mean?"

"It means that if your left hand moves any closer to the South Pole, it could trigger an avalanche. Unfortunately, I always sing when that happens, and I'm not known to be very good at that— singing, that is."

'V'h'Neek'qQ"WA'a Smith glared at me. "Are you trying to be funny?"

"No, ma'am. I *am* trying to remain celibate."

The Virginia hams stopped their needless probing. "For all I know, you're packing a gun down there."

I sighed, anger and relief mingling like smoke from a freshly doused fire. "Do I look like the type?"

"There isn't any one type. And since you're in that strange getup, with that little hat thing on your head— Hey, where are you from anyway?"

"Hernia?"

Ms. Smith howled. "Are you putting me on?"

"I fail to see the humor in this. At least I don't have seven apostrophes in my name."

"Hey! Don't be making fun of my culture."

"Your culture? Where are you from?"

"Da hood."

"Is that near Dahomey? My church supports a missionary

family there—the Sapersteins. You wouldn't happen to know them, would you?"

"Oh, sure, I know them; I have them over to dinner every other Sunday."

"Really?"

"Look, you fool, Dahomey is now Benin, and 'da hood'— Well, I was just making that up on account of my mother got a little apostrophe crazy. I admit that. But I'll be watching you in there; this glass is one-way. Don't you be slipping your sister anything, or taking anything from her. You're allowed to hug her—but no kissing on the mouth."

"Ugh."

"You'd be surprised what people try in order to get stuff in or out."

"Stuff? Like what?"

"Cocaine mostly. One woman who normally wore a glass eye came in wearing a fake eye made of coke that had been painted with food dye to look like the real thing. But when she left I noticed that her hair was pulled down. I asked her to pull it back and whoa! You could practically see her brain."

"Well, my body parts are all real—as I think you know by now."

"And protected by the most insane underwear I've ever encountered. Where did you get that stuff—that crazy bra, in particular? From the Army Surplus Store? I mean, is that like for combat, or something?"

"It's sturdy Christian underwear, although clearly it is not invincible. I'm going to have to surf the Net for a more unassailable model."

"Girl, you have definitely lost it; I shouldn't even be letting you in here. Although"—she paused and cocked her head as she pursed her lips—"I like you."

Alarmed, I took a step back. " 'Twas only a fleeting thought, put there by Lucifer the Lustful. I beg thee, kind miss, please do not misconstrue my sexual preference."

"Say what?" 'V'h'Neek'qQ"WA'a laughed. "Go on through, before I change your mind. When you're done—or if there's any trouble—rap on the glass."

Susannah looked better than I'd ever remembered seeing her. She was dressed in orange scrubs—perhaps not her most flattering color—but at least one could see that she had legs. Also quite visible, and rather new on the scene, was the presence of a bosom. The latter was, no doubt, a result of boredom; my pseudo-anorexic sister had been packing on the pounds since her incarceration almost five years ago because she had nothing more interesting to do than to eat.

"You look positively voluptuous," I said.

My baby sister grinned. "Mama would have hated it. Right?"

"Absolutely. In fact, when I get home I'm going to drive up to Settler's Cemetery and give her the bad news."

Susannah giggled. "How fast do you think she'll spin in her grave?"

"Hopefully fast enough, and long enough, to make the U.S. less oil dependent on the Middle East."

"You see! And you said I'd never amount to anything."

"I never said that!"

"Well, you thought that."

Few things annoy me more than being told what it is I think or feel. I'm not in the habit of letting folks inside this thick skull of mine. I especially hate it when I'm being justly accused, and the injured party knows that I can't wiggle out of his or her accusation.

"And look how wrong I was; for surely you are an exemplary inmate. I mean, if not in deed, at least in your animal appetites."

"Thanks—I think. Was that sarcastic?"

"What matters is, what do you think? As Dr. Phil would say, perception is everything."

"Mags, you're still weird. You know that?"

" 'Tis a badge I choose to wear with honor. Okay, Susannah, tell me the purpose of this so-called emergency visit."

She had the temerity to blink. "Who said anything about an emergency?"

"That's what your message read. Shall I call the warden to collaborate it?"

Susannah sighed. "All right. There's no need to get snippy about it. Just promise me you won't freak out, that's all."

I gasped. "But you've been in here five years; you can't be pregnant!" I gasped again, as reality sunk its baby teeth into my overnourished skull. "Oh no, don't tell me it was one of the guards. Clyde? Houston? What's his name with one eyebrow and no chin?"

"Eric? Give me a break! For your information, Miss High and Mighty, I'm not nearly the slut you think I am. I have never once cheated on my Melykins. Not once. Not ever."

I must have been staring at her incredulously because she waved a long, but otherwise shapely, hand in front of my eyes. "Earth to Magdalena, are you in there?"

"I'm here," I said. "I'm just having a hard time processing the fact that marrying the Mantis might actually have been good for you."

"He was my salvation, Mags—and I don't mean that in a sacrilegious way. Mama was always so strict, and let's face it: you weren't any better. It was all or nothing with you. If I didn't toe the line a hundred percent, you got furious. Remember the time you threw me out because I wore a low-cut blouse and fire-engine red lipstick?"

"I didn't throw you out; I made you choose between dressing

like a hussy and living on the street, or showing some respect while enjoying the comforts of home."

My baby sister opened and clenched her jaw several times, and frankly, I was surprised by just how much the issue seemed to affect her. Then, much to my astonishment, she threw her arms around me and began to sob. Furthermore, since folks in our family are genetically incapable of touching one another for more than two seconds without resorting to some vigorous backslapping, I was stunned when she let herself go as limp as a dishrag and simply hung from my neck like an Art Deco gewgaw.

"Hey, break it up, you two!" 'V'h'Neek'qQ"WA'a rapped sharply on the glass with her billy club.

Susannah slumped into the nearest chair and began to sob. Neither of us is a pretty crier— Well, is anyone? But what I really meant to say is that my sister is uncommonly unsightly when she boo-hoos. Her nose turns bright red whilst emitting viscous fluids, her cheeks mottle in a multitude of unappetizing shades, and her eyelids immediately swell into something resembling half-baked puff pastries stuffed with spinach. It is barely an exaggeration to say that a lesser woman than I would have run from the room screaming.

Much to my credit I simply handed her a wad of tissues from my oversize pocketbook. "What is it, dear? I'm your big sis, remember? You can tell me *anything*."

She had to swallow before speaking. "*Anything?*"

"*Anything*. And just so you know, now that I'm married, and well acquainted with the sweet mystery of life—so to speak—I am no longer the prude I used to be."

She snorted, drenching me in the process. "Yeah, you were pretty awful. That time when we saw the horses—"

"That was then; this is now," I said, using a favorite expression from her younger years.

She began to blubber again. "It's—M-M-Melvin."

"He's *dead*?" Oh woe is me. There was far too much hope in my voice. There was too much hope in my soul as well. What kind of a Christian was I? How could I be happy to hear about someone's death? Didn't that, in a way, make me just as guilty as a murderer?

"No, stupid," my sister croaked, "he's not dead. My Melykins is about to do it again, and this time I have a feeling he's going be caught."

Melvin "the Mantis" Stoltzfus was not only Susannah's husband, and my biological brother, but he was an escaped convict, a *real* murderer, who'd been on the lam for five years. Given that he had a pea-size brain, it was a miracle that he'd been able to elude the authorities for so long. I'd almost assumed that he was dead, or that perhaps he was lying somewhere in a coma, unable to convict himself with those thin bloodless lips of his—and oh how I judge!

"Caught doing *what*?" I practically shouted. "And where?"

"Pulling another heist," she whispered, her voice now hoarse. "Somewhere in Somerset County."

"*Heist?*"

"Don't be such a *dummkopf*, Mags; you know what I mean."

Except that I didn't. I was, however, happy that Susannah had reverted to our ancestral tongue to dress me down.

"A heist is a robbery," I said, reasonably, stubbornly, and, of course, quietly. "Has Melvin ever robbed anyone before?"

She was quiet for a moment, her ragged breathing aside. "Yes," she finally mumbled. "That bank job in Bedford—the one you had to go and interrupt."

It was then that every hair on my head stood up, forcing my prayer cap to reach new heights. "Those faux-Amish men, like the one who shot Amy and could have killed my Little Jacob, one of them was Melvin Stoltzfus?"

"Shhh, Mags!"

"Don't you shush me, Susannah. Unless you want me to rat you out like the Orkin man, you better tell me everything—and I mean every last detail."

"I can't."

18

"What do you mean by 'I can't'?"

"Mags, you know if I tell you anything, then you'll try to do something to stop it, and you'll get hurt this time. I just know it. I feel it—kind of like a premonition. That's why I had to see you."

I took my time processing this new batch of information. "You're in contact with that cold-blooded killer, and you know when he's going to strike again?"

"He's not a cold-blooded killer, Mags! He only kills when he's very stressed—when he has to. Otherwise, you know that my Sweetykins wouldn't hurt a flea."

"I think the expression is 'fly,' dear, but in this dirt bag's case, flea is just as appropriate."

Shame on me. I'd never used such harsh language; I'd never called anyone such a vulgar name. But Melvin had actually tried to throw me over a cliff once, and if it hadn't been for the grace of God and my sturdy Christian underwear—which got caught up on a tree branch—my head would have broken open on the rocks at the bottom of said cliff like a jack-o'-lantern hurled in front of a speeding automobile. And for the record, I only did that once, and I was only ten years old, and after the licking Papa gave me behind the barn, it is a wonder I still have a bottom with which to fill out my Hanes Her Way cotton briefs, which are, of course, plain Protestant white.

My words seemed to have struck a nerve in Susannah. In the blink of a bloodshot eye, her demeanor went from being limp and weepy to resembling that of an alley cat caught in a net. Out came the fangs and claws, which, frankly, I much preferred.

"How dare you call my Woosty-Bootsy names? He's a lot more of a man than that mama's boy you're married to. At least my husband can cut his own meat!"

I must admit that it is rather pitiful that a heart surgeon has to pass his steak to his mother first so that she can saw it into manageable bites, but doesn't each family have its own idiosyncrasies? I'm sure that the Obamas do things behind the White House doors that they would rather not be made public. In fact—and I say this as a woman who voted for Barack—what was his wife thinking when she selected her inaugural gown? From the picture I saw in the paper, it looked like it had wadded balls of toilet paper glued hither, thither, and yon. Frankly, a little less hither and a lot more yon might have been in order for that *schmatta*.

"Susannah! Do you *hear* yourself? You're defending a murderer. You are, in fact, a convicted accessory to murder. Oh where, oh where, did I go wrong?" Not knowing quite how to wring my hands, I rubbed them together vigorously.

"Stop being so dramatic, Mags. If you loved someone as much as I love my dingleberry pie, you wouldn't be asking yourself that question."

Not being a great fan of dingleberries, I let the argument drop. "Let me get this straight, sis. All you wanted was for me to listen to your premonition as regards what's his name in an upcoming heist?"

"His name is Melvin Lucretius Stoltzfus III."

"*Lucretius?* The poor dear never stood a chance—but still, that's no excuse for cold-blooded murder."

"Guard, guard!" Susannah shouted. "I'm through in here!"

"Oh no, you're not," I hissed. I was so angry I was able to do it without an "S"—a feat usually reserved for sloppy novelists. "You're not through until you promise me that your little nephew is safe."

Susannah waved the guard back, but her eyes were as flat and lifeless as the buttons on my old wool coat. "Why wouldn't he be?"

"Because if what you've intimated is true, then the Son of Satan was in the bank that day and saw my Little Jacob. If he thinks that Little Jacob can identify him then—"

"*Can* he?"

"Of course not! If he could, don't you think he would have told me? And if he'd told me, do you think that I'd be this shocked to learn that he was still around?"

"You've always been a good actress, Mags—which is the same as being a good liar."

"Well, I'm telling the truth this time. Listen to me, I'm not even wailing. I'm just being quiet and earnest. This is a mother talking, not your sister."

"You sound cagey to me, sis."

"Save the life of my child," cried the desperate mother. "Honestly, Susannah, Little Jacob didn't see anything."

"Guard," she called again.

"So help me, Susannah, if Melvin touches one hair on my baby's head, that little rat of yours is going to—"

That was when Susannah threw back her head and screamed like a banshee with its tail in a vise. I'd been referring to her lap rodent (was it *really* a dog?) named Shnookums, who was quite safe with my daughter, Alison, who was away at college. Besides,

I'm the sort who scoots earthworms off the sidewalk and ferries lost ladybugs outdoors. I only step on fleas by accident. So you see, there was no need for her to carry on like that, and she ding-dang well knew it.

Unfortunately the lady linebacker guard jumped to a wrong conclusion, and woman-handled me in the worst possible way. It wasn't the least bit fun and offered me absolutely no fodder for romantic daydreams—not that I was in the market for any. It's just that as I get older, I try harder to keep an open mind.

By the time I got to the car, I was shaking like the paint mixer at Home Depot. 'Tis a cliché, I know, but one that originated with me, so I feel free to employ it. Very little of my intense emotion came from the rude way in which I'd been treated; to be honest, I was just plain scared. I feared for the life of my son, who was my flesh and blood, my pride and joy, the crowning achievement of my life.

Take the inn, Melvin. Strip everything from me, but leave my son be. He *is* my life. Yes, I know, Gabe was my life as well, but my husband had already lived a good many years, and had a vast range of experiences under his belt. Little Jacob, on the other hand, was just starting out. He was just beginning to be curious about everything. It was "why" this, and "why" that, and he was innocent—he didn't know what death was; how could he possibly comprehend his own?

Ordinarily, logic would dictate that I contact the sheriff with the information that Susannah had given me, and I intended to, but not until my little darling was safely out of harm's way. But first I needed a plan—a way to get Little Jacob out of Hernia without being followed.

I couldn't very well hide him in the trunk of my car. Who would that fool? If indeed Melvin was back in Hernia, he probably had a telescope trained on my inn. He had, after all, made his supposed escape from our town on the bus with the Sisters of Perpetual Apathy, who were now living in a convent just across the road from me. Perhaps he was back with them, disguised again as a nun—or maybe one of the self-styled nuns was in ca-hoots with him. After all, they were all a bunch of whackos—and I say that with Christian love.

The Babester would face the same problems that I would, so there was no use going that route. Besides, he'd want to confide in Ida, who was Sister Superior to the Super Deluded—again, I say this with Christian charity. It did occur to me to enlist Freni and Mose; perhaps Little Jacob could be smuggled out hidden in the bottom of their buggy. However, despite the fact that both septuagenarians have hearts of spun gold, their lips could sink all the ships in the Gulf of Aden, thus causing a global oil short-age of epic proportions.

No, there was only one person in all of Hernia with whom I could entrust the life of my precious little boy.

"You want me to do *what*?" Sam said.

"Shhh, I don't want him to hear you," I said.

"No need to worry about that," Sam said. "Even Superman couldn't hear us with the volume up that loud."

He was right. We were standing up by the register, at the front of the store, and Little Jacob was at the back in Sam's office watching cartoons. As we don't have a TV set, he seldom gets to watch it. Needless to say, he was utterly entranced.

"Sam," I said, "you're my last resort. You've got to help me think of a way to get him out of town—out of state—without anyone suspecting until he's long gone."

"Yes, but why me?"

"Because you love him, and because I can trust you."

"You can?" Sam's watery blue eyes attempted to lock onto mine.

"Yes," I said wearily, "but don't be reading anything into that. I'd sooner cheat on Gabe with a drunken henweigh than allow you to plant one kiss on these ruby red lips of mine."

"Uh—is that so? What's a henweigh?"

"About four pounds if she's plump."

Sam roared. "You see? That's what I love about you!"

"Well, then love me from afar, but help your godson close up—you know what I mean."

Sam sighed. "Yeah." Then he closed his eyes and scratched his balding head with the stub of a number two pencil that lived behind his ear. "Wait a minute—what time is it?"

"According to that enormous clock behind you—courtesy of Blough Brothers Butter—now *that's* a mouthful—it's two fifteen. And a few seconds."

"That's it!"

"Sam, that is indeed the largest—and ugliest, I might add—clock I've ever seen not attached to a tower, but even my somewhat diminutive offspring couldn't fit in there. Besides, even if he could, how long do you propose he stay sequestered? And of course, you'd have to remove the works—"

"Magdalena, there you go again, getting all sorts of exercise from jumping to conclusions." There were no customers in the store, but Sam did a visual of all three aisles first just to be sure. "You see, Henry Blough, the owner, is my second cousin once removed on my father's side of the family, and something else—but I forget—on my mother's side. He's related to you too, for your information. Anyway, I've been stocking his butter for the past twenty-three years. It's the only kind of 'store bought' butter my Amish customers will buy, and you know why?"

" 'Cause it's the best?"

"You're darn tooting."

"This is all very nice, Sam, and remind me to buy some more soon, but what does this have to do with saving the life of my child?"

Sam flipped his fingers from his forehead to indicate what he thought of my highly developed intellect. "It has everything to do with it. You see, the butter truck is due to arrive just about now—always before two thirty. They unload my butter, the last order of the day, and then zip on down back to Maryland and the family farm."

"The farm's in Maryland?"

"Yes, and surrounded by three other farms that are all owned by relations of some sort, and they have every animal you can think of—even llamas. Little Jacob's going to love it. Trust me, Magdalena, I wouldn't suggest this, unless I was a hundred percent sure that the boy would be safe."

I knew Sam believed his own words, but could I? "What exactly is your plan?"

"We put Little Jacob in an empty butter carton and carry him to the back of the truck—he can get out as soon as he's in the truck, but he has to stay out of sight. Meanwhile you stay visible up here; pretend you're shopping. Of course, the TV will be blaring cartoons the whole time. After the truck has pulled safely away, I'll fix up a dummy of sorts— Hey, I can use the scarecrow from last year's Halloween display. We'll wrap it in a blanket and you'll carry it to the backseat of your car and lay it gently down. Pretend it's him. Then you drive straight to Agnes Miller's house."

"*Agnes's* house?"

"Yes, it will buy you more time. Everyone knows you hang out there. After a while you can call Gabe from there. But make him come over to Agnes's before you tell him what's really going on. Dollars to doughnuts, the inn is bugged."

I shivered. "Sam, you're a genius. You'd be a diabolically evil criminal if you had chosen to go that route."

"The only reason I didn't is because of you."

"Stop it, Sam! Not now." I put my face in my hands and prayed. Then I walked assuredly back to where my son was enjoying himself more than he had in perhaps weeks, and kissed him on the forehead, both cheeks, and even on the corners of the lips.

"Mama!" he said, pushing me away. "I can't see."

"You're going on a trip," I said. "You'll see pigs, and sheep, and goats—even llamas. It's going to be lots of fun."

"Do the llamas have TV?"

"I'm sure somebody there has TV."

"Will I get to watch cartoons?"

"You know what? I hope that you can! But first we have to play a little game of hide and go seek."

The truest love of my life looked up at me for the first time since I'd entered the room. "Do I get to hide?"

"Oh yes, dear. Uncle Sam and the butter man are going to hide you in a cardboard box and put you in the back of the butter truck. That way the others can't find you."

"Who is the others, Mama?"

"Everyone, dear. This is going to be our little secret until you're out of Hernia and on your way to this special farm."

"Are you coming with me?"

"If I come with you, someone might see us, because I'm too big to fit in a box. But I'll be there as soon as I can to get you."

"But I don't want to go without you."

He threw his arms around my neck, and put his head against mine. His little-boy scent of sweat, as yet unsullied by puberty, nearly broke my heart. This was the human I had actually grown inside me—from scratch! I'd almost sooner cut off my arm and send it away in an empty butter box, except that such a ghoulish act would do nothing to keep my progeny safe from the maniacal Melvin.

"Lots and lots of cartoons," I said. I didn't care if it turned out to be a lie. I needed to keep my boy safe.

"Okay, Mama." He kissed me on the lips and then leaned back in my arms. "Why are you crying?"

"Because I want to fit in a butter box too," I said in an exaggerated pout. I tousled his hair. "Hey, do you think President Obama has a llama? A llama with drama?"

Little Jacob giggled. "Mama, you're silly—you know that?"

While my heart went south to Maryland in a butter box, I drove north to see Agnes. My dearest friend remained remarkably composed when I poured out my anguish, and although they didn't help anyway, she remembered to serve me hot chocolate and ladyfingers. It was Agnes who told me how to break the news to my son's father; she even got him on the phone.

"Gabe—"

"Hon, where have you been? Are you all right?"

"We're fine as a frog's hair split three ways, dear."

"Frogs don't have hair."

"It's so fine you just don't see it."

"They don't have hair."

"Okay, if you're going to split hairs—"

"I'm not; you are."

"Gabe, just shush up and listen. *Please.*"

"Huh?"

"I'm leaving you, Gabe."

"*What?*"

"Our marriage is over. Surely you've seen this coming."

"The heck I have!"

"Well, I have. Our differences are just too great; we're never going to get past them. The best thing we can do for Little Jacob is to go our separate ways now and get on with our lives while he's still young enough to adapt."

"Adapt? To *what*?"

"To whichever path we decide to head down—individually, I mean. I imagine that you wouldn't mind it if he learned more about Jewish customs and—"

"Ding dang dong," Gabe shouted into my ear. "Frumpy Felicity feverishly fricasseed fryers!" Of course those weren't the actual words he said, but they do alliterate with them. The real words were boringly repetitive and I would never repeat them.

"Look, we can discuss this better face-to-face," I said. "I've decided to stay at Agnes's tonight. Little Jacob is in her bedroom watching cartoons, so I haven't told him yet. Why don't you come over right now and we can discuss this more in person?"

"*What?* In front of Agnes?"

"No, silly. I'll send her over to visit her weird uncles."

"You serious, babe? Because you've just socked me in the gut with a punch out of nowhere and—"

"Come," I said and hung up.

19

First Gabe was incredulous. Then he was angry that I had not consulted with him before shipping our beloved son off to the butter farm— No, angry is an understatement. But I'd expected some of that, so I was as ready as one can be on that score.

It was, however, the fear he felt and the torrent of tears it brought on that came as a surprise. Nothing in my life had prepared me for an experience of this nature.

I'd never seen anyone cry like that, male or female. In my culture we are reserved, stoic even. We bear up under our burdens or give them over to the Lord, who shoulders them for us. Yes, there are times when we are overwhelmed, and Satan is nipping at our heels, when we might succumb and weep quietly—but always in the privacy of our own bathroom or bedroom. We never, ever sob openly—in a living room, and most certainly never with streams of water cascading down our cheeks.

Agnes, dear friend that she was, prepared for Gabe his own version of hot chocolate and ladyfingers. I knew that Agnes belonged to the First Mennonite Church of Hernia, which was vastly more liberal than Beechy Grove Mennonite, but just how liberal, I had no idea. Gabe's hot "chocolate" turned out to be "Irish coffee," and his ladyfinger was a shot glass of straight-up liquid comfort served on the side. Considering how distraught he was, I held my counsel like the good little wife I was supposed to be. *For the time being.*

It was decided that I would spend the night with Agnes on the pretext that Gabe and I were still fighting. Surely by the morrow we would receive word that the eagle had landed and I could return home, but with lips sealed so tightly that even waterboarding couldn't pry them open.

Sure enough, around seven a.m.—I'd already been up for three hours—I got a call from my little one.

"Mama?"

"Darling! Are you all right? Are you safe?"

"I'm at Cousin Hilda's farm and they have every kind of animal, just like you said. After breakfast we're going to feed the Obamas."

"Uncle Sam's cereal?"

"I don't know, Mama, but then we're going to hunt for eggs in the barn, 'cause they don't keep their chickens penned up like we do."

"That's wonderful, dear. So you *are* all right?"

"Yeah, kind of."

"What do you mean, 'kind of'?"

"Well, I gots a boo-boo on my foot on account of something bit me."

First I panicked. "When was *that*?" Then I took a deep breath. "Show it to Cousin Hilda!"

"It's all better, Mama. You put a Flintstones on it, remember?"

"Oy veys meer." Was that all? But you see what had happened? The stress had caused my brain to crosswire. If it kept up, the next thing I knew Swahili might come flying out of my mouth.

"Mama?"

"Yes, dear?"

"Can I stay here for a while?"

"Yes, dear, but you have to brush your teeth."

"But I don't gots a toothbrush."

"The word is 'have,' dear— Never mind, dear. Cousin Hilda will get you one."

"Mama?"

"Yes, darling?"

"I love you."

In the final analysis, it didn't matter to me if loving little Jacob was really nothing more than loving myself. What mattered is that I did, and that I would do anything to protect him—even brave Freni's wrath. Although it must be noted that Freni, being a good Amish woman of an essentially peaceful nature, was slow to anger. Relatively speaking, that is.

"Magdalena, I cannot believe that you would leave our little one with Agnes Mishler."

"Agnes is my best friend—after you, of course. And Gabriel."

"Yah, but she does not have children."

"Nonetheless, the little shaver adores her."

Freni, who was rolling out dough, gave my future cinnamon buns a sharp whack. "Maybe, but what will he do there?"

"Watch car—s go by," I said, compounding my lie. Freni, even more than I, disapproved of television of any kind.

Freni dropped the rolling pin, which promptly rolled onto the floor. Instead of picking it up, she vigorously smeared a handful of butter across the flattened dough. It was like watching her give a Swedish massage to an enemy.

"Agnes Mishler lives on a dead road, yah?"

"Oops. Yes, she does live on a dead-end road— Look, Freni, you're going to find out, so I may as well tell you now. Melvin Stoltzfus is back."

Freni froze. Given that the woman abhors alliteration, I hastened to elaborate on the entire situation. I left nothing out; I even told her about the Irish coffee. I did not, however, reveal my son's location.

Freni seemed remarkably blasé about my revelation. "The Irish are a sensible people."

"What?"

"A lot of prayer, a little whiskey—not such a bad combination."

"But you don't drink! The Amish don't drink! That's of the Devil!"

Still a prisoner to alliteration, Freni flinched. "Ach, not me personally, but there are many among us who might take a sip now and then—to calm the nerves. But no, we do not get drunk like the English; this we do not permit."

"Wow, and I thought I knew everything about the Amish."

"Sometimes it is you Mennonites who are too strict, Magdalena. You have thrown out the baby oil with the bath salts, yah?"

"Close enough."

"So now you tell me where my little boy is."

"Sorry. No can do."

Freni tossed a handful of sugar over the dough, and then dusted it with cinnamon. The whole time she clucked to herself like a hen about to lay an egg.

"Magdalena, you are like a daughter to me. When you were little, I washed you in the tub. When your mama was sick, I changed your poopy diapers. I was here for you when you married Aaron Miller—the man who led you into bigamy, yah?"

"I was an inadvertent adulteress," I wailed. It was the last time I was ever going to wail, or respond to any comment pertaining to that unfortunate part of my life.

"But now you do not trust me?"

"You bet your bippy I do trust you," I said. It was stress—and of course, Satan—that caused me to lapse into the pagan prose of the vernacular. And to lie.

"Ach! What is this bippy?"

"It's just an expression, dear; it's something I heard Susannah say. By the way, she needs our prayers more than ever. She's not at all the carefree spirit we used to know."

Freni, who'd picked up the rolling pin by then, began to roll the dough into a log. "She *is* in prison, Magdalena, yah?"

"But it's more than that. This obsession with Melvin—it's taken over her soul. She could barely bring herself to tell me that her little nephew was in danger. I hate to say it, Freni, but I think she's mentally ill. Maybe it's depression, maybe something I've never heard of. But as her closest living relative—not on the lam, that is—I'm going to ask that she undergo a thorough psychiatric evaluation."

The Amish, like we Mennonites, do recognize that there are times when people need assistance from the outside world. But especially for the Amish, it can be difficult to determine where the line between poor mental health and weak faith lies. If only one were to submit more fully to the will of the bishop, and the *Ordnung* of the community, one would surely find the peace one was missing.

Freni loves Susannah as much as she loves me—well, almost as much. I could tell that at that moment she loved my sister enough to struggle with the rigid belief system in which she'd been raised and to consider alternative possibilities. As she grappled with her conscience she brought a butcher knife repeatedly down on the dough log, expertly rendering it into cinnamon buns of equal size. These she plopped into greased pans which she essentially threw into the oven before slamming the oven door.

"So now the truth, yah?"

"Okay, but you don't need to get so bent out of shape. The truth is that although you are the dearest woman alive—a surrogate mother to me *and* my best friend—at least of your generation—you do engage in a fair amount of— Well, shall we say 'news sharing'?"

The Coke-bottle-bottom glasses fixated on me. Thank Heaven the lenses were so greasy I couldn't see her eyes.

"What?"

"Tongue wagging, dear."

"Like a dog?"

"Like a woman who gossips. Loose lips sink ships, et cetera. You have a heart of gold, dear, but you just can't help yourself from sharing with your friends. If I tell you today where our precious one is, by tomorrow at this time all of Hernia will know, and half of Somerset. Besides"—I lowered my voice to a whisper—"these walls have ears."

Freni slowly wiped her hands on her apron as the truth hit home, as surely it must.

"I quit," she said after a dramatic pause.

"Okay. But please take the apron home and wash it before you bring it back. Remember that dinner is a half hour early tonight because the gang wants to drive into Pittsburgh to see some movie. Now there's an opportunity to engage the Devil if you ask me."

"No, Magdalena, I really quit."

"Yes, Freni," I said patiently. "Just be sure that you're back in time to make dinner."

She untied her apron and, and covered as it was with sugar, flour, and cinnamon, she folded it neatly and laid it theatrically in the center of my rough-hewn kitchen table. Then, without saying another word, she got her coat and started walking home.

*   *   *

I would have run after her—*eventually*—and made amends. At the very least I would have sent Gabriel to give her a ride home, had I not been so rudely imposed upon. Besides, Freni was taking the shortcut to her farm that led through the woods, and it was only a footpath, unsuitable for automobile travel. By the way, those were the same woods in which I'd once lain in a bush, from whence I'd untied one of Freni's shoelaces as she passed in front of me. (I've long been of the mind that if a bird in the hand is worth two in the bush, then surely a hand in the bush is quite desirable.)

But I digress. My day had only gotten worse by the sudden appearance of Mother Malaise. In addition to being Mother Superior at the Convent of the Sisters of Perpetual Apathy, she's my husband's mother, which makes her my mother-in-law, so one might say that Ida is the mother of all— Well, I won't say it, because I've been practicing loving-kindness as of late. If I do say so myself, this effort at self-improvement has really paid off.

"It's you," I groaned, having opened the door to some fierce pounding.

"So now you lock zee door on me?"

"Melvin's on the prowl in these parts again; I suggest you do the same over there at the Funny Farm."

Ida wagged a finger so close to my nose that it trimmed a few hairs. "Eet eez a convent, not a farm, und you should be so lucky to join. But enough about dis; I vant to know vhere my grandson eez."

"So you heard already?"

"Of course! Vhere do you tink I leef? In zee shtetl?"

"Uh—"

"My Gabeleh told me. Who else? But not to vorry. I haf not told a soul; I am zee model of eendeescreshion."

I smiled generously. "I'm sure you are, dear. But I'm not telling anyone—and neither is your son telling anyone. Even Freni's being kept in the dark. As a matter of fact, she quit over it."

"Und your friend?"

I offered her a face as bland as noodles on mashed potatoes, which, I hear, is a Hoosier delicacy. "Which friend, dear? There's Gwen, Mignon, Kay, Georgia Ann, Daisy, Carolyn, Gene, Janie, Janet—"

"Ugh-uh-nuss."

"Excuse me.

"Zee von mitt zee naked brodders. Ughuhnuss."

"That would be *Agnes*. And what she knows is only on a need-to-know basis."

Even a wolverine will stop digging if you pave over the wilderness. Sadly those animals are quitters compared to Ida. She glared at me and rubbed her shoulders with hands the size of tea bags while she considered her next move. The woman is tiny— or she *would* be tiny, were it not for Dollyesque bosoms, which even the nastiest of habits couldn't hide.

"Nu," she said at last, "eet eez gut that you protect my grandson, but who vill protect dis Agnes und her meshuggeneh brodders? Eef Melvin tinks dat dey know too much, und dey leef out in zee boonies by demselves—den boom, he vill kill them, yust like I kill de rats in my barn mitt zee firecrackers I buy at Crazy Joe's down in Maryland."

"But you don't have a barn over there anymore; you converted it into dorm rooms for pseudo-postulants, who pensively postulate apostasy in part due to only partial alliteration."

"Boom!" This time Ida mimed an explosion.

"All right, all right," I said. "Perhaps you have a point. I'll talk to Agnes about seeking safety in numbers. But while I'm on the subject, Ida, I have a suspicion that one of your de facto dingalings is spying on me."

She blinked. "Vhat are my dingalings?"

"Your self-proclaimed, so-called sisters. How nuts is it to join a group wherein the only common bond is apathy? That means as soon as you start to care about the group, or even just another individual, you no longer qualify for admission."

"Und?"

"*Und?* That's all you have to say?"

"Vhy should I care vhat happens to the group?"

"But you're their Mother Superior!"

"So?"

"Come on, even you can't be *that* apathetic! Besides, you seem to care about what happens to the Mishlers."

"Zee Mishlers vas only a suggestion. So now I tell you a secret: I care about my grandson, and my Gabeleh, of course." She paused to look studiously at a zigzag crack in the kitchen floor. "Und mebbe you."

"Does that warm the cockles of my heart, or what?" I cried. "Let me clasp thee to my bosom from henceforth and forevermore!"

Ida could move like a prizefighter—I should know; I've had a few of them stay here at my inn. And 'twas true: she could float like a butterfly, whilst stinging like a bee, and after a few stings, I decided to let go of her and leave well enough alone. It was nice knowing that she cared. In fact, silly me. Having a mother-in-law who cared from a distance, and from beneath the cloak—literally and figuratively—of apathy, was really the ideal situation.

I patted her wimple fondly. "When it's safe to tell you where the little shaver is, you'll be the first to know, Idaleh."

20

Thai Coconut-Ginger Sticky Rice Jumbles

Ingredients

1 cup (2 sticks) butter, softened
1¼ cups firmly packed light brown sugar
1 cup granulated sugar
1 teaspoon pure vanilla extract
1 teaspoon salt
2 large eggs
2 cups all-purpose flour
1½ teaspoons baking powder
1 cup shredded unsweetened coconut
1 cup candied ginger pieces, diced*
4 cups crispy rice cereal
Optional: 2 tablepoons sesame seeds

*Candied ginger (also called crystallized ginger) can be found in many supermarket produce or spice sections or in a health or gourmet store.

Cooking Directions

Preheat oven to 350°F.

In a mixing bowl, beat together butter, sugars, vanilla and salt until light and fluffy. Add eggs one at a time and beat until smooth.

In a separate bowl, whisk together the flour and baking powder. Add the flour mixture to the butter mixture and beat until blended. Stir in coconut, ginger, and cereal, mixing until just blended. Using a teaspoon, drop the dough onto parchment-lined cookie sheets about ½ inch apart. Sprinkle the top of each cookie with sesame seeds, if desired.

Bake until edges just start to turn golden but centers are still moist, 10 to 12 minutes. Remove to a cooling rack to cool completely.

Store in an airtight container for up to one week.

Courtesy http://www.eatwisconsincheese.com/

21

Oh, what a *dummkopf* I can be. I don't know what made me think that the gang from the Garden State would be satisfied with a supper of scrambled eggs and franks and beans. The Babester and I often made do with just such a repast on Freni's day off. A couple tubes of jumbo-size biscuits and a tossed salad, and what more does one need? Why, throw in a vitamin pill, and one has a veritable banquet!

"This isn't what we paid for," Olivia Zambezi said.

"You paid for a filling meal," I said evenly. "Now fill up."

"We paid for authentic Pennsylvania Dutch cuisine," George Nyle said.

"I am an authentic Pennsylvania Dutch woman, and I made this cuisine; thus it is authentic Dutch cuisine."

"It's crap," Peewee Timms said. "My grandma used to serve this on Sunday nights when we visited. Neither she nor my mother could cook worth a darn."

"Yet somehow you didn't starve," I said, and not nearly as unkindly as I might have.

"Hon," Gabe said under his breath. He is always the conciliator, although it's not because he believes in peace, so much as he fears conflict.

"Yes, that was mean," Tiny said. "I thought you were nicer than that."

"I am nice. Look, our Amish cook quit, and since I really don't need your money, I'd be happy to give you all refunds."

"Please, if I may," Surimanda said, by way of breaking into the conversation. She was dressed in a black velvet blouse with kimono sleeves, a black velvet ankle-length skirt and high-heeled black suede boots. Around her waist was a gold chain belt. Her blue-black hair was gathered in a chignon and adorned by a single silk rose the color of fresh blood.

"Certainly, you may," I said. "And just so you know, in this country April showers bring May flowers, and I'm told we can look forward to a very soggy April."

Miss Baikal brushed aside my attempt at obfuscation. "Miss Yoder, I like this food. Is good sturdy peasant food."

I beamed. "Indeed! Peasant food, that's what it is, only I shall call it 'peasant fare' and charge an extra twenty dollars per meal for it."

"Why, that's highway robbery," Olivia said. She was obviously quite livid.

"I don't know," Barbie Nyle said. "It sounds reasonable to me. You try ordering peasant fare in a fancy Manhattan restaurant and see how far you'll get. This is a one-of-a-kind experience we're getting here, and I say let's go for it. Miss Yoder, what do you call these things again?"

"They're biscuits, dear. They're like rolls, but they come from a tube. And those," I said, taking the liberty of pointing at her plate, "are beans. And that's a frank."

"What fun," Carl Zambezi said, and although his wife scowled at him, she dropped her objection to my meal.

However, the woman had the eyes of a hawk, and the manners of a vulture. "Where's the boy at?" she demanded abruptly, her mouth filled with masticated yellow egg.

"He's staying at a friend's, dear."

"Is that so? Isn't he a little young for sleepovers?"

Now that was rude, challenging my parenting style like that. "Not in my culture, dear," I said facetiously, which really is not the same as lying, because it is teaching someone a much-needed lesson. "We institute mandatory sleepovers at six weeks of age as part of an initiation process. That way, if we're invaded by the Russians and—God forbid—a mother is killed, the child will be used to other adult caretakers." A little late, I remembered Surimanda's presence. "Oops, those would be bad Russians, dear, not your kind."

Nevertheless there were gasps of awe and disapproval from my rapt audience. But, more important, Olivia looked like she'd been put in her place.

"She's only kidding," Gabe said. "Little Jacob just started having sleepovers; in fact, this is his first one."

If my arms had been long enough, and if I hadn't had five hundred years of pacifist breeding to overcome, I'd have reached the length of the table and throttled my dearly beloved. What was he thinking! Someone in this bunch could be in cahoots with Melvin. At the very least, there was bound to be a bug somewhere, and the dining room seemed like a likely location.

Yes, I'd conducted a thorough search before supper, but surveillance systems these days are extremely sophisticated. Short of taking a torch to the room, there was no way I could be sure of disabling everything anyway.

"Miss Yoder," Olivia said, a new bite of egg familiarizing itself with her dentures, "I don't find you in the least bit amusing. It's a shame, you know, because at first I thought we might really get on, given the fact that we are roughly the same age. But you are rude, crude, and generally very abrasive; you are not any-thing like what I expected a Mennonite woman to be like."

"I think she's delightful," Tiny said.

"Me too," Barbie said.

I looked at the men, one at a time. *"Well?"*

"Sorry, but I'll have to agree with my wife," Carl said.

"And I'll agree with mine," Peewee said, "even though you did insult me with your 'didn't starve' comment."

"Which was true," Tiny said. "You promised me you'd go on a diet."

"Yeah, yeah."

"What about you, George?" I said.

"You're a hoot, Miss Yoder."

I turned to Surimanda. "And you?"

"I adore you, Miss Yoder."

"Then it's settled," I said. "I will continue to be myself, we will continue to feed you sturdy peasant fare, and you will butt out of our family business. *Capisce?"*

"Hon!"

But everyone except Gabe laughed—even Olivia snickered.

I used to have lofty dreams. Often in them I flew without the benefit of wings. Since the birth of Jacob, my dreams tend to be darker and have, in fact, included a few in which he is somewhere far away, and I am trying to reach him. In these dreams there are always insurmountable obstacles, such as the road keeps disap-pearing, or Jacob's whereabouts continually change. I've even had a few dreams in which I can no longer remember what he looks like or, worse yet, I see Ida's head on my dear son's body.

This particular night I was dreaming that Agnes and Dorothy Yoder were one and the same person. Agnes was actually Dor-othy's fat suit, which she could take off and put on at will, *or,* to look at it another way, Dorothy was Agnes's skinny persona, the soulless slattern she could slip into anytime she wanted to experience a mindless mattress mamba. Given that Agnes was my best friend and still a virgin, this dream was disconcerting to say the least—especially since I was supposed to be her business manager.

"But you can't quit on me now," Agnes pleaded. "You were supposed to arrange a sleepover with the Royal Moroccan Marching Band. They're only going to be in town one night."

"What?"

"Magdalena, you're getting very forgetful. My rendezvous with the Shriners was Saturday night in Somerset; it was my breakfast in bed with the Jaycees—"

"No, no, I won't!"

"Magdalena, it's only me—Gabe."

"Gabe? Best friend or not, you get your hands off my Cuddle Buns!" I lunged for Agnes with both hands, claws bared.

"Hon!"

"What?" I popped up in bed as the bad dream drained away like the remains of a large soap bubble.

"You were having a nightmare, hon, and were fighting back at something tooth and nail; I have the scratch marks to prove it."

"I'm so sorry! There's some hydrogen peroxide under the sink—"

"Don't worry about me. There's someone here to see you."

Unconsciously my hands balled into fists.

"Agnes?" I bleated guiltily. Now that's a fine "how do you do" for a woman with five hundred years of pacifist blood flowing through her veins. Clearly I was in need of a vacation somewhere: just me and my hunkylicious Babester and my precious little Babykins—preferably someplace far away from Hernia. The Marquesa Islands in the South Pacific came to mind.

"No, not that busybody; it's the police chief."

*   *   *

Chief Jerry Memmer is a pleasant, mild-mannered man who hails originally from somewhere near Indianapolis. So far his sensible Hoosier ways seem to be just what Hernia needs.

During the year and a half that he's been running the show, our crime rate has fallen substantially. There have been no murders committed, no horses stolen, and no overpasses painted. The only case of a "malicious mischief" reported involved slit diaper bags on the horses tied up outside Yoder's Corner Market one morning. Either someone had it in for Sam, or the Amish who were shopping inside, but apart from a few spilled "road apples" there was no real harm done.

It helps that the Memmers are good Christian folk of the conservative bent, who put noodles on their mashed potatoes. They have blended into the fabric of Hernia almost seamlessly, and that has been a blessing for me, because at this stage in my life, I would like nothing more than to leave civic responsibility behind. Jerry Memmer is an avid model-train enthusiast, and his wife, Marilyn, can quilt along with the best of our local quilt masters, which is saying quite a lot. In short, I couldn't ask for more qualified and congenial replacements.

Jerry is even pleasant to look at, albeit a bit shy. Perhaps my appearance in a bathrobe was too much for the devout man, because he squirmed in his parlor chair, like a grub on a weenie roasting stick—not that I've roasted many grubs, mind you.

"Yes, Jerry, what is it?"

"I'm sorry to bother you, Mrs. Rosen—uh, Miss Yoder— uh—"

"How about Magdalena, like I've asked you to call me a million times?"

"Yes, ma'am. I'm sorry to show up at three in the morning. Honest—"

"Ding dang dong! Is that what time it is?"

"Magdalena! You have the mouth of a truck driver!"

I slapped the offending lips. "So I do; and I assure you that they are ever so contrite. Now, tell me, what is the problem? Has your wife overdosed on chocolate again?"

"No, it's about a woman named Amy Neubrander—up in Bedford."

Although nowhere near a standing body of water, much less one with a current or influenced by tides, I felt the undertow. "What *about* Amy?"

"She's dead, Magdalena. The sheriff asked me to tell you, on account of I know you better than he does."

I felt my way to a straight-backed chair—all the chairs in my parlor are purposely uncomfortable—and sat. "How did she die? When?"

"Apparently just hours ago. A neighbor in her building heard a shot, but by the time he got the super to open up— Well, there was nothing to be done by anyone. She was shot at close range in the back of the head."

"Dong dong dong," I said slowly, letting the cussword roll off my tongue like a seasoned pro. "What a cowardly schmuck!"

"I beg your pardon?"

"Melvin—Melvin Stoltzfus. It was an execution-style murder, performed either by him or one of his band of not-so-merry robbers."

Chief Memmer's eyes bulged and he swallowed hard. "*The* Melvin Stoltzfus? Your brother? Elvina's son?"

"We supposedly share some genes, but the jury's still out, as far as I'm concerned."

"Have you been tested?"

"This is hardly the time for idle chitchat, Chief." The truth of the matter was that I feared the outcome of such a test. I would rather go through life living with the possibility that what Elvina said was true—Melvin was my brother—than with the certainty that it was so. The latter would cause me to seek a complete blood transfusion, comprehensive flesh replacement, and universal bone substitution. The last I've heard is that one or more of those procedures is still impossible.

"I'm sorry, Magdalena. Is there anything I can do for you?"

"Yes, actually there is."

"Anything."

"Keep your guard up. Melvin hates authority of all kind. It wouldn't surprise me if he stages an attack on you—either at home or at the station."

"But my wife! Marilyn has nothing to do with my job; she's a retired nurse who gave back so much to the community in Indiana."

"Then you might see that she returns there until Melvin is caught. Believe me, I know firsthand how this monster's mind works, and it ain't pretty—pardon my use of the vernacular."

"I see," he said, but I'm not sure he did. In any case, he sent his pretty wife packing the next morning.

22

I knew that the sheriff wouldn't let me get anywhere near Amy's apartment at that hour, so I returned to bed. It was with a bit of a jolt that I awoke the next morning and recalled that Amy had been senselessly murdered—but then aren't all murders senseless? I hadn't known the girl well enough to form a personal attachment, but the fact that she was so young, and died at the hands of someone I did know well, haunted me.

My long-suffering husband took it upon himself to cook breakfast for the gang from New Jersey, because he makes an almost-edible Southwestern-style omelet. Meanwhile I set out some boxes of cornflakes and two platters of toast that were sure to please: one pale and the other bordering on burned. Then I rang my five-pound dinner bell.

Tiny Timms was the first to appear. "Good morning, Miss Yoder," she said, just as perky as Katie Couric after a good night's sleep.

"And good morning to— Oh no, you don't, missy! Not again!"

"What? What's wrong with this one?"

The tiny woman with the enormous assets was dressed in what has been described to me as a baby-doll negligee. Over that, she wore what was supposed to be a duster, but both were constructed from fabric so sheer that I could tell she wasn't a natural blonde.

"It's heathen—that's what. Even *National Geographic* wouldn't photograph you in that. Now go upstairs and change before a good Christian man like my husband sees you and is led astray."

"Your husband is Jewish, Miss Yoder."

"That's all the more reason, dear. Now am-scray."

She reluctantly did as she was told, and I prematurely breathed a sigh of relief. Perhaps the morning would go smoothly after all. But then, of course, along came George and Barbie Nyle.

"Not you too," I wailed. "Now you see what you've done? I've officially given up wailing—given that it's both annoying and unnatural—but this! What is this? Some kind of pajama game? We put on clothes for breakfast here at the inn, and, George, the sight of all that chest hair is— Well, it brings to mind all the brambles I need to have cleared away in the north pasture before I can let the cow in there to graze come spring."

Chastened, the Nyles scurried back up my impossibly steep stairs, but they must have squeezed past Olivia Zambezi, who was on the way down. At least she was in proper attire: a blue knee-length frock, long sleeves, mock turtleneck. Her prematurely aged face was freshly spackled, but her thick gray locks were askew. Who knew the woman wore a wig!

"Good morning," I said, perhaps a bit too cheerily. One has a way of overcompensating when one is uncomfortable, doesn't one? Or was it just me?

"Is it just you, or does everyone in Hernia shout in the morning, Miss Yoder?"

"Oh, it's our local custom, all right. In Pennsylvania Dutch we call it *shout-an'-Freud*." Okay, so it was a small lie; but I had to say something, or else I was in danger of blurting out something that might embarrass her.

"Funny, but I don't recall being deafened yesterday morning when I came down to breakfast—then again, I was greeted by the pleasant Mrs. Hoffenstetter."

"Her name is Hostetler, dear," I said through clenched teeth, "and she isn't all that pleasant all of the time—not that I'm telling tales out of school, mind you."

Olivia raised a thick black eyebrow. "Oh?"

"Well, you know, the usual. She's human—that's all. We all get grumpy from time to time."

After arranging her thick features in a skeptical mold, she pulled out her chair and plunked her patooty down without further ado.

"We're not going to eat until everyone is here and the blessing is said," I informed her crossly. It wasn't as if she didn't already know the rules.

"What if I'm an atheist?"

"Then it's even more important that you hear grace."

"What about your husband? How does he feel about having to sit through one of your interminable prayers?"

"Would everyone just leave my husband out of it?" To say that I wailed would be too kind; "braying" would be a more apt description. From the distance of a good mile away, I could hear Kaye Cornmesser's pet mule bray in response.

Olivia smiled. No doubt she was happy that she'd struck a nerve.

"It must be hard for your husband, living in this closed, judgmental community."

"Your wig's on crooked."

"What?"

"It looks like someone tried to scalp you last night, but got stopped in the middle of the act. You haven't seen a tomahawk lying about, have you? It would be an awful thing to stub one's toe on, don't you think?"

Olivia flushed as both hands flew up to her head. "You are a wicked woman, Miss Yoder. A wicked, wicked woman." Then she was gone.

But, in the end, everyone returned, hair in place, or properly clothed, as the situation warranted. I said my interminably long grace, after which they were rewarded with one of Gabe's fabulous omelets—well, part of one, at least.

We were halfway through the scrumptious repast when who should fly in the front door but a nun on a mission. The truth be known, I am loath to refer to the Sisters of Perpetual Apathy as nuns, since none of these so-called nuns has had any theological training, nor are they required to believe in anything except the philosophy that apathy is the best approach to dealing with the stresses life throws one's way. Some of the pseudo-sisters are even too apathetic to subscribe to that concept.

"Whoa," I said, to the flying nun. "Hold your horses. A truly apathetic person would never be in such a hurry."

"*Ma?*" The Babester can instantly recognize his mother, no matter how many times she changes her habits.

"Ya. Who else?"

"Is something wrong?"

"You tink mebbe I come to twiddle my tumbs?"

My husband was on his feet. "Ma! What's the problem?"

"Yes, dear," I said with remarkable patience. "What is so urgent that you had to storm in here—without knocking, I might add—and disturb our breakfast? Especially on a day when I have a particularly unruly lot from the Garden State that I have just now managed to calm down—"

"'Subjugate' is more like it," said Carl Zambezi. For the

record, he hadn't been too thrilled by the toast selection, preferring as he did a medium brown hue.

I prayed for a patient tongue. It was a very brief prayer, as I have learned over the years that it is not cost effective to pray for things that are unlikely to happen.

"We serve food family style here," my tongue said. "You would be wise to remember that I am the mama in this family."

"Is that some sort of a veiled threat, Miss Yoder?"

"Oh, not at all, dear. I think it's quite clear: if you continue to complain, you'll have to leave the table."

I fully expected there to be an uproar, but everyone fell silent except for Mother Malaise, aka my mother-in-law. "You see, dis von's a tyrant."

"I am not!"

"Eet's a good ting," the *real* tyrant had the chutzpah to say. "Das vhy I vant you to be my replacement someday."

I couldn't believe my ear pans. "You *do*?"

"Of course! Who else? You're meshuggeneh like me, no? Und you like to control zee people around you, ya? Bossy, dat is vhat vee are. Dat eez our God-given talent."

"I think she might have a point," the Babester said.

"But I'm not apathetic!" I wailed.

"I thought you were going to stop wailing." The Babester looked away when he spoke, which was a wise move on his part.

"I *am*, but there is a time and a place for everything. It's in Ezekiel—that's in your Bible too."

"Dun't vorry," Mother Malaise said, exhibiting remarkable generosity. "Someday you vill be apathetic, and by den Sister Disgruntled vill heff moved on to greener pastures, so you can heff her name. Eet vill feet you pearfectly."

I turned to the guests. "Eat, dears. This isn't a floor show." I turned back to mother-in-law. "So, you ran all the way over here on your—uh—petite—legs to recruit me for that distant day when Sister Disgruntled will stand before her Maker and account for her time spent in your loony bin?"

"Mebbe not so distant, ya? Sister Disgruntled is eighty-four and loves bacon—fey! But you are right dis time; I heff come here because of a very beeg problem."

"What is that?" the Babester asked.

"Zee ooncles!"

"Zee vhat?" I said. It was unconscious on my part, believe me.

"Zee ooncles!" Ida shouted. "Zee brudders of zee modder of Agnes."

"Ah, the uncles," the Babester and I said together. "What about them?" I added.

Ida inclined her head toward my guests, as *if* any of them would have what my mama referred to as "gentle ears." She waggled a brow that could have used a good trimming with hedge clippers.

"Dey are in zee boof."

"Ah," Gabe and I said, again in unison.

There followed a moment of silence, after which my dear husband dared speak first. "Ma, what is a 'boof'?"

Mother Malaise clapped her liver-spotted hands in annoyance. "Dey are nekkid."

That I understood. "Holy guacamole," I cried, swearing like a sailor, "they promised to keep their robes on! They said that they looked forward to having fun playing monk midst all your nuns."

"My, my," Olivia opined, "monks running amok amongst nuns. Isn't that a bit risky? Sort of like having a rooster loose in a henhouse?"

I glared at her. I couldn't help it.

"They're more like capons, dear—not that it's any of your business."

"What's a capon?" Tiny asked.

"Just a kind of chicken, dear. Which reminds me"—I turned back to Barbie Nyle—"I read on your guest survey that you play the piano. As you can see I have no Steinway, but I'll do my best to get you a henweigh by three o'clock."

"What's a henweigh?" Olivia demanded rudely.

"About four pounds—plucked. But I've had some old fryers that have topped the scale in the six-pound range. Tough old birds though."

It was Olivia's turn to glare. "I suppose you think that you're funny."

"Au contraire, dear. I don't have a funny bone in my body. In fact, I eschew humor. Now, about those ooncles—Have you spoken to Agnes?"

"Oy vey," Mother Malaise said, and rolled her eyes. "Do I look like a cabbage? Of course I speak to her."

"Nu," I said, just a tad impatiently. Sometimes learning a foreign language comes in very useful.

"Und she said that dis is America, de land of de free, und dat her ooncles vere yust exercising der rights."

"Rights, shmights, she's wrong. It's your convent, and you make the rules. Besides, they could be a bad influence. Who knows? Maybe some of your nuns will bare all, and pretty soon the place will turn into a nudist colony. Boy, wouldn't that just be a fine "how do you do"? Movie stars can officially check in here, but spend their time there gawking. Maybe even a few will shed *their* clothes. If that happens, and you get some good pictures— Well, it wouldn't surprise me if the *National Enquirer* would be willing to pay millions."

"You tink?"

"Too much, it seems."

"Hon," Gabe said, "I know what you're doing, and it isn't fair to her."

"She's a grown-up, dear. Ida, you're old enough to make up your own mind, aren't you?"

"Ya?"

"You don't sound sure. Either you are, or you aren't. If you aren't, you can always come to me for advice, and my advice is to throw Agnes and her funny ooncles out on their respective ears. The last thing you need to see is Brad Pitt or George Clooney in the altogether, if you know what I mean"—I paused to waggle my eyebrows—"because at your age such a sight could precipitate a heart attack. Besides, if you were successful in selling some photos to the tabloids, you'd be so rich that you'd probably move back to New York, and then what would I do about my most reliable—if somewhat kooky—babysitter?"

"Magdalena!" Gabe said sharply.

Ida spent all of ten seconds pondering my weighty words. She then threw her small, but pudgy, hands in the air—a sign that either she has conceded one of your battles, or else she believes that she is victorious.

"I vill return to my convent," she trilled, "but vee vill no longer be apathetic. From now vee vill be passionate about embracing our outer selves. Vee shall be known as zee Sisters of zee Complete Package."

"Ma! That has certain connotations."

"Ya?"

I hadn't a clue, but that buttinsky Olivia whispered in my mother-in-law's ear. The stout nun recoiled in surprise.

"Oy! Not gut. Den vee vill be called zee Nude Nuns of Narnia."

"Nix! C. S. Lewis put a lock on Narnia decades ago."

"Vell, I vill tink of something."

"How about the Sisters of Subcutaneous Inflammation?"

"Hon!" Gabe protested, but to no avail.

"I like," said Mother Superior. "Vrite that on a piece of paper for me, Magdalena. Tell me, vhat should my new title be?"

"Well, since you'll be *head* of the convent, and you are Caucasian, how about if the *pus*tulants just call you Mother Whitehead? You will, of course, wear a white headdress."

"Mags," Gabe bellowed.

I scribbled the convent's new name on an embroidered hankie I pulled from my dress pocket and handed it to her. "As the others will be merely pimples with wimples, it might be easier to have them revert back to their given names. There will be less confusion that way—and less paperwork. And less paperwork always saves one a passel of money."

The five-foot-tall thorn in my side took off with the speed of a space probe. Frankly, I was so relieved to get rid of her that I didn't much mind the dressing-down I received from Gabriel in front of my guests, or their added clucks of disapproval. Only Tiny seemed to find any humor in what I'd done—no doubt because she was the youngest, and my actions had been so immature.

I must add, however, that the mysterious Surimanda Baikal wisely held her tongue, and for that, she endeared herself to me.

23

As usual, Mary Berkey's myriad children were delighted to see a car drive up to their house. It was a miracle I didn't accidentally run over any of the urchins as they pranced joyfully in front of my moving horseless carriage. If I was to be their day's entertainment, then I was glad to be of service.

Their mother, however, was a mite less enthusiastic. "Oh, you are back way too soon. I cannot possibly have the dress ready—there are too many pleats, yah?"

"Yah—I mean, yes, I'm sure there are more pleats in it than there are in a polka band worth of accordions."

Her blank look was not encouraging.

"I understand," I said. "I'm not here for *that* dress. I'm here to buy your dress."

The children giggled.

"*My* dress?" she said.

"Not the one you're wearing, of course, but another one—just as long as it's clean or only lightly worn. It's for me, in case you're wondering. And no, I'm not about to switch over to the horse-and-buggy side; I merely want to look the part for a special occasion. It just so happens though that the special occasion is today, which really limits my options. Fortunately, you and I are approximately the same size. My bosom might be a tad larger, but it's hard to tell given that you don't wear a b—" I stopped, having remembered the kids, although I needn't have worried.

"A bridle," said Veronica, finishing my sentence. "She said that Mama doesn't wear a bridle!"

Of course our vertically challenged audience found this immensely funny. Some of them even neighed like horses and pawed the air. Frankly, if they were my children I'd have told them to am-scray because we were having an adult conversation. But the Amish are far more indulgent than I am, and Mary, being a widow, is especially loath to discipline her offspring lest they abandon her someday.

"But, Miss Yoder," she said, seemingly oblivious to their antics, "I have only two other dresses: my Sunday-meeting dress and another such as this."

I gave her the once-over. "Is it clean?"

"Yah. But I have yet to iron it."

"Then time's a-wasting." I dug my wallet out of a very uncooperative purse, and from its parsimonious mouth pulled three twenty-dollar bills. "Here, this should cover it, don't you think?"

She waved the money away.

I smiled kindly. "You only own three dresses, dear, and you have more mouths to feed than your average breakaway Mormon family. I wouldn't feel right accepting the dress as a gift."

Mary Berkey covered her mouth with one hand as she laughed softly. Around her the children giggled like her very own backup choir.

"Oh, Miss Yoder, I do not want just sixty dollars for the dress. It is all handmade. It is worth much more."

"Hmm. Okay, I'll give you eighty. I can buy a nice spring

dress at JCPenney's in Monroeville for $79.99. And that's before any kind of sale."

"Yah, maybe. But you cannot buy an Amish dress in Monroeville."

"Touché. Well, I can see that we're related."

She nodded solemnly, as did the pack of urchins. "There are many Yoders in my family tree."

"And isn't family what it's all about?"

She continued to nod, and so did her cheering section.

"So then," I said brightly, "how about giving your cousin a special price."

"I think one hundred twenty-five dollars is a fair price for you—my cousin."

"For just one dress?"

"Yah, but I will sell you a bonnet to go with it for two hundred dollars."

"You have got to be kidding!"

"I do not joke, Miss Yoder. And, of course, you will want the beautiful traveling cape; every Amish woman must have her cape, yah?"

"Yah? How much?"

"Only three hundred fifty dollars."

"Why, that's highway robbery!"

"Miss Yoder, the bonnet has many more pleats than does the dress. Also, both it and the cape have been worn by me, so they will give the outfit an authentic smell."

"You want me to pay *extra* for the scent of a woman?"

She had the chutzpah to look me right in the eye, without a bit of shame. "This is my offer. Take it or leave it."

"Okay," I groused, "but let it be known that Magdalena Portulacca Yoder Rosen doesn't drive the hardest bargains in the state. That honor is yours, my dear."

Mary Berkey, like me, was trained to be humble about her accomplishments, but I saw a competitive glint in her eyes, if only for a second. Well, she did have a lot of mouths to feed, and the Amish do not accept public assistance, such as welfare. I was in a hurry, so she could win this time, but when I returned to pick up clothes for the English, *then* we'd see who was better at this game.

"When I come back in a couple of days, I plan to play hardball."

Mary smiled. It was obvious she'd heard that expression before, which just goes to show you that most folks are more complicated than we give them credit for.

There is only one road to take from Mary Berkey's farm into Bedford. Since I didn't want to risk being spotted in my Amish garb, I had to come up with an illusion of some sort—rather like David Copperfield, I should think. Susannah dragged me into Pittsburgh to see him when he was on tour, and I'll admit that, even though I was reluctant to go—magic is not a healthy Mennonite preoccupation—he managed to knock my socks off. That alone was quite a feat. But how he managed to get my woolies off and to the top of a flagpole in the arena without me knowing—that *almost* made a believer out of me.

At any rate, everyone who knows me knows that I have a penchant for speeding. But no one would think that an Amish woman driving a slow car was me. And just for the record, there are Amish who *do* drive cars—but they're black cars and mine is silver. Still, it isn't the sinfully red BMW I had a few years ago, and for which the Good Lord made sure I paid my dues.

However, when I got into the city itself, I parked my car in front of a Laundromat and called a Yellow Cab. The driver's name was Amir Hashish, and he'd been in the country exactly three weeks.

"This is my third anniversary," he said in a Scottish lilt, which also happens to characterize—to my untrained year—the English of the Indian immigrants I've encountered. Other than his accent, his vocabulary and grammar were as good as mine, perhaps better. It was obvious that Mr. Hashish was an educated man, and probably had not been a cabbie in his country of origin.

"What is it you used to do in India?" I asked.

Amir sighed deeply. "Madam, if I told you, I'd have to kill you."

I squirmed. "Please don't say that. You *are* kidding, aren't you?"

"Do you mean joking, madam?"

"Yes."

"Very well, I was joking. I was an aeronautical physicist working on the Indian space program, but"—he laughed sardonically—"suddenly they no longer had space on their team for someone like me."

"I see. Well, welcome to America." I gave him the address to which I wanted to be delivered, but he didn't know it from a hole in a wall in Calcutta. That meant I had to direct the poor fellow while I lectured him on the good and ill in American society, and warned him that there were some folks about—who shall remain nameless—who are capable of bargaining just as ruthlessly as Yours Truly.

By the time I got to my destination, poor Hashish looked a bit like a beaver that had been submerged behind its dam and was forced to come up for air. Frankly, whilst I wouldn't want to listen to my own spiel after just three weeks in the country, I must say that I do dispense a lot of important information and a few tidbits of wisdom as well.

"Don't say you plan to knock someone up, when your intent is to rap on their door. And in lieu of loo, you might want to try restroom or even bathroom—that is, if you want to be understood—although frankly I've never rested or bathed in a public loo before."

"That is excellent advice, Miss Yoder. Thank you."

"My, what a pleasant fellow you are."

Since we were stopped, he turned and faced me full-on. "Is that not a bit condescending?"

"I beg your pardon?"

"That the foreign cabbie is courteous: this should somehow be extraordinary? I mean, really, you of all people should be beyond such judgment."

Why is it that when my heart begins to race, my blood temperature drops? Aren't cold liquids supposed to congeal and move slower?

"What do you mean by 'me of all people'?" I demanded. In all honesty my voice was so shrill that a lonesome magpie outside in a spruce tree began a mating call in earnest.

"Well," he said, waving a hand much too close to my face, "this getup of yours—it might be authentic, but you're not one of those Aye-mish ladies."

"It's pronounced *Ah*-mish, dear. And how would you know? You've only been in the country three weeks."

"Because I am able to see auras, and you do not have the same color of aura as the Ayemish women I have had the pleasure to meet."

"It's Ah-mish," I said through gritted teeth. "I wouldn't say 'Mum-bay,' even though it's spelled like 'bait' without the 'T.'"

"Touché, madam." He turned to face the front of his cab again. "Whatever your reasons for the illusion, it really is none of my business."

"Life is an illusion, isn't it?" I said, as I dug around in my oversize handbag to locate my wallet. "Take the most beautiful woman in the world, drape her in the finest silks, have her do nothing but lounge on a daybed as she eats chocolate-covered bonbons and watches reruns of *Project Runway*—I hear that it's very good—but then turn off her electricity for a week and see what happens. After two days without a hot shower, she'll start to get irritable. After five days, the shimmering silks will be as ripe as last week's fish, and at the end of the seven days, the raving beauty will be ready to trade her firstborn for the chance just to wash her face."

"Miss Yoder, in my country hot showers are a luxury, and there are many for whom even cold water is scarce—at all times."

"Well, I don't believe in auras," I said, "and neither should you."

There was nothing to be gained, and perhaps a lot to be lost, by betraying the immense amount of irritation I felt. Instead of saying another cross word, I wrested money out of my exceedingly reluctant wallet, and gave Mr. Amir Hashish a very handsome tip.

He nodded up and down and sideways as he thanked me profusely. "You are very generous, madam," he added, "so I feel that it is my duty to warn you that I sense imminent danger in your path."

"Poppycock."

"Pardon?"

"Balderdash. Isn't that what they say in England? I thought perhaps that they say that in India as well. At any rate, I don't believe in fortune-telling."

"Very well, madam," and then he practically threw me out of the cab. Perhaps he expected a tree to fall on me, or a meteor to zero in on my newly acquired, very expensive bonnet as its landing place.

I'd asked Mr. Hashish to drop me off at a location that was a full two blocks away from Pernicious Yoder III's house. I'd already called the house and gotten the answering machine, so I assumed that the man was either at work, or at the police station being grilled like a weenie about his professional relationship to Amy. Margaret—aka Mrs. Pernicious Yoder III—was already busy at her volunteer job, which was tutoring reading in the public elementary schools— Well, at least she didn't answer their home phone.

One might think that the sight of an Amish woman on foot in an upper-middle-class neighborhood such as this might cause an eyebrow to rise, and one might be right. Such an action, however, required the presence of at least one eyebrow—something that seemed to be missing from the contemporary scene. Gone were the days of coffee klatches and the Fuller Brush man; here to stay were the days of two working parents and deserted streets at least between the hours of nine and three. In any event, I was pretty sure that I wasn't seen during my brief highland stroll, and my "forced entry"—thanks to the myriad bobby pins that hold my bun in place (not to mention more than a dollop of experience)—went even smoother than I'd expected.

I'm only a partial fool. Upon closing the door soundlessly behind me, I called out softly into the shuttered gloam.

"Anyone home?"

Silence.

"Yoo-hoo, anybody here?"

Dead silence.

"Yoder to Yoder: calling once, calling twice, calling thrice, then shall I wander, as quiet as mice."

A deafening silence prevailed.

"Let's not all speak at once, dears. And just so you know, this wasn't really *breaking* and entering, as I didn't break anything. My hairpin merely found its way into the keyhole, and when I twisted and turned it— Well, can I help it that I have a gift? But enough about me; I'm here to see if I can discover something—

anything—that will shed some light on the horrible bank robbery, of which I was a victim—and have yet to sue anyone about—and also on the death of Amy, who was also traumatized that day."

I'd slipped in through the kitchen door (for some reason they're always the easiest locks to pick) and was working my way through the formal dining room. It was obvious that Pernicious and Margaret took their meals elsewhere; on the dining room table were four color-coordinated, dust-covered place settings. That fact, and the elaborate centerpiece, indicated to me that Margaret took her decorating cues directly from the showroom.

The formal living room was also very much decorated, with no sign of life: not a magazine or gag-me-green afghan to be found. Just to be thorough, I located the spot where Pernicious and Amy had stood the night before when I'd hid in the bushes. In the daylight I could see quite clearly into the overgrown Japanese yews; I also had a better appreciation for what it might be like to be spied upon. Shame on me for lurking about in anyone's bushes.

Frankly, it was hard to imagine that a cold-blooded killer could live in such harmonious surroundings. No, that wasn't quite right. What I meant was that such a pleasant environment— Uh-oh, was that someone coming? I thought that I heard a snurffle. A snurffle, by the way, is a distinctly male sound, as opposed to snuffles and sniffles, which can be attributed to either sex. Oh shoot, there really was someone coming!

I glanced madly around the elegant room. Where could a tall, curvaceous, but still lithe, woman in traditional Amish clothing possibly hide? Not behind the drapes, which although quite beautiful, hugged the walls like newlyweds. And certainly not under the pair of facing sofas, not unless I could magically compress myself into the stick figure I always thought that I was whilst growing up. The only possible option was inside the large oak armoire in the corner opposite the kitchen door. But Heavens to Murgatroyd, who knew if the cabinet door was even unlocked?

The snurffles were followed by a snort and a loud footstep. At that point I flew across the room—literally—I'm sure of it. Fear got me airborne and the voluminous cape kept me aloft, and I will not be dissuaded of this notion. Anyway, much to my relief the armoire was unlocked, so clutching my cape to me, I leapt into it and pulled the door shut. Unfortunately, not all of the fabric made it inside with me. I tried yanking it in beneath the door, but to no avail. Besides, it was too late.

24

"Now where did she go?" a familiar voice said.

"Beats me."

"I swear I saw her headed for this room."

"Yeah, but she's a cagey old woman." The second voice was familiar as well, in addition to being cheeky.

"She's downright stupid—that's what she is," the first familiar voice said.

"Yeah," said the second voice. "But what do you expect? She's supposedly some kind of cousin of his. Them Yoders is all alike if you ask me. Couldn't none of them find their way south from the North Pole without a compass."

That did it! That hiked my hackles so high that they dug into my armpits, forcing me to fling open the armoire doors to defend my honor. It's one thing to pick on me personally, but to disparage the entire clan? I won't stay stuffed in a portable closet on that account.

"You take that back!" I shrilled.

The men stepped back, but they didn't seem at all surprised to see a woman in a black cape fly out at them from an oaken armoire. In fact, they doubled over laughing.

I stared angrily at them for a full minute before realizing that they were the security guards from First Farmer's Bank. Almost immediately then I wised up and tried a sweeter approach.

"Talk to your ma lately, Johnny?" Okay, so it was mean of me to call him by his nickname in front of his bud. But for the record, I did it in self-defense, and I have since confessed this sin. The only reason that I bother to mention it now is that I have since come to believe that full disclosure is good for the soul.

At my snide comment the man called Johnny immediately clammed up. He balled his fists and a vein popped out on his temple.

Alas, John's buddy was no more sensitive than was I. "She got your goat, eh, *Johnny Boy*?"

"Shut up, the two of yinz."

Instead of shutting up, his companion turned and offered me a hand the size of Connecticut. Normally I eschew handshakes on the grounds that they are unhygienic, but there times when one is simply caught unawares.

"This is a good way to catch a cold," I said, as I pressed the flesh. "Besides it's an archaic custom dating from the days when men commonly carried weapons, such as swords. Extending an open hand was a sign of neutrality."

"Yeah, and my name is Bill—not Billy *Boy*." He laughed briefly. "We seen you get out of that cab and break in. Decided to follow ya."

"I didn't break in! I merely entered uninvited."

"Hey, don't get your panties in a bunch there, Miss Yoder, 'cause I ain't judging. We was gonna break in anyway."

"Shut up, Bill," John said even more forcefully.

Bill turned to his friend. "What's wrong with being up front with her? Ain't she that famous detective from Hernia? If we were ta throw in with her, we just might figure something out? There's answers in numbers; ain't that what they say?"

"If you ask the right questions, dear. And speaking of which: why were you two going to break in?"

John nudged Bill aside. "Same reason as you, I imagine: we don't think that Mr. Yoder killed Amy. We think it was a setup. If they get away with this, and he gets sent to the pen, then there go our jobs."

"Yeah," said Bill. "Ain't no one gonna take a chance on me the way Mr. Yoder did—me not having a high school diploma and all."

"I told you to get your GED," John said, "but all you wanted to do was party."

"Quit yer complaining," Bill said.

"No, you quit," John said.

"Shut up," Bill said.

I clapped my hands. "Children! Focus, please. Who is this 'they' that you referenced?"

Bill stepped forward and gave his buddy a not so playful tap on the biceps. "Hey, what's with this refer—whatever? You been holding out on me?"

John shook his head as he rolled his eyes so far back they resembled two freshly peeled hard-boiled eggs. "You see what I gotta put up with? What she's *talking* about, Bill, is the people I was *talking* about who really did kill Amy."

"Yeah?" said Bill. "So you *do* know who they are! Like I said, you were holding out on me."

John growled. "No, you dumb piece of—"

"Stop it!" I commanded. "Put a zipper on it, the both of you." Believe me, it was the first and last time a Mennonite has ever uttered such strong words. "Bill, your friend John and I think that someone other than Mr. Yoder killed Amy, but we don't know who. That's why I'm here—to find out. So, for now, I'm going to ask the questions and you two are going to supply the answers. *Capisce?*"

"No, thanks," Bill said. "Mama made that stuff once and I threw up."

"Hunh?"

"He thought you meant 'quiche,' " John said.

I quickly did some mental gymnastics, converting run-of-the-mill questions into pointed queries that Bill might understand. "What did the men look like who tried to rob the bank last month?"

"Two of them was old."

"What?" I would have fully expected the word "Amish" to be part of any one-sentence description.

"To Bill anyone over thirty is old," said John.

"What else?" I coaxed.

"One of them was—uh—I guess they say 'overweight' these days," said John.

"But I call them 'fat,' " said Bill. "He was so fat that he was sweating in them fake Amish clothes of his."

Finally, there it was; the A word. "What do you mean by 'fake'?"

"Well, maybe them clothes was real, but he weren't no real Amish man; I could see that he was wearing a Spider-Man T-shirt under that white shirt of his. And red socks. Ain't no Amish man that wears red socks."

"You're right about that," I said.

"And they was mean."

"Of course, they were mean," John said, and shook his head again. "One of them shot little Amy, didn't he?"

"Yeah, but I could tell they was mean a-fore that. There was something in their eyes, something you don't see in no Amish man. These fellars was out to get what they wanted, come hell or high water."

I shuddered. "Please, dear, watch your language. 'Fellars' is such a bastardization of the word 'fellows' that it offends me to no end."

"Yes, ma'am."

"Is there anything else you two can think of that set these men apart from real Amish men?"

"No," said John.

"Their shoes," Bill said.

"*What?*" I said.

"Two of them was wearing Amish work shoes—like the kind you might wear if you was gonna plow some field, but one of the men was wearing a fancy foreign type—maybe Eye-talian."

"Bill is very fashion conscious," John said, without a trace of irony.

"I'll make note of that," I said, without a shred of sarcasm. "Was it the heavyset man who was wearing the fancy shoes, or one of the other two?"

Bill scratched his head as he pondered my brain teaser. "I think it was the fellar with the mustache—yeah, that was him. Them shoes had little tassels on them. I always wanted to get me a pair of shoes with tassels, but my mama said no. Now she's dead, but I still have to answer to John."

"Why is that?"

"Because I ain't so smart, that's why."

"I won't argue that, dear—" I slapped my cheek for being so cheeky. "But why John?"

"Because I'm his older brother," John growled. "You have a problem with that, Miss Busybody Yoder?"

"Not at all. In fact I stand here chastised."

"We ain't Catholics," Bill said.

Whilst I was intrigued by his enigmatic statement, we hadn't another moment to waste in idle prattle. "We need to fan out, men, and look for evidence."

"What kind of evidence?" John said.

"What do you mean by that? What kind were you looking for when you broke in?"

"We were going to look for something we could use as black-mail if we lost our jobs."

"Yeah," Bill said. "I told ya John was smart."

Thank heavens irritation has very few calories, because I had to swallow enormous chunks of the stuff before I could speak. "What *we're* going to look for now is something—possibly a let-ter, or a document—that shows that Pernicious Yoder III is al-ready being blackmailed. That's why he hasn't pursued the robbery case any further. Perhaps it was even an inside job."

"Hmm. What you say makes sense, but we can't both be help-ing you."

"Why not?" I said. "Are you in need of a coffee break?"

"Bill can't read."

"Oh. Excuse me for a minute while I eat crow."

"Ya ain't really gonna eat a crow, is ya?" Bill asked. The con-cern in his voice was touching. "Them's nasty birds that eat roadkill and the like. Mama said that eating them will make ya sick. Except she weren't right about that—but it still don't taste good."

"You ate *crow*?" John said. "When?"

"When you was off in the army," Bill said, without a second's hesitation. "We didn't have nothing to eat and it was Thanks-giving. I plucked them birds before I brought them home and told Mama they was pigeons." He started to sob great wrenching sobs that shook his body and made me feel like I hadn't eaten nearly enough crow.

"Now you see what you've done?" John said. "How could you?"

"I didn't mean to!"

"Miss Yoder, I'd just as soon that you and us don't work together. You go your way, and we'll look for stuff on our own. If we find anything I'll let you know. But if you don't hear from me, just stay the St. Louis International Airport, Concourse A away from us."

I gasped. "You've heard of that place too?"

"St. Louis International Airport, Concourse A, yes," he said. Then, with his arm around his brother's jerking shoulders, he led him away from me.

If one deigns to root around in a strange man's drawers, then perhaps one should not complain too loudly about what one finds therein. *That* is an opinion I might well have offered *before* the fact.

"Help, help! Turn on the lights! I've been violated."

To their credit both John and Bill came thundering into the room, and a second later the overhead light came on.

"What is it?" John's tone was one of pure concern.

"It's that—that disgusting thing!"

"That *thing* is a flashlight," he said. He picked it up, flipped on the switch, and shone it full in my face. "Let there be light," he said smugly. "Miss Yoder, you have a very active imagination. Anyone ever tell you that?"

"I plead the Fifth. Still, I don't like searching alone—not when we can search together. I mean, there's safety in numbers, right?"

"Yinz never makes any sense," Bill whined.

"Oh, all right," John said. "But I still think we oughta be looking for something to blackmail that old coot with."

I sighed. "Separate searches, same room?"

"Works for me," John said.

And it did. Not five minutes later he found exactly what he'd been looking for: something with which to blackmail Pernicious Yoder III.

25

Sea-Salted Coffee Toffee Bars

Ingredients

First layer
1 cup (2 sticks) butter, softened
1 cup dark brown sugar, firmly packed
½ teaspoon salt
2 cups all-purpose flour
1½ tablespoons instant coffee crystals

Second layer
1 can (14 ounces) sweetened condensed milk
2 tablespoons butter
2 teaspoons pure vanilla extract or dark rum
1½ cups whole pecans*
½ to 1 tablespoon large crystal sea salt

*Hazelnuts, almonds, or other mixed nuts may be substituted.

Cooking Directions

Preheat oven to 350°F.

In a mixing bowl, beat together butter, brown sugar and salt until light and fluffy. Add flour, 1 cup at a time, stirring between additions. Add instant coffee crystals and blend until well incorporated. Pat batter into ungreased 9x13x2-inch baking pan in an even layer. Bake until edges are lightly browned and center is puffy, 12 to 15 minutes.

Meanwhile, in heavy saucepan, stir condensed milk and 2 tablespoons butter over low heat until butter melts. The mixture will thicken and become smooth. Stir in vanilla or rum, remove from heat, and let sit until bottom layer is done baking. Sprinkle nuts over baked bottom layer and pour hot condensed milk mixture evenly over nuts using a spatula to spread.

Return to the oven and bake until top is golden and bubbling, 10 to 12 minutes.

Immediately sprinkle desired amount of sea salt over bubbling toffee top. Cool slightly in pan and cut into bars. Bars can be kept up to one week in an airtight container.

Courtesy http://www.eatwisconsincheese.com/

26

I stared enviously at the briefcase full of one-hundred-dollar bills. Why couldn't I have found it first? Now John was going to get credit for preventing yet another crime by Pernicious Yoder III. I say "another" because, even though I believe that betting is a sin, I'd almost be willing to bet my dining room table that it was this distant cousin who had snuffed out the life of his pretty young cashier.

My dining room table, by the way, is the only possession that I hold dear. It was built by my ancestor Jacob the Strong Yoder in the early 1800s. It is the only thing to have survived the great tornado of 1998—the one that picked me up, sent me flying through the air like a sliver of barnyard straw, and then just as quickly, and capriciously, dropped me facedown in a pie of cow doo-doo (a technical term I recently learned from Little Jacob).

It is possible that I've digressed. The point I was intending to make was that John and his brother, Bill, were destined to become Bedford heroes. This wasn't just my assessment, either. Both the chief of police and the county sheriff agreed. What's more, they both agreed to sign a letter that was to be distributed to the board of trustees of the First Farmer's Bank recommending that the Ashton brothers be given a reward—perhaps even as much as ten percent of the amount that Pernicious had stolen.

After that serving of crow, I didn't have much room for humble pie, so as soon as I could—without appearing to be ungracious—I made tracks, as they say, back to Hernia. At least there I was somebody, even when I was a nobody. Besides, it was one thing for law enforcement officials to come up with a story for the papers on how the Ashton brothers happened to be snooping around in a banker's house, but quite another if they had to explain the presence of a faux-Amish woman.

But while I fully expected to find the inn in a hubbub and Gabe frustrated to the point of pulling out his beautiful dark curls, I could not have dreamed up the scenario that greeted my world-weary eyes.

"Freni!" I cried. "What on earth are you doing here? You quit, remember?"

She shrugged, which of course took a great deal of effort. "The sun sets, but it also rises, yah?"

"That sounds like it would make a great book title."

"The English and their riddles," Freni said. That's her way of explaining anything and everything enigmatic about the outside world and we strange folk who inhabit it.

"That could probably be another book title," I said pleasantly. "But seriously, why are you back?"

Freni glowered through glasses that needed a cleaning when Mary Magdalene was a little girl. "*That* one—she gets on my nerve, yah?"

"And which nerve would that be?" Okay, so I was being mean, but it irritates me that Freni so dislikes her daughter-in-law. I find Barbara Hostetler to be utterly delightful—all six feet of her—even if she is from Iowa.

"On the nerve that would break down if I stayed home,"

Freni said, without missing a beat. "This morning she tells me that times have changed and that it is no longer the Grossmudder's place to punish the child."

"Indeed."

"So you agree?"

"Well—I guess it all depends. If Ida—aka Mother Malaise—were ever to hit Little Jacob, I'd be tempted to hit her back. And I'm a dyed-in-the-wool pacifist like you. But if she was living with us, and told him that he wouldn't get dessert until he finished his veggies, well, then I'd back her."

Freni nodded vigorously, which took even more effort than shrugging. Those of us blessed with necks would do well to ponder the plight of the neckless, especially those of that ilk who must bear the double whammy of sporting enormous bosoms. After all, there is always the danger of hurting oneself whilst expressing vigorous agreement.

"Yah," she said, "it is exactly this kind of thing!"

"Hmm. The thing that matters is that you're back. Little Jacob will be so happy to see you."

"Where is he?"

"Across the road with *her*." That he was still on the butter farm was a fib told only to save my son's life. So you see, they were wholesome words, just told incorrectly, so as maintain the secrecy of my son's location. If you ask me, the occasional misstatement of fact, like fresh dairy products, often gets a bad rap.

A sly smile spread slowly across Freni's lips, leading me to consider the possibility that being Amish does not exempt one from the fleeting, but very real, pleasure one derives from schadenfreude. I smiled sweetly back at her.

"It's not quite the same, dear. You see, in this paradigm I'm Barbara and you're Ida."

"More riddles," Freni said, and turned to stir the homemade butterscotch pudding.

"Freni, have I ever told you that I love you?"

"Ach!" Tears welled in my elderly kinswoman's eyes, and when she attempted to wipe them away with the corner of her apron, she knocked her glasses up onto her forehead in the most endearing way.

Truly, I had so much for which to be thankful, most especially the love of someone like Freni. I *kvelled mit goyishe naches*. At the same time, the centuries of inbreeding amongst austere, pietistic ancestors had left me incapable of appreciating the moment without making some sort of deflecting wisecrack.

"Now you're going to make me cry," I said, "and I'm a really ugly crier. Once Bigfoot looked in the window and saw me bawling, and he's never been seen in Bedford County again."

Apparently that was the wrong thing to say; Freni let loose enough tears to float Noah's ark.

"Just so you know, dear, there really isn't such a thing as Bigfoot, but if you think there is, I can try and get him to pay you a visit—although frankly, I would think that your six-foot daughter-in-law would satisfy that itch."

Freni was supposed to laugh, but instead she put her stubby hands on her broad hips and glowered at me beneath her pushed-up glasses. "Have you no respect, Magdalena?"

"Uh—well, of course, I do. You know that I respect you. I was only making a joke."

"Ach, not about the big feet! I shed maybe some tears, but they are for the children of Mary Berkey."

"Yes, it is very sad how the community treats their mother." It was not a personal indictment, because Freni is one of the few Amish in Hernia who has always given Mary the benefit of the doubt.

Freni paled. "Then you do not know?"

"Of course the rumors: suicide, murder—it happened so long ago, I don't see why folks can't let it go. The kids, for sure, didn't have anything to do with it."

"Ach, not the father, Magdalena." Freni moved toward me, and her short arms encircled my waist as the smell of chopped onions and bell peppers filled my nostrils. "It is Mary now who has gone to meet the Lord."

I pulled loose. *"Excuse me?"*

"Yah, she was run over by a tractor this morning."

"An accident, then. How awful! Forgive me, but which one of the children was responsible?"

Freni's eyes flashed. "The children were all in school, and the babies were in the house. It was the mailman who discovered Mary lying under the tractor."

"Then it was an accident!"

"Yah, maybe, but there were three sets of tracks on the body. The tractor very much wanted her dead."

I gasped as I groped for a chair. "Or somebody else did—somebody with the initials MS."

Freni shook her head solemnly. "Meryl Streep is a fine woman. When she stayed here, she had only good things to say about my cooking. She would make an Amish man a good wife."

"Oh, please. She's *such* a good actress that you'll believe everything that she says—whether it's accurate or not."

"Harrumph," Freni said, giving it a Pennsylvania Dutch accent. It's one of her favorite new words.

I smiled, happy for just a couple of seconds of diversion. Speaking with Freni of death in the kitchen was becoming an all-too-frequent pastime. Just a month before this, Freni and I had been standing in the exact same spots that we were now, discussing the recent passing of Silas Coldfelter, our town's most accomplished builder of multiple-passenger buggies, when all of a sudden Little Jacob walked in from the dining room.

"Hi, Mama," he'd said, almost blithely. "Hi, Aunt Freni."

I'd hugged and kissed him, and Freni had patted his head affectionately and offered him a gingerbread man with a glass of milk. Being the fruit of my loins, he'd accepted the snack gratefully, but had demanded a piece of fruit as well.

"It will spoil your lunch," I'd said.

"Mama, what happens when you die?"

"Uh—well—remember that baby sparrow we found underneath the barn eaves yesterday morning?"

He'd taken a big bite of milk-softened cookie before posing his next question. "Mama, we're not birds. What happens to people?"

"Well, their souls go to be with Jesus, but their bodies are put into the ground." There is no use trying to shield a child from death in a farming community. It would be like trying to keep an ice-cream cone from melting on a hot August day.

"I know that stuff about Jesus and the ground," said my precocious four-year-old, "but what happens to *them*?"

"Them who, dear?"

"The people who died," he'd cried impatiently. "You know, the *them* part!"

"Ach, he asks an ex-intentional question," Freni had said reverently. Sometimes she is in awe of the little tyke and sometimes it is understandably so.

"Maybe the 'them' part is the soul," I'd said. "Little Jacob, will you still love your mama when you're all grown-up and can think circles around her?"

My darling son had thrown himself at me and locked his little arms around my neck. "Don't be silly, Mama. I'll always love you."

"And don't be cheeky, and call your mother silly," I said, before kissing his eyelids until he begged me to stop.

"Earth to Magdalena," Freni said, bringing me back to the present. "So now will you tell me who really killed poor Mary Berkey?"

"Only if you promise not to use idioms from the eighties that were annoying even then," I said.

The expression Freni assumed made her look like a sheep that had been asked to solve the national debt. "Yah, whatever. I promise."

"And quit being a teenager as well. It doesn't become a seventy-nine-year-old Amish woman."

"*Oy veys mere.*"

"Who pretends to be Jewish when it suits her."

"Ach!"

"Now where was I? Oh, yes—I believe that Amy and Mary were both murdered by Melvin Stoltzfus."

"*Our* Melvin Stoltzfus?" Freni's hands flew to her throat as she fought for her breath.

"One and the same. Like I've always said, the man is evil personified."

Freni staggered over to the nearest straight chair and dropped heavily on it like a sack of spuds. "Does his mama know?"

His mama. She was my mama too—that was the kicker. Elvina Stoltzfus was my birth mother. Given the circumstances surrounding my conception, and the social climate of the time, I don't blame her. I do, however, blame her for the way she continues to treat Melvin, even after he's been convicted of first-degree murder, as if he were a prince, deserving of every consideration. No doubt Elvina has broken every law in the book, aiding and abetting that son of a gun-toting, hunting, deceased husband of hers. If there's any justice in this world—but I'm beginning to doubt that there is—Elvina will end up in the slammer as well.

"Freni," I said, "this is just my theory. Susannah warned me that he was back and would try something. How these two deaths are connected, I don't know—but I intend to find out. And believe me, you'll be the first to know."

*   *   *

Police Chief Jerry Memmer was polite as he could be. He listened to everything I had to say and took reams of notes, in addition to recording our conversation. But when it was all said and done, there was really nothing anyone could do but sit and wait.

Aside from the tractor prints, Melvin had left no tracks at the scene of the crime. Yes, Elizabeth Gastelli had seen a tractor driving along Ebenezer Road, but she couldn't remember exactly when. Besides, trying to identify a tractor in Hernia was like looking for a drunk in a St. Patrick's Day parade in Boston.

Amy's death also remained a mystery. I wasn't supposed to know the facts, but Chief Memmer filled me in anyway, given that I used to be mayor of his new hometown and was still its unofficial crime solver. At any rate, the young woman had been strangled to death by a bubble gum pink pashmina, which is a kind of scarf, I'm told. There'd been no prints left behind, and no signs of forced entry. The supposition was that whoever had so brutally murdered the girl had either been an acquaintance or in possession of a gilded tongue. The second idea made perfect sense to me: young women that age are easily flattered by the hairier sex into believing that they alone are the special one, and that said relationship will inevitably lead to the altar.

I had just stepped outside into the street, in front of Hernia's police station, when my cell phone rang. I have chosen as my ringtone the dulcet sounds of Pachelbel's Canon, so you see, it really is not at all obnoxious. In fact, I have been known to hold up my phone in public places when it rings so that others may be blessed by hearing this classic. It is my fond hope that one day, at the Monroeville Mall, a rapper will fall to his knees in awe and forsake his base ways.

Because there was no one else about at this particular moment, I answered after the first ring. "Yoder's House of Fun and Frolic, the owner herself speaking."

"I need your help," a desperate voice said.

27

"And a gracious hello to you too, Agnes," I said. "The answer to eighteen down is 'fubsy.' According to Merriam-Webster's Collegiate Dictionary, Eleventh Edition, it means 'chubby and somewhat squat.'"

"I'm through with the crossword, Magdalena. This is about my uncles; they're running amok."

"Yes, I know. Ida was over here yesterday and I jokingly told her to start a nudist colony."

"Which she did."

"She didn't!"

"Oh, but she did. Just before this morning's meditation—which was supposed to be on the meaningfulness of mediocrity—ten of the sisters assumed the lotus position au naturel!"

"Look on the bright side, dear: the lotus is a beautiful flower that—"

"That means that they sat with their legs crossed so that their feet were tucked up against the opposing knee. You can imagine what happened next."

"If I do, I'll have to perform my own lobotomy, and that can be a laborious process when one is using a number two pencil—or so I've heard."

"This isn't funny, Magdalena. After the meditation ended, these ten sisters decided to spread the Gospel of Physical Freedom—that's what they're calling it—to the good folks of Hernia."

"Uh-oh. Exactly what does that mean?"

"They're following Hertzler Road into town as we speak. They plan to go door to door, in pairs, kind of like Mormon missionaries. You've got to do something to stop them."

"Okay," I said. "I'm right here at the station, so I'll alert the chief—"

"No, you can't!"

I could practically feel the vehemence in her voice coming through the airwaves. "What do you mean by 'you can't'?"

"I mean you can't tell Chief Memmer what's happening because if my uncles get arrested, they'll get locked up for a year—minimum. That was the deal they cut with the judge last time. So give me a chance to talk to them first. Someone put them up to this missionary business. I just know that's the case."

"That could be, but in the meantime a whole lot of Herniaites are going to have to ruin their number two pencils, and that's just not fair. Some of these folks have led really sheltered lives. Why Edith Wharton confessed to me on her deathbed that she had never even gotten a look at her own nether region, much less anyone else's. That was her one big regret in life,"

"Edith Wharton—wasn't she like ninety-eight years old when she died?"

"Ninety-three. Still, despite what she said, I don't think she could have handled an impromptu visit from one of these loonies— Oops, I'm not referring to your uncles, of course."

"Yes, you are. And you're absolutely right. We both know that they're as nutty as a Payday bar, but they're all I've got—except for you."

"Aw," I said quite seriously. "I'm touched."

"I mean it; you are the best friend I've ever had. *Ever.*"

"Thanks, but although I'm touched, I'm not 'teched.' I know you're trying to butter me up, and I can't promise you that your uncles are going to get off scot-free. In any case, you're going to need to find a home for them—maybe on a ranch out in Montana where the deer and the antelope play."

"But it gets cold in Montana; they'll freeze their little whatsits off."

"Well, when that happens, their nudity will no longer be so much of an issue. In the meantime, how do we prepare the good citizens of Hernia for an invasion of cellulite and varicose veins—not to mention whatsits of every size and description?"

Agnes is a quick thinker; you have to give her that much. "Who are Hernia's biggest gossips?"

"Present company excepted?"

"Ha-ha."

"Well, that would have to be Marlene Reenkle, Catherine Ayebagg, Estelle Waystrohl and Naomi Bakkphat."

"Good. We call them and tell them that the IRS is on their way to do surprise audits on anyone that they find at home. That should send everyone to their basements. Hopefully we'll get the nudes rounded up before our terrified citizenry has the nerve to venture back upstairs."

"Like I keep saying, Agnes, you should have worked for the state department."

"Oh, I spotted one of the uncles!" She hung up.

The invasion of unfettered flesh might have been far more time-consuming for me, and traumatic for most Herniaites, had it not been Fred and Alice Rosenthal. The couple are retirees, refugees from the Big Apple, who've sought out small-town living because of our clean air and quaint old-fashioned ways. Imagine their surprise to look up from their *New York Times* and spot a horde of pasty white bodies running down the road in their direction, whoosits and whatsits flopping joyously, just as freely as the ears on a cocker spaniel.

But instead of being scandalized, the Rosenthals went out on their porch, where they commenced laughing. And laughing. And laughing. By the time I got there, poor Fred had practically laughed himself sick, and Alice, bless her heart, found that she needed to change her designer blue jeans.

The nude missionaries, however, were not amused. The laughing duo offended them so much that they stopped in their tracks to argue, the whole bunch of them. Then along came a buggy, driven by Amish teenagers. The occupants hooted and jeered at the escapees with the Haight-Ashbury frame of mind. One by one the nudists hung their heads in shame, and that was how another cult bit the dust.

It wasn't until I got home and saw the ship's clock on the parlor mantel that I realized just how time-consuming it was to have the Sisters of Perpetual Apathy directly across the road from the PennDutch Inn. If it wasn't nude nuns, then it was plumbing issues—either Ida's own or her establishment's—but there was always something coming along that demanded the full attention of either Gabriel or myself.

I slumped onto a hard, unforgiving Victorian chair. Following my great-granny Yoder's example, I kept the furniture in my sitting room as uncomfortable as I could and still have it appear cozy. Great-Granny believed that a body should rest only after death; I merely see the value in keeping guests from congregating. Heaven forefend they should collect in numbers and conduct a full-scale revolt over some imagined mistreatment at my hand.

At any rate, I was so upset by that time, I didn't see Olivia Zambezi enter the room from the other direction. In my defense I shall hasten to explain that the woman favored pastel dresses that hung nearly to the floor. Today it was pale gray, with darker gray crosshatches. Her hair was steel gray and, frankly, so was her complexion. While I'm hardly a proponent of makeup, if one is going to wear it, one should at least pick a flattering tone, shouldn't one? In short, Mrs. Zambezi resembled the battleships I'd once seen while on a cruise of Norfolk Harbor more than she did a flesh-and-blood woman her age.

Not that I'm a fashion icon, to be sure. However, one can never go wrong with a modestly cut navy blue broadcloth dress, and one's hair—it is after all, a woman's crowning glory—braided and then swept securely into a bun, over which is pinned a white organza prayer cap. This simple way of dressing flatters every body type, and women of every walk of life and religious persuasion could do worse than adopt it as their daily uniform.

Now where was I? Oh yes, in my understandably self-absorbed state of mind, I got up from my chair and ran smack into Olivia Zambezi with enough force to knock Arnold Schwarzenegger on his keester.

"Dang you, Yoder," she swore in a shockingly deep voice.

"I am so sorry, Mrs. Zambezi." I would have asked her if she was all right, but I didn't want to plant any suggestions in that old gray head.

And speaking of her old gray head, I seemed to have knocked it a bit askew. That is to say, her noggin was no longer sitting directly on top of its pedestal— No wait, silly me—of *course*! Olivia Zambezi wore a wig, and I had knocked the dang thing practically off her head. Suddenly she no longer resembled Olivia from New Jersey at all. Still, she was very, very familiar.

But what to do? What to do? The poor woman seemed entirely oblivious to the hair-raising situation at hand. Perhaps her face stung too much from slamming into mine. Should I say something to her, or just reach out and give the rug a tug—taking care not to burn my hand on her whiskers. Her *whiskers*! Land o' Goshen! Olivia Zambezi was sporting five o'clock shadow, and here it was only six minutes past three—give or take a minute.

I've known some hirsute women in my time—Gloria Crabtree comes to mind—but none quite as hairy as the one I beheld. Then again, her face was missing a swath of pancake makeup an inch thick where mine had swiped it, which meant that half of me undoubtedly resembled a Kabuki performer. I pulled the collar of my shirtdress out to where I could see it.

"Oh Fudgsicles," I cried. "Now see what you've done!"

"Me?" Olivia boomed. "Yoder, it was you who ran into me."

It was the way "she" said Yoder that tipped me off. The person masquerading as Olivia Zambezi managed to make my maiden name sound like a curse. Factor in her large feet, large hands, odd stance, and eyes like those of a lobster on steroids, and even a heavily sedated zombie would be able to tell that I was face-to-face with none other than the maniacal Melvin Stoltzfus.

28

My blood froze. I know that's just a figure of speech, and I have a tendency to embroider mine at times, but I'm not exaggerating now—well, sort of almost not. It really did feel like I had icicles in my veins. But at the same time, my frozen limbs were anything but stiff; my legs, for instance, felt like they'd been sculpted from whipped butter. (Although, to be honest, it's very hard to determine whether or not these feelings are accurate. I have never actually had even one leg sculpted from whipped butter, and seldom, if ever, do I insert icicles in my veins.)

"Oh my gracious, oh my soul," I said. "There goes Alice down the hole."

"Where?" Olivia, aka Melvin, glanced around the parlor. His panic was practically palpable, just like my shock.

"It's just a kid's rhyme," I said. "I couldn't think of what else to say, and since I'm never speechless, something had to slip out."

"Yeah, you've got a tongue that can cut cheese. But this time, Yoder, I outsmarted you. Admit it."

"I will admit nothing to you!" There is a theory that cold

water boils faster than warm. It may not be true, but the ice in my veins had turned to steam in a matter of seconds. "You killed Amy, didn't you?"

"She was a nosy girl who deserved what was coming to her."

"She was a young girl just getting started in life."

"Boo-hoo. Your sister rots in jail and you waste emotion on a kid from the wrong side of the tracks?"

"And what side would that be? We don't even have tracks in Hernia!"

"You want to get riled up about someone, Yoder, get riled up about Mary Berkey. Now there was a fine woman—good breeding hips on her too. It was a shame she had to go."

I couldn't believe my ears. The evil man was making a full confession, but there were no witnesses besides Yours Truly. My kingdom for a tape recorder. Or even just a number two pencil!

"Why did she have to go?" I said, as I edged for the back door. "*She* wasn't nosy. She had nothing to do with the bank robbery."

I'd already figured out that Melvin had been one of the three armed robbers. If he could convincingly pass himself off as a matron from the Garden State for several days running, pulling off the role of a hit-and-run Amish man must have been a piece of cake. (In for the penny, in for the pound of makeup, it seemed.) As much as I hate to admit it, his ability to disguise himself had kept him a free man for past five years.

Melvin pulled his wig back into place before answering. "Yeah, too bad. Mary was a class act. And with all those kids to support. How many were there? A dozen?"

"Six," I hissed.

"Yeah. She ought to have thought about them a little more and a little less about what I was up to."

I was flabbergasted. "So it's her fault that she's dead."

"Yeah, basically. For starters, she should have refused to make you that silly outfit that you've got on now. Don't think you fooled anyone, Yoder. You look like the Halloween version of a Beverly Lewis book cover."

I thought I heard footsteps in the kitchen. In any case it was to my advantage to keep the kook yammering on as long as I could.

"I didn't think that you could read, Melvin, *and* just so you know, this outfit happens to be very authentic. You said 'for starters.' What else did she do to irritate you?"

"What do you think, idiot? She saw through *this* getup! Well, not exactly this getup, because she made me strip down to my bra and panties when she measured me for my Amish dress."

"*Your* Amish dress?"

"Pretty smart, huh? Local banks might be suspicious of Amish men for a while, but no one would suspect an Amish woman. And I have you to thank for it, Yoder. You're the one who put the idea in my head."

"And here I thought it was impenetrable."

"But Mary had to go and ruin it, on account of she had eyes like a hawk."

"On either side of her head?"

"And all because she saw my hairy chest. Somehow that got her attention right away. It was like she got fixated on them."

"Three hairs will do that to a gal. Trust me, four hairs and she would have swooned."

"Very funny, Yoder. No need to remind me why I hate you so much." He reached down the front of his frumpy frock and pulled out a pistol, which he aimed at my head.

"But, Melykins, I'm your flesh-and-blood sister, remember? Our birth mother, Elvina, was quite sure of the gory details. And if that's not enough, please cogitate on the fact that I am the only sister—and friend—of your darling wife, Susannah."

I've often (quite unkindly, I admit) likened Melvin to a praying mantis because of his bulging eyes, which operate independently of each other. I was wrong; I should have compared him to a chameleon—one from the island of Madagascar. That's because apparently he did cogitate, and while he did, the longest tongue I'd ever seen came slithering out between slightly parted and extremely pointed teeth. This serpentlike appendage proceeded to lick his dry lips and clean crusted bits of lunch from the corners of his mouth before slithering back into its den.

"Does Jack Hanna know where you are?" I said. Sometimes I just can't help myself.

"What's that supposed to mean? Was that a put-down?"

"Is a put-down like a touchdown? Does it count for, or against, me?" One can always be hopeful, can't one?

"I'm going to put you down, Yoder, and Susannah's never going to know that I did it. Now move!"

I read somewhere that one should never, ever go with a gunman. Apparently the odds are that what happens after abduction is invariably worse than what would happen if one tried to make a break for it while at the original site of the crime. After all, it is extremely hard to hit a moving target. This is excellent advice, but it's better suited to areas other than small Victorian parlors.

Much to my dismay the chameleon was able to move with lightning speed. I felt the barrel of the gun against my back while in midlunge. By the time my size elevens hit the ground, I was indisputably his prisoner and his temper was nowhere to be found.

"Now you've done it, Yoder. Any mercy I might have shown you at the last minute, you just threw away."

I could definitely hear someone else moving about in the house. Was that a chair scraping in the dining room?

"I can't believe you used to be the chief of *police*," I said, speaking just as loud as I dared. "When folks were in trouble, they would *call the police*, and that was you."

"Shut up, Yoder, and get moving." He used the gun barrel to push me toward the dining room door.

I needed no additional prodding. Perhaps if I stumbled in the doorway, whoever was in the room would see the gun and might think fast enough to make a run for it. Or I could just fall backward on top of Melvin. After all, he was a spindly thing, mostly arms, legs, and misshapen head—not to be unkind. My overly active brain came up with other scenarios as well (some of them far-fetched, one even involving duct tape), but before I even reached the ding dang door, it was opened from the other side.

"Tiny Timms!" I couldn't help but gasp. Her presence was literally a godsend, because I had been praying for deliverance. Since the Good Lord sent an angel to shut the mouths of lions for Daniel, it seemed perfectly logical to me that He would send a small but big-busted woman to help me fight a chameleon.

Tiny smiled. "Hello, Miss Yoder. Hello, Olivia."

"Yinz are wearing out my name," I said, whilst gesturing madly with my eyes. Unfortunately my eyes neither bulge nor swivel dramatically in all directions; hence, any gestures I make with them are somewhat limited. And since Tiny was not an astute enough observer of regional dialects to pick up on my uncharacteristic usage of Pittsburghese (I never say "yinz" unless compensation is involved), I was unable to warn her of the sure and present danger behind me.

"Tiny," Melvin said, "the jig is up. She knows."

"What?"

With his free hand, the chameleon must have pulled off his wig; I'm certain that I heard Tiny gasp. A second later a very expensive head of hair sailed into the dining room and landed on the table, where it lay like a road-kill centerpiece.

"Oh, my," Tiny said slowly. "I thought you were going to wait until her husband got home and then we would get the two of them together."

"She wouldn't let me," Melvin whined. "She had to go and spoil everything by outing me."

"What did you say?" I managed to rasp. Tiny's words had shocked the bloomers right off me and so filled me with despair that I could barely catch my breath.

"We're going to kill you," Tiny said calmly. "Really, Miss Yoder, you've become quite a liability."

"But first," the Chameleon said, "we're going to learn where you've hidden that kid."

Adrenaline is an amazing thing. In an instant my fear had been replaced by anger. "That *kid* is your *nephew*," I growled. "And he has a name—Little Jacob—in case you've forgotten."

"Oh yeah," the Chameleon said. "How do I know that you're even his mother?"

I looked Tiny straight in her tiny eyes. "The fact that my son emerged from my womb means nothing to a man of your leader's intelligence. Apparently only a 'made in Magdalena' stamp on my son's backside will satisfy this man's unusually high standards."

"You're darn tooting," Melvin said. He was deadly serious.

"Well, Mr. Stoltzfus *is* a genius," Tiny said. She was deadly serious as well.

"Where is Chicken Little when I need him?" I cried. "At least *he* was sane!"

"You see what I had to put up with all those years?" Melvin had the nerve to say. Then he prodded my shoulder with the pistol. "Now move it, Yoder. I want you to exit your dump of an inn just as calmly as you would under more normal circumstances. There is a white van waiting for us in the driveway. I want you to climb in the back. Don't even think of running. If you do, I'll shoot you from behind, and Tiny here will shoot you from in front. One of us is bound to hit a vital organ. Personally, I'm hoping that we don't kill you right away; I'd like to see you suffer a good bit before you join our birth daddy and your adoptive parents in their mansions in the sky."

I'm all for procrastinating—as well as fact-finding. "Tiny has a gun?"

Tiny reached between her enormous bosom and withdrew the largest handgun I had ever seen. She also removed a small hand mirror, which she laid on the table behind her, and two sandwiches.

"What the heck?" Melvin said. (He actually used a much stronger invective.)

"Don't swear in my house," I snapped.

"Turkey or ham?" Tiny said, just as casually as if she was laying out a picnic.

"I prefer cheese," I said. "A well-aged baby Swiss with weensy-teensy tiny holes. Oh dear, did I use your name in vain?"

"You were right, Melvin," Tiny whined. "She's every bit as sarcastic as you said she would be. But she's not at all afraid."

"Actually, I am," I said. "I'm shivering in my brogans—can't you tell? And you would be too, if you were trapped between a crazed chameleon and Tinkerbell."

"*Tinkerbell?* Oh, Miss Yoder, you don't realize how much that burns my bum! All my life I've been called that, and for something I can't help. How would you like it if I called you Queen Kong or something like that?"

"Ha-ha, that's a good one," Melvin chortled.

"Sticks and stones may break my bones," I said, "but words will forever hurt me." I know those aren't the real words, but they're much more accurate. Besides, when folks are that familiar with a saying, they seldom listen to its recitation closely.

"Well, you just have to shut up, Miss Yoder," Tiny said, "because I didn't offer the sandwiches to you. Only Melvin gets lunch."

"I don't get to eat?"

"Oh no," she said calmly. "What would be the point? You're going to be dead within the hour; that's barely enough time to get the digestive process started. To feed you now would be a waste of this planet's precious resources."

"Hmm," I said, "that does make some sense. But you can't get away with this—you know that, right? You fire that gun and someone is bound to hear it. Your husband, for instance."

"Ha, that's what you think. Tell her, Melvin."

"Yes, tell me, Melykins."

"I'm not your Melykins! Only your sister gets to call me that."

"Sorry," I said, "but you look so adorable in that outfit. All I want to do is to hug you."

"You see, Tiny?" Melvin cried. "What did I tell you about her?"

Tiny's clenched fist was barely larger than a brussels sprout. "For your information, Miss Smarty-pants, the others aren't going to help you, because we're all here together."

Now that took the wind out of my sails. *"Together?"* I asked in a tiny voice. (To be sure, it was my own tiny voice, not hers.)

"Together," they said in unison.

"Chew on that," said Tiny triumphantly.

I did. A million years later, I had the courage to speak again.

"So in that case, dear, there is absolutely no reason why you can't tell me how this brilliant plan of yours was supposed to work. First and foremost, are you supposed to be an organized crime gang, and secondly, why on earth would you return to the scene of the crime? Especially to the home of a witness?"

Melvin thrust his scrawny chest out like a bantam rooster out to impress a rival. No, wait—that was one animal metaphor too many. Suffice it to say, his hackles were hiked and his dander was raised.

"Of course, we're an organized crime gang, Yoder. Haven't you ever heard of the Mafia?"

"*You're* Mafia?"

"Don't be an idiot, Yoder. Of course, we're not *the* Mafia— you have to be Danish or something to belong to that; we're the Melfia."

"*Mel*fia," Tiny said, in case I'd missed it. "Isn't this man awesome?"

"Yoder," Melvin said, "if you had half a brain, you'd know that a good criminal always returns to the scene of the crime."

"*Oy vey,*" I said. "Elvina must have had two wombs; I can't believe that we're products of the same one."

"You think you're so smart, sis, don't you? Well, you don't deserve an answer, but I'll tell you anyway. I had to see if there were loose ends that needed to be tied up—and there were. Like your kid, for one."

"Don't call me 'sis,' but do call him 'nephew.' He's your nephew Jacob. And just out of a dead woman's curiosity, why did you wait so long before you— Well, what I mean is that you could have gotten to your nephew right away."

The bantam's chest deflated just a tad. "I wanted to get to know him first. Is that so bad?"

"Stop listening to her, Melvin," Tiny said. "She's trying to make you feel guilty. To establish a human connection."

"Would that were possible," I said.

"Yeah, I read about that connection thing somewhere," Melvin said. "I think it might have been in my Policing 101 textbook."

"Remember, Melvin," Tiny said, "that we're a proud crime family—the Melfia—and you're our godfather."

I tried to stifle my nervous laugh, but it came out as a snort, and not as a human snort either. From out on Hertzler Road, I could hear an Amish horse neigh its lovesick response.

"Ahem," I said against my better judgment, "the way a certain someone is dressed, wouldn't that make him your god*mother*?"

Tiny stamped a doll-size foot. "Make her shut up, Melvin, so that we can eat."

29

Now wait just one apple-picking minute! Why hadn't I seen it before? Timms, Zambezi, Nyle—they were all names of important rivers, although in some cases the spelling was not the same as the actual body of water. And the mysterious Russian? Surimanda *Baikal*? Wasn't Baikal the name of the world's deepest lake?

One may wonder how a mere Mennonite woman stuck in the hinterlands of southern Pennsylvania would have such a grasp of geography. I would be inclined to let one rudely wonder, were it not for the fact that this presumption sorely vexes me. In all modesty I summarily report that I am extremely well-read. I read primarily nonfiction books—books that feed my mind. I see little point in reading fiction, as it is all made-up. (I find comedic mysteries to be the least satisfying, as they rely too much on clever wordplay and not enough on plot.)

Now where was I? Oh yes, it couldn't possibly be a coincidence that all my guests had great water features for names. But now that I knew something very strange was going on, what was I to do? At the moment, nothing, of course, but in the future—

Well, maybe I should not be so quick to despair. I had one small advantage in this cat-and-mouse game—unfair as it was, with seven cats and just one rat—er, mouse—I'd just figured out from their aliases that they were all in this together, and power always comes with knowledge.

Melvin picked the ham sandwich, which left Tina the turkey, but neither took the time to eat just then. With guns poking in my back, they hustled my bustle out the seldom-used rear hall door, the one located right next to the root cellar.

"Oh, please, please, don't put me in the root cellar. It's dark down there and it's cold."

"Listen to her beg," Melvin said gleefully.

"I'm not begging; I'm imploring. Melvin, I'll do anything you want. I'll forget this whole thing, if only you don't put me in the root cellar. There are spiders down there. You know how I feel about spiders."

"She hates them," Melvin chortled. "Once I sneaked up on her when she was reading a book, and I dangled a plastic spider in her face, and you know what she did? She peed in her pants!"

Alas, it *was* a true story, but Melvin had neglected to mention that it had happened when we were kids—a very long time ago. No matter. In the interim I'd gotten over my arachnophobia.

What mattered now was that I convince Melvin that putting me *alive* in the cellar was the worst form of torture he could possibly devise. What Melvin apparently didn't remember was that my root cellar had survived the tornado of the 1990s completely intact. Also still intact was the secret tunnel that led from the root cellar to the floor of my current henhouse. The tunnel had been dug by the original owner of the house, my ancestor Jacob the Strong Hochstetler, whose father had been taken captive by the Delaware Indians when Jacob was a boy.

"Melvin, have I ever told you that you're as dumb as a post?" the teensy Tiny said.

Melvin stopped pushing me and grunted. "Hunh?"

"Miss Yoder *wants* you to put her down in that root cellar. She's playing you."

"Don't be an idiot, Charlene. Magdalena never plays."

Charlene? Who would have thought that such a petite young thing would have such a long, old-fashioned name? She was obviously named after her father—Charles. That was heartening in this day and age when so many don't even know who their fathers are.

"Yoder, I asked you a question," Melvin snarled. I'm sure it's very hard to imagine a chameleon snarling, but one must keep in mind a very big one, the size of a runty man.

"What question would that be, dear?"

"You see? You always tune me out. I asked you where you stashed the kid."

"You mean your nephew?"

"Says you; how do I know you weren't sleeping around?"

"Charlene, dearest," I purred in a conspiratorial tone, "Melvin and I are biologically siblings—albeit of different species. Wouldn't my son be his nephew, no matter who the father was?"

Tiny Timms tossed her golden ponytail. "Beats me. I failed biology in high school—*twice*. They finally let me graduate using double credits from health class because I was the captain of the cheerleading team *and* sleeping with Mr. Gawronski, the principal." She giggled.

"You see?" Melvin said. "Now tell me where he is!"

"Not even if you throw me into a den of spiders—of which I'm terribly afraid. Of course, after a few hours in there, I'm sure I'd tell you everything. Maybe even give up my PIN number."

"Then that's where you're going." He grabbed me by the elbows and began to manhandle me toward the cellar door. "Keep your gun on her, Charlene."

"Melvin, wait," Charlene said, sounding suddenly focused. "She *wants* to go into the cellar, I can tell."

"I do not!" Oops, I'd responded way too soon and with too much force.

"You see: she does. She's just pretending she doesn't. Let's take her with us."

"But she'll slow us down. Besides, she stinks."

"I most certainly do not!"

"Shut up, Yoder with the odor."

"That was in junior high, for crying out loud, and I couldn't help it. Mama thought that real Christians shouldn't wear deodorant on account of we shouldn't be ashamed of the way God made us smell. I can assure you that I use a good deodorant now—an antiperspirant in fact."

"Yeah, well, I still don't want to drag you along. You always think you're so much better than I am."

"Then I say we kill her," Tiny said.

"What?" Melvin and I chorused.

"Throw me in the hold," I wailed. "Toss me in the dungeon filled with spiders; I beseech thee, dear brother."

"I'll shoot her if you want," Tiny said.

"And then what will Susannah think of you," I said, playing my trump card. "My baby sister and I are all you have now that our mother is gone. And, of course, Little Jacob."

"She wasn't your mother; she was *mine*!"

"Nonetheless—which ever universe you choose to inhabit— my sister will hate you if you kill me or her beloved nephew. Do you want that, Melvin? Do you want the love of your life to hate you?"

"She's playing you," Tiny said.

Despite being a good Christian, and a pacifist to boot, I could have kicked the miniature woman down the cellar stairs; that was how mad she made me. But instead of acting out, I prayed that Melvin would listen to reason for once in his life and do the right thing.

"But it's too late," Melvin wailed, proving once and for all that we were indeed blood kin. "You know too much, and Little Johnny can ID me."

"He *can*?"

"Do you know how much that wig cost? And these breast forms?" He tugged at his matronly bosom. "I'm telling you, Yoder, that kid had me pegged as a dude the minute he saw Olivia Zambezi."

"He *did*? Where was I?"

"Somewhere off in *your* parallel universe, Yoder."

"Good one," Tiny said. "By the way, kids that age are notoriously good at seeing through disguises. It's because they still take the time to read all the information available to them, and not jump to conclusions based on a few obvious cues."

"Thank you for the psychology lecture, Dr. Timms," I said. "By the way, Melvin, the kid in question is named Little *Jacob, not* Little Johnny."

"Whatever," Melvin said.

Tiny must have consulted her watch. "We gotta get going, Melvin. If you don't want to kill her, then I will. Just go on ahead and get the car started. I'll catch up in a minute."

I could hear the chameleon cogitate; that is to say, he sucked in noisily, like he was slurping hot coffee. "Oh heck, all right. But do it quick and easy. Here, like this." My brother—my very own flesh and blood—had the chutzpah to take Tiny's hand and guide it so that the end of her pistol nestled in the soft spot behind my right ear.

"Say your last prayers," Tiny said mercilessly.

"See you in Heaven, Yoder," Melvin said, and then slipped around on my left and loped across the lawn.

30

Lavender Sugar Cookie

Ingredients

1 tablespoon fresh or dried lavender flowers*
⅔ cup granulated sugar
1 cup (2 sticks) unsalted butter, softened
1½ teaspoons pure vanilla extract
2 cups all-purpose flour
⅛ teaspoon salt
Sanding sugar (natural, white or colored) for decorating

Cooking Directions

In a small food processor (or with a mortar and pestle), grind lavender flowers with the granulated sugar.

*Fresh or dried lavender flowers can be found in health food stores, herb and spice markets, or through online baking supply retailers.

Combine the butter and lavender-sugar in a medium bowl. Using an electric mixer or wooden spoon, cream together until light and fluffy. Beat in the vanilla. Add flour and salt and blend until combined taking care not to overmix (dough should be soft but not sticky). Separate dough into two balls and wrap in plastic, flattening each into a flat disc and refrigerate until firm, about 2 hours or overnight. (The dough can also be frozen for months and baked in batches by bringing it to temperature in the refrigerator overnight.)

Preheat oven to 325°F and line baking sheets with parchment paper or leave them ungreased.

Remove only one disc at a time from the refrigerator, and roll dough on a lightly floured surface with a floured rolling pin to approximately ¼ inch thick. Cut into desired shapes with cookie cutters and place on prepared baking sheets. Decorate with sanding sugar and/or lightly press a lavender sprig or leaf into the cookie and top. (To keep intricate shapes intact, refrigerate baking sheet with shaped cookies for 10 minutes before baking).

Bake 12 to 14 minutes or until cookies are just beginning to lightly brown around the edges. Carefully remove and cool on wire racks. Repeat with remaining dough.

Courtesy http://www.eatwisconsincheese.com/

31

"Don't I get a last meal?" I said. "I want Swiss steak, mashed potatoes, baby peas with onions—frozen, not canned—pickled beet salad, hot yeast rolls with real butter and strawberry jam— Hey, aren't you going to tell me to shut up?" My plan wasn't going to work without getting her temper up to its boiling point.

"I want to hear what you'd have for dessert—*if* I were to feed you your last meal."

"That depends; are you a good cook?"

"This is theoretical, Miss Yoder. Now tell me."

"No can do, dear. For something as important as the last part of my last meal, I need to deal in facts. Can you cook?"

"No! But I can get something from the bakery, ding dang it!"

"I'll thank you not to swear in front of me, Tiny—although in this case, it is behind me. Which is exactly where I tell the Devil to go stand whenever he tries to tempt me. Tell me, Tiny, do you see the Prince of Darkness back there?"

"Hunh?"

"Don't worry; you will soon enough. Would it be a Mennonite bakery, or one owned by someone from another denomination?"

"What difference does that make?"

"In all modesty, Mennonites excel when it comes to cooking. Eating too. If you want the very best, go to a Mennonite bakery—but you probably won't find a devil's food cake there. Ha-ha."

"Very funny—not! And now you're babbling. Just shut up, Miss Yoder, or I'll shoot. I swear that I will."

"Well, that *is* your intention, isn't it?"

"Yes," she hissed. Good, she was getting up a proper head of steam, of the kind that made her less likely to see straight, much less shoot straight.

"Say, Tiny, I've been thinking: if you shoot me at this close range, it's going to be really, really messy. Brains and blood everywhere."

"That's okay; I'm washable."

"No doubt that you are, but did Melvin tell you that bleached blond hair absorbs blood like a sponge, and that unless you do something to protect those beautiful locks of yours, you'll be carting my scarlet DNA around in your ponytail until you snip it off, or it grows out. In fact, you're going to have to shave your head starting in about five minutes if you don't want my murder to be traced back to you. You see, the *hypoglucimides* in the hemoglobin travel right up the bleach-stripped hair shafts and into the *facaelumgaefolicum* of the *aqualuminatorus* resulting in the condition known as *Pincus scalptorium*. In layman's terms it's called pink scalp."

"Why, that rat," she said, hissing again, despite the dearth of "S"s.

"Indeedymouse." I think it's important to point out that lying to save one's life is a whole lot different from lying just for the sake of lying; it certainly isn't as much fun. Besides, I really can't be faulted for the fact that Tiny was so gullible.

Or was she? "Where did you learn all that medical terminology, Miss Yoder?"

"I've donated extensively to the Bedford County Memorial Hospital," I said. At least that part was true.

She thought a moment, and all the while the gun barrel never left its soft nest behind my ear. "Well, if you think—even for an instant—that I'm going to go after Melvin now, instead of you, you've got another think coming."

What *was* it about that man that gave him so much power over women? Allow me to amend that: *some* women?

"Very well," I said. "Suit yourself. I'm sure, what with your moderately good looks, you'll have no trouble making friends in prison."

"Well, I'm not going to prison, so there! You're going to help me protect my hair."

"And *then* you'll kill me? That hardly seems fair!"

"You do a lot of whining, Miss Yoder. It's no wonder your cousin doesn't like you."

"Why, that is an absolutely true, but unnecessary, thing for you to say! But, since I'm at your mercy, what choice do I have, but to protect those bleached blond locks of yours?"

"Miss Yoder! That's the second time you've referred to my hair as 'bleached blond.' How dare you be so presumptuous?"

"Hey, if it looks like a dead woodchuck— I mean, what are the chances it's not, right?"

"Grrr!"

I reckoned that was the precise moment that Tiny was at the zenith of her tizzy. Keeping my hands straight down to my sides, I leaned back, slowly and stiffly, a veritable sinking tower of Yoder—and I mean sinking, not stinking. The farther back I went, the more I felt the tip of the pistol barrel move in relation to my ear. First it seemed to be caught in the soft spot, and then it slid over the hump to graze along my temple.

There are only so many degrees a body can lean without falling altogether, but it wasn't until I came close to reaching the critical point that Tiny seemed to notice what was going on. "Hey," she yelled. "What the—"

"Timber!" I cried, and took her down with me as I plummeted backward.

As for what happened next, I owe it all to my parents, who were dairy farmers. You see, what most folks don't realize is that the milk you buy in the supermarket is taken from a cow that has given birth in the not too distant past, and that is being kept in a perpetual state of nursing. We refer to these cows as "freshened." At any rate, in order for there to be milk available to sell, the calves must be removed from their mothers and weaned early. It was my job, after school, to care for these unhappy "orphans," and more often than not, this job required a good deal of wrangling.

Papa had an uncanny ability to communicate with his cows. Most of this communication was unspoken, although he used a few grunts and hand signals. Occasionally, he had to deal with a wayward calf by throwing it to the ground and dragging it to where he wanted it—all by just using his bare hands. (Papa eschewed ropes.) I, on the other hand, had to get a headlock on my charges just to turn them around in their stalls so that they faced the feed bucket.

But Papa never had to manhandle a bank robber*ess* from New Jersey. Particularly one like Tiny.

"If you've broken my implants, I'll sue," she screamed from beneath me.

I could see the gun glinting in the grass about a dozen feet away, so I was no longer in any physical danger, but I still gave her tit for tat. "Well, I can sue *you*; I expected a softer landing."

"Get off me, you big oaf! You Mennonite country bumpkin."

I sat up on her sternum, just south of the Rockies, with my legs splayed outward to hold her arms down. "Why, Tiny Timms, how you talk! And I always thought you were the sweetest of the bunch."

"You were a fool! Melvin said that you once married a biga-mist, and I read in the *National Revealer* that you had a love affair with a real-life Bigfoot."

"It was inadvertent adultery," I wailed, and this was my very last wail—I promise! "And as for Bigfoot, what they say about men with big feet is absolutely true, so how could I resist?"

"*Huh?* You don't deny it?"

" 'If you read it in black-and-white, it must be right.' Stories written in colored ink are not to be trusted."

"Yeah, I guess. Hey, what you doing?"

I'd done a complete about-face so that I could hold both her tiny hands in one of mine, while the other performed a necessary function. "I'm removing my over-the-shoulder boulder holder," I said, exhibiting far more patience than she would have, had the tables been turned.

"What? You're taking off your bra?"

"Don't worry; I'm just going to tie you up with it."

"But you can't! I'll absolutely freak out. In fact, I'm freaking out now with you holding my hands."

"Well, dear, you should have thought about that before you embarked on a life of crime." I emitted a long, drawn-out sigh. "And if I can't even hold your hand, what chance do we have?"

"*What?* Miss Yoder, are you—"

"I suppose we could move to Iowa; gay marriage is legal there now. Plus which, I hear that folks are more taciturn there—especially out on the farms. We could get ourselves a nineteenth-century farmhouse with a working windmill—I've always wanted one of those—and raise pigs and corn. Do you know how to call pigs, Tiny?"

"Miss Yoder, you're crazy! I mean like *really* crazy—over-the-top nuts. Are you supposed to be on some kind of medication?"

"Oh phooey on pills. All I need is clean Midwestern air and—ding, dang, St. Louis International Airport, Concourse A!"

I wasn't getting very far in removing my flopper stopper. Not without letting go of Tiny's hands for a second or two. Not all of the petroleum by-products Tiny owned had been affixed internally. Attached to her tiny fingers were the longest fake nails I'd ever seen in all my born days. Ruby red garden rakes—that was what they were! If I let go of Tiny's hands, those claws could grate my flesh like a head of cabbage.

"Miss Yoder, you just swore!"

"Indeed, I did. Please remind me later to apologize."

"But you have such a foul mouth! I've been to Terminal A. On a Sunday evening. I had three hours to wait before my next flight. I'm not religious, but I prayed that God would take me—that's how boring I found the place."

"You too?"

She nodded vigorously. "So maybe we can make a truce?"

"A truce?" I said. "Like what?"

"I'll promise not to struggle, and you can take me somewhere and lock me up—but just don't tie me up, because that will really freak me out."

Sometimes one has to go with one's gut. (Judging by what I saw at the shore last summer, there sure are a lot of people going very far in life.) Call me silly and ship me off to boarding school, but I had a feeling—in my large intestine—that Tiny was so terrified of bondage that she would indeed cooperate. Of course I would have to hold the gun on her. However, she did not have to know that, as a practicing Mennonite, I would never, ever use it.

I got a death grip on one of her frail wrists and we both stood up. After a couple of steps, and a quick bob to get the gun, I dragged her straight into my laundry. I swung her up in front of the dryer and pried open the door with the end of the gun barrel.

"Climb in, dear," I whispered. The laundry room is an add-on behind the kitchen and has its own rear door so that one can head directly out to the clothesline if a genuinely fresh scent is desired. (I particularly love the faint smell of nearby cow patties.) You can be sure that I immediately shoved a chair under the doorknob that led to the kitchen.

"*What?*"

"It's a jumbo-size, commercial machine; there's plenty of room."

"But I'll suffocate!"

"No, you won't. I just cleaned the lint trap; stick your nose up against it. By the way, I clean all my lint traps before and after using my dryers, don't *you*? A lot of people are lazy about cleaning them, which is a good way to get your house burned down."

"I don't *do* laundry," Tiny said. "I get Peewee to do it."

"Well, I'll be dippety-doodled! How on earth do you get a man into the laundry room?"

"Look at me, Miss Yoder; I could have any man I want. Why would I be with someone like Peewee unless there were some perks—you know, special services?"

"Hop in," I said, "and start praying that I don't send you for a short spin."

The Good Lord knows that I was sorely tempted to do just that. But I behaved. I merely shoved the folding table up against the dryer, jamming it against the lid in such a way that Tiny would be unable to open it by herself.

Then I did exactly what I'd begged Melvin and Tiny not to do to me. I made myself go down into the cellar.

32

I wasn't lying about the spiders. They're everywhere in the cellar. Fortunately most of them are fairly benign, and since I would walk through fire—slowly—if it meant putting Melvin behind bars forever, so what if they weren't?

By the way, I feel compelled to distinguish fire walking from mere coal walking. The latter, in my not so humble opinion, is a gimmick. I shall herewith attempt to elucidate. Hot coals (aka embers), are by their nature covered in a layer of ash. A person walking quickly across a bed of coals is protected by that ash, and will not get his feet burned. To perform this feat, one does not need to be in a trance or be the object of a miracle. One need only walk quickly.

Contact with actual flames, on the other hand, will certainly result in injury. Although it may appear that I have digressed, I assure you that this is not the case. I am stating, unequivocally, that I would endure great pain, if it meant that the Murdering Mantis, that the Conniving Chameleon, was no longer a threat to humanity and to my family in particular.

If this were not the case, if my resolve had not been so strong, believe me, I would never have dared tug open the little round metal door on the north side of the cellar and squeezed blindly into it, like a bottlebrush into an opaque rose vase. Once I was fully inside, there was barely enough room for me to wiggle my way forward, with my arms stretched out in front of me. I felt like a giant earthworm— Well, I don't mean that literally, having seldom, if ever, been a giant earthworm.

This tunnel, incidentally, was constructed at the height of the French and Indian War, shortly after my Hochstetler ancestors were taken captive by the Delaware Indians in eastern Pennsylvania. It was intended solely as an escape route that led from a log cabin on this site to the nearby woods. Comfort of the escapees was not taken into consideration.

At any rate, as I have many times stated, adrenaline is a wonderful thing. Oh that it were available for purchase in pill or liquid form. Because I was focused on my destination, and because of what I intended to do when I reached it, I didn't feel the many cuts and abrasions I collected along the way, nor did I particularly notice the myriad insects I squashed. Some insects, of course, bit me, as did some spiders, but I honestly wasn't aware of this until long afterward.

Nowadays the far end of the tunnel surfaces smack-dab in the middle of my henhouse. As I understand it, the tunnel has been closed and reopened several times in its long history, but Papa was the last person to reopen it, and that was during the Bay of Pigs invasion.

In the event of a nuclear war, we were to take refuge in the root cellar. Should the house tumble down, or the surrounding trees topple, and we were trapped inside, we could always escape via the tunnel and the henhouse. Frankly, it wasn't such a bad idea then, and given the way things have been going on the international stage since then—well, I've not been motivated to spend the time or money to block up the tunnel.

The henhouse exit is a simple wooden trapdoor that blends in nicely with the floor, and under a layer of straw is virtually unnoticeable. Thus it was that when I finally flung open the door and hoisted myself up into the broad light of day, I caused quite a bit of commotion.

For one thing, the hens that had been skulking about, waiting for a chance to lay their eggs, became highly emotional. That is to say, each clucking chicken had been instantly transformed into a five-pound ball of airborne feathers and earsplitting cackles. Then there was the not so small matter of Peewee Timms and Barbie Nyle, who had unwisely chosen the henhouse as the location for their romantic rendezvous— No, I take that back. This was adultery, pure and simple.

What a disappointment that was! Barbie had always treated me nicely, and although I don't know why, I'd had this feeling that maybe Peewee was secretly Jewish. Well, Peewee, although aptly named, was certainly *not* Jewish. Still, who was I to judge, and why should I even entertain the idea? After all, the zillion mites and fleas resident in my henhouse were going to do the judging for me, although most of the misery would come a little later, once Barbie and Peewee started scratching.

Of course I was shocked to discover two naked people fornicating amidst bits of straw and chicken poo, but I was nowhere near as shocked as they were to see me suddenly rising from the floor, covered as I was in slime and squashed spiders. They were literally breathless for a spell, and frozen with fear, and when they did react, the first sounds they made eerily resembled chicken squawks. Fortunately by then I had exited the well-built shed, slammed the hasp into its place, and closed the Yale lock on their sinfulness.

Now to catch the evil Melvin—although I had a sinking feeling he'd already gotten away by car. I started running and was halfway to the parking area in front of my barn, just passing under the old swing tree, when George Nyle appeared out of nowhere. Well, to be fair to myself, George did have mousy brown hair, a mousy brown mustache, and a deep tan, and he was wearing a khaki safari suit—even a Maasai could have walked right past without noticing him.

"Hey," George said, "where are you going so fast?" He sounded positively genial, but then again, he might have been putting on act. After all, I had become Alice in Wonderland; nothing was as it should have been. Until I figured out just how much he knew about what *I* knew, I'd best play along as though everything were normal.

"It's been a long day," I said, "and I still have miles to go before I sleep."

"Ah, a fellow lover of poetry."

"Not especially—unless you're talking about the Song of Solomon. Now *that's* poetry. 'Thy hair is like a flock of goats, going down from Mount Gilead. Your teeth are like a flock of shorn sheep which have come up for the washing.' No modern poet could touch lines like that with a ten-foot pole."

"And I wouldn't want to touch a girl like that with a ten-foot pole. *Where* did you say the poem was from?"

"The Bible."

"It figures. Look, Miss Yoder, I don't mean to be rude, but you're not exactly touchable at the moment, either. Where the heck have you been?"

"Well—you see—one might say I look like a sewer rat."

"That's not what I asked."

Uh-oh, his tone was a lot nastier than I'd hoped for. If I didn't think fast on my size elevens, I might well perish whilst covered in a shroud composed of squished arachnids. It would not be a pretty way to go. Personally, I was hoping to hold out until the Second

Coming, because I have never been a big fan of pain. Just about every day I give thanks that when I gave birth to Little Jacob, I practically shot him out like a cannonball. Of course, it hurt like St. Louis International Airport, Terminal A, while it was happening. . . .

"Miss Yoder! This is no longer a game! How did you get out of the cellar?"

Aha! So he *was* in on it. Indeed, just like Melvin said, they all were.

I pointed to the upper branches of the tree behind him. "Is that an owl up there? They usually come out about this time of day."

Surely a question, no matter how misleading, cannot be a lie. And even though I didn't see an owl, there might have been one up there somewhere, hidden by the foliage, and it was true that they did come out about that time, which was about an hour before sunset.

"Where?" he asked, and foolishly turned.

That was when I grabbed the old wooden swing and swung it practically as high as it could go. Yes, it was a dangerous weapon in my hands, and it was a violent act that I performed, but I have since repented of this. In my defense— Well, I really have none, do I? My ancestors submitted to being scalped, rather than killing the Delaware with their muskets when they had the chance.

To sum it up, I may have been a poor pacifist, but I was an excellent markswoman. The wooden seat caught George just above the nape of the neck and gave him a nasty concussion. He survived, but for a long time—something like six months— he thought Peewee was his mother and Barbie was his sister. Frankly, it was just as well.

With four down, there were still two more to go, and that didn't include the mysterious Surimanda Baikal. One can imagine my astonishment, followed by enormous relief, when I beheld one of the rental cars from New Jersey idling empty in the parking area in front of the barn. It was if the Lord had sent an angel down to start it for me. After all, my car keys were in my purse, which was still in the house, and the Good Lord only knew who was still in there.

I gaped at the idling vehicle for a few precious seconds. It should not have amazed me, and in that regard I was a faithless woman. After all, I was on side of Good, battling Evil in the guise of a spindly man with an ill-fitting head and bulging eyes that could rotate 360 degrees. Since Heaven had sent me a chariot—a horseless carriage, if you will—I should have immediately credited it to the Man Upstairs and given thanks.

But give thanks I eventually did, and then as the Good Lord expected of me, I took action. However, as I tried to climb into the driver's seat of the monstrous black SUV, I was met with a great deal of unexpected resistance.

33

"Put your hands up, Yoder, and get in the back."

"Mantis—I mean Chameleon—I mean Melvin! Where did you come from?"

"I've been sitting here the whole time, Yoder—slouched, of course."

"And you didn't see me either," the craggy Carl Zambezi said, "although I was barely slumped."

"Right. Well shame on me for not seeing either of you!"

"What's the matter, Yoder? You going blind in your old age?"

"Au contraire, I have fifty-fifty vision. I see the half of the world that is good and kind and nourishes my soul, and the scum-sucking evil elements—like you—I just naturally overlook."

"Now that was hurtful, Yoder," Melvin said.

"Yeah, we watched you kill George Nyle," Carl Zambezi said.

My heart leapt into my throat. As hard and small as my heart is, there's always the danger that I'll accidentally disgorge it, perhaps during a phlegm-producing cough. I shudder to think of the consequences. Besides the obvious physical difficulties this would present, what about the emotional and theological ramifications? For instance, it would put a whole new spin on Valentine's Day—

"Yoder, are you in even in there?" Melvin barked.

"Of course, I am; and shame on you, because you should know by now that I engage in rather lengthy inner dialogues. That's what makes me so interesting—at least to myself. And I didn't kill George Nyle. I mean that if I did, it certainly wasn't intentional. Shall I go back and see?" For the record, I still hadn't as much as stuck one foot up into the SUV.

"George can take care of himself. Now get in before I blow your copulating head off!" Melvin actually used a far more vulgar term to express his anger, one that has never passed these lips.

"Double shame on you, Melvin," I said, as I grudgingly climbed in. "Are those the same mandibles with which you kiss your mother?"

"Oy, such a smart mouth on you. You'll get us both moidered yet."

I jerked my head around to look at the seat beside me and then did a double take. "*Ida?*"

"No, it's da Queen of Sheba."

As my eyes and brain adjusted to my new surroundings, I could see that it was indeed my scrappy little mother-in-law, and that her hands were bound behind her, as if she were a hostage or a prisoner of war. Ida was a survivor of the Holocaust, and to be restrained like that had to be torture for her. Whilst she is not my favorite person—she is perhaps number twenty-six down the list—I cannot stand to see someone truly suffer. To say that my hackles were hiked is like saying that Hitler was a bad boy.

"Melvin Lucretius Stolzfus III! What have you done to this poor woman?"

"She tried to scratch me," he whined.

"Untie her!"

"You can't tell me what to do! You're *my* prisoner."

"Then I'll untie her," I said. Which I did.

Melvin's response was to press the pedal to the metal and peel out of my long driveway amid curtains of gravel. Thank Heavens he wasn't driving my car.

"Are you going to let her get away with talking to you like that?" Carl snarled, once we were on Hertzler Road and headed for the bridge over Slave Creek.

By the way, this is the only route out of Hernia, unless one has the patience to meander all the way over to Somerset past myriad Amish farms. Passing buggies might be fun for tourists, but believe me, it gets old—as do some of the buggy drivers, and as a consequence, they don't hear one coming up behind them and so don't move away from the center of the road.

"Heck no," Melvin said. Again, he used extremely foul language. "Yoder, don't you ever talk to me like that again."

"Yes, sir," I said. Melvin was immune to sarcasm. (Try it on either a praying mantis or a chameleon sometime, and you'll see what I mean.)

"T'anks," Ida whispered when I released her bonds.

"What happened?" I whispered back. "What did you do?"

"Don't whisper," came the command from the driver's seat. "Speak so that we can all hear."

"I vas doing nutting vrong. I vas only coming to see eef my Gabeleh vas home. Your phone eez not vorking, Magdalena, und az you know, I dun't haf a cell."

"The woman is a menace," Carl said.

"No comments from Olivia's erstwhile spouse, dear," I said.

Melvin laughed long and hard. That is to say that for at least a minute, it sounded like there was a cicada loose somewhere in the car.

Most folks respond better to pleasant speech than they do to inflammatory words, so for once I decided to give that tact a try. Besides which, I had both the "brother" and the "local" cards going for me. After all, most folks root for the home team, don't they?

"Where are we going, *brother* dear?" I asked sweetly.

"Shut up, Yoder," Melvin snapped.

It was Carl's turn to laugh long and hard; he sounded like the Bontragers' male donkey come the first warm days of spring. He can be glad that Melvin was driving with one hand and holding a gun with the other, and that I was a good Christian woman. Honestly, I was tempted to lunge over the seat and smack the hee-haw right out of him.

But Carl answered my most burning question for me as soon as we turned right on Route 96, going away from Bedford. "Melvin says he knows this cool place that has lots of sinkholes where someone almost died last year. We're going to throw you guys down one of those holes, but not before we torture you first to find out where that brat of yours is hidden."

Ida jumped to her feet, her head still not touching the roof of the SUV. "You vant my *grandchild*? For vhat?"

"Because he witnessed the—"

"Sinking of the *Titanic*," I said loudly.

"No, Yoder," Melvin said, disdain dripping from all three syllables, "the *Titanic* sank in the nineteen fifties—your kid isn't that old."

"My kid is your nephew," I said. "Remember?"

"Yeah, yeah," Melvin said, waving the gun impatiently. "Anyway, the little brat was there when we—"

"Ate all the chocolate brownies," I said.

"What?" Melvin barked. "Yoder, you're nuts."

Ida clapped her wee spotted hands to her weathered cheeks. Not to be judgmental, but the woman really ought to consider wearing sunscreen, given the amount of time she spends gallivanting outside.

"You ate all zee brunies und he had *nahsing*?" she said.

I could have called Melvin a ding-a-ling, but I prayed for patience—yet again. I pity the Lord on account of He's had to listen to this prayer a billion times; it's no wonder that He so often chooses not to answer it. However, this time, a sweet peace seeped into my pores as an idea formed in my weary brain.

"Ee-shay oesn't-day oh-nay at-thay ou're-yay obber-rays."

"Darn it, Yoder, we've had this conversation in the past. How many times do I have to remind you that I don't speak Pennsylvania Dutch?"

"It isn't Pennsylvania Dutch, you ding-a-ling. Think again."

"Oh, I get it now—you're talking Jewish to your mother-in-law."

"And it isn't *Yiddish*, you numbskull!" You see what I mean about my prayer for patience going unanswered?

"You're really trying to tick me off, aren't you?" Melvin said. He was actually exhibiting more of the P word than was I at the moment.

"It's Pig Latin," Carl growled impatiently. "I can speak it."

"Then you whisper in his ear," I said.

Much to my surprise, he did as I directed. He may have said a few other things—things that Melvin vehemently disapproved of—because the car weaved back and forth across the road several times, throwing me up against poor little Ida, and almost provoking me to throw up *on* her as well.

Finally Melvin turned his attention to me. "Yoder, are you speaking from the perspective of an ex–law enforcement officer?"

As thrilling as it was to hear him say those words, they weren't true. I acted—and still do—as a liaison between the community and the Hernia Police Department. The unofficial post was created back when Chris Ackerman was chief. Young Chris hailed from California—the land of fruits and nuts—and he had no idea how life in a barrel of sour Krauts was lived. (During Melvin's administration, I was the brains.) But it behooved me naught to set him straight. In fact, it could be the difference between life and death.

"Yes. As far as I know, I'm the only one who knows the whole story: I've connected all the dots, and I know who all the players are. Little Jacob doesn't know that—he doesn't even remember your name."

"He *doesn't*?" Heavens to Betsy, I almost felt sorry for the Murdering Mantis; that was how sad this bit of misinformation seemed to make him.

"Of course, he doesn't. Why should he? You've been on the lam his entire life. And you've been staying at the inn; did you see any pictures of you around?"

Would that the little munchkin had never seen a likeness of his evil uncle, but, alas and alack, he had a Granny Stoltzfus who insisted on showing him snapshots of his "flesh and blood." Truthfully, I've considered raiding her assisted-living apartment and confiscating this album in the name of human decency, but two things hold me back: the love of my son (prison would keep us apart) and the fact that I look hideous in stripes.

"Shoot, Yoder," Melvin said, a tremble in his voice, "it isn't right; a boy growing up and not knowing about his uncle."

"That's why you don't want to compound any possible charges. Look, I've got an idea."

34

―――♦・♦・♦・―――

"Yeah?"

"Don't listen to her," Carl said.

I clenched my teeth but, other than a short-lived growl of my own, said nothing offensive. "Melvin, what you do is release Ida—just dump her along the road, anywhere here is fine—and the three of us immediately head for the West Virginia border. You know I've got enough money to qualify for a government bailout. You get me to a bank in West Virginia, and I'll make a series of withdrawals that will set you up for life."

"Yeah? And then what?"

"Then you kill me, of course," I said. "Two's company. Three's a crowd—isn't that what they say? Of course this is all predicated on you swearing—on your mama's life—that you'll leave Little Jacob out of this."

"Why West Virginia?" Carl said. "You have to get provisions if you're going there, and all we have is half a roll of tropical-flavored Life Savers and a warm can of Diet Coke."

"Because, dear," I said, not even making an attempt to mind my spittle, "West Virginia is a wild and woolly place. It's got all those hills and forests and who knows what stretching as far as the eye can see. The long white arm of the law will never find you there."

"Yeah, but it's the 'who knows what' that's got me worried, Yoder," Melvin said. "Remember that girl in ninth grade whose father had to have a hole cut in the back of his pants so that his tail could hang out? Wauneta somebody. She was from West Virginia."

Melvin forgot that I was eleven years older than he, but yes, I remembered Wauneta Beecher. How could anyone forget a girl with a father like hers? I read somewhere that, briefly, in utero we all possess tails at some stage of our development, and that this is a legacy of us having evolved from lower creatures. This article went on to state that in a certain percentage of the population this tail gene does not get switched off, and that's why certain individuals are born this way. But since evolution is pure fiction, and the Devil is not— Well, what other conclusion can a reasonable person draw from this?

"Melvin, dearest," I said, "if lasses who look like Lassies have you worried, then simply keep right on driving. Before you know it, you'll be in North Carolina, a state that has the highest mountains east of the Mississippi, hundreds of miles of beautiful coastline, and inexplicably still finds itself in the clutches of the tobacco companies."

"So what are you saying, Yoder? You want me to die of cancer?"

"No, no! I want you to live happily in a beautiful place."

"Can Susannah join me?"

"She's got a lot better chance of doing that if I stay alive," I said, "and work it from this end—but I meant what I said before. You can kill me, if that means that you spare Ida's hoary head."

"*Vhat?* You hear how dis von talks about me?"

Melvin also gasped. "And you had the nerve to criticize my mouth! Ha, what a hypocrite you are."

"It means 'gray,'" Carl said. "Like from old age."

"Yeah? That's a good one, Yoder. I'll have to remember it." My would-be killer with the seventh-grade sense of humor turned his attention to his partner in crime. Mind you, this was while we were hurtling down a winding road at a speed so fast that the shadow cast by the SUV we rode in was now several car lengths behind. "Carl," Melvin said, just as coolly as if he'd been discussing whether to hang up flypaper on the screen porch, "what do you think? Shall we kill her outright by throwing her down a sinkhole? Or tie her up in the woods somewhere and let her starve to death? Then again, maybe we should try to hold her for ransom."

"Vhat about me?" Ida bleated like a little lost lamb.

"You keep your mouth shut," Melvin said. "That's if you want any mercy."

"This could be a movie," Carl said. The bizarre change of subject, coupled with his burst of energy, belied his etched features and heretofore-mature demeanor. "I see Drew Barrymore playing the part of Miss Yoder."

"Much too young," Melvin said. "It's got to be Meryl Streep."

"Und vhat about *me*?"

"*Oy vey*," I said.

"I say we kill them now," Carl said. "Just pull over on the first little side road, park off in the trees, and blow her brains out. Ka-boom. What a rush that would be. And then, like she said, we collect money from her the rest of our lives."

"That's not how it would work, *dummkopf*," I said, exercising extreme restraint. "I have to set up an automatic-payment system first. Otherwise you'll get zilch, nada, nothing, zero. *Capisce*, compadre?"

"I don't like her," Carl whined. "Has she always been such a smart mouth?"

"Always," Melvin and Ida answered in unison.

"Let me see that gun," Carl said, and just like that, he grabbed it from the waistband of the mantis's trousers.

"What the heck?" said Melvin, and nearly ran off the road again.

"Pull over and stop," Carl said. When the mantis refused, Carl brought the gun up level to Melvin's oversize head. "Do it, or it will be your brains scattered from here to uh—uh—"

"Eternity," Melvin said.

"The correct answer is 'Kingdom come,'" I said. "Honestly, guys—"

"Shut up, Miss Yoder," Carl said.

Then much to my disappointment, my little, little-loved brother pulled over, first onto a dirt fire lane, and then into a small clearing in the pine trees. Waving the gun around like it was a conductor's baton, Carl Zambezi made us line up with our backs to him. Ida was in the middle.

"Well, well," Carl said, walking back and forth, "now I have my choice of who to kill, don't I?"

"Don't be an idiot, Carl," Melvin said. "I'm the brains of this outfit. I'm the one who brought you out of retirement."

"Retirement?" I said. "Whereabouts? Florida?"

I'd read somewhere—as I don't watch TV on principle; I do a lot of reading—that one should always attempt to make small talk with one's kidnappers. To do so humanizes the victims, and thus the criminal has a more difficult time dispatching them to their final destinations, wherever that may be.

"He retired in New Jersey," Melvin said. "But it wasn't where that I meant; he retired *from* being a pickpocket in Atlantic City, on the boardwalk."

"Down by da sea?" Ida rasped. "I vas picked der vonce!"

"I thought you looked familiar," Carl said. He continued to pace behind us. "Okay, Melvin," he said at last, "we can go back to bank jobs, but we have to get rid of these two first."

"Maybe the short one," Melvin said, "but I'm not so sure about my sister."

"The short one is the hen who will lay the golden eggs," I said quickly.

"*Oy*, the insults," Ida said.

"Explain," Carl barked.

"Well, speaking of retirement, not only does my husband have access to my money, but he is a rich, retired doctor. You keep the short one alive—put her on the phone now and then—you'll be able to milk him for a huge fortune."

"It might work," Melvin said with far too much enthusiasm.

"All right then, it's settled," Carl said. Suddenly the barrel of the gun pressed against the back of my skull. It was getting to be quite a familiar feeling.

"On your mark," Carl said. "Get set. . . ."

Get set for what? To meet my Maker? I *was* set; that didn't mean, however, that I wanted to go *now*. I still had a little boy to raise, for Heaven's sake.

The events that happened next transpired so quickly that in retrospect they seemed to happen simultaneously. First, I heard a loud grunt come from Carl, followed by a bellow of pain.

"Dat is vhat you git for trying to keel my Magdalena," Ida roared.

"Ouch, ouch, ouch! Oh please, Mommy, Mommy, help me! Ouch, ouch, dang it!"

By then I'd turned to witness Carl hopping about like a crazed wallaby, his hands cupped over his privates, his face screwed into an expression of intense pain.

Ida stood several feet from where we'd lined up, with her hands on her hips. Her large, broad face wore a small, satisfied smile.

Melvin too was watching. He was still decked out in a size fourteen dress and size twelve shoes—not that there is anything wrong with those measurements—but without Olivia's wig, I appreciated for the very first time what a truly unconvincing woman he made. Why hadn't I noticed that before? For one thing, he had absolutely no waist (although many insects do!). It was his stance, however, that should have tipped me off.

Most women carry themselves forward with their hips, for that would appear to be their center of gravity. For men, I have noticed, it is the chest that leads the way. That is why they stride; they are essentially trying to catch up with runaway rib cages.

Melvin saw me watching the curious scene unfold. "Yoder, that woman is crazy; you need to *do* something."

I saw that the gun was lying in the leaves, practically at my feet. "Indeed, I do need to do something," I said, as I stooped and picked up the pistol. "Ida, thank you for saving my life."

"You're velcome," my dear, sweet mother-in-law said.

"That's *it*, Yoder?"

"Of course not, *Mrs. Zambezi*. Now it's time for you and your hippity-hoppity husband to climb back into the car and we'll take it from there." I waved the gun at each man in turn.

The man who as yet went by the name Carl Zambezi, whilst still clutching his family jewels—if I may be so crude—moved obediently toward the SUV. But just as he was about to climb in, a sleek black car came flying around the curve, screeching to a stop inches behind the SUV's back bumper.

As I said, it all happened so fast that the details remain fuzzy in my mind. The more I try to sort them out, the more convoluted the situation becomes, and more absurd in its telling. But the truth is the truth, and it deserves to be told. And anyway, even someone who has been known to embellish the truth a tad— such as myself, for example—will find that there are enough bizarre happenings in life to supply good stories even when all is stripped to the bone.

I do remember that Carl Zambezi had tremendously quick reflexes. He took advantage of the sudden distraction by darting into the woods, and even if I had been inclined to shoot him, he was soon too far away to make that a possibility.

As for Mrs. Zambezi—aka Melvin Stoltzfus—he too tried to bolt, but running in pumps down a hill covered with thick leaf litter was not his forte. He twisted his left ankle not three yards from where he started, although he continued to hobble for another ten. But it was the fetching blue frock in the tiny flowered print that hung him up. Literally. When I caught up with Melvin, he was swinging by his jeweled neckline over a small gulley. The man was perfectly fine, something that could not be said for the young sycamore from whose broken branches he swung.

Having satisfied myself that there was nothing else that needed to be done vis-à-vis the bank robbers at that moment, I turned my entire attention to the cause of their great distress: the occupant of the sleek black car.

35

Sour Cream Pound Cake

Ingredients

1 cup butter, softened
2¾ cups sugar
2 teaspoons vanilla
6 eggs
3 cups flour
½ teaspoon salt
¼ teaspoon baking soda
1 cup sour cream

Cooking Directions

Cream butter and sugar until light and fluffy. Add vanilla and eggs, one at a time, beating thoroughly after each addition. Sift flour, salt and soda together 3 times. Add dry ingredients to creamed mixture alternately with sour cream, beating well after each addition. Stir in pecans. Pour into buttered 9-inch tube pan or two 9x5-inch loaf pans. Bake at 350°F for 60 to 80 minutes. Cool 5 minutes in pan. Remove and cool thoroughly.

Courtesy http://www.eatwisconsincheese.com/

EPILOGUE

———◆×◆———

"Do you remember that beautiful long coat that the Russian woman had?" Agnes said. "You know, the one who was spying on us from the hill opposite my house?"

This was, incidentally, four years after the Melfia paid a visit to the PennDutch Inn. They say that time flies by when you're having fun. I'd like to add that it can also seem to pass by quickly—especially in retrospect—even when you're alone and miserable. Not that I ever am; I can usually manage to drag at least *one* person down in the dumps with me.

"She wasn't Russian," I said calmly, as I refilled the cookie plate for the third time. "She was an FBI agent and as American as you or I, or these butter cookies. I thank the Good Lord she was spying on me the day I climbed into the SUV containing Mr. and Mrs. Zambezi and the not so helpless Ida. She was doing a good job of following us that afternoon until she ran out of gas. Fortunately she kept a jerrican in her trunk. Better late than never, they say."

"Yes, but do you remember her coat?"

"I remember that she dressed beautifully—and that she was

beautiful. You know, the Bureau had been on the trail of this gang of six for almost a year with no results, and then they assigned her, and within a week she not only had proof of their culpability—she had everyone in custody except for Carl Zambezi."

Agnes is a portly woman who doesn't gain weight by osmosis. For every two cookies I'd been putting on the plate, she'd been putting one in her mouth. She is, however, my very best friend in the entire world, and I would never say a word against her.

"But, Magdalena, it wasn't Suri—Sura—whoever—"

"Surimanda."

"Yeah. It wasn't her who apprehended all those gang members; it was you. You even stuffed one in the clothes dryer. You know, Magdalena, you're my hero."

"Hero, shmero," I mumbled, feeling my face turn red. "Agnes, dear, I *am* going to miss you."

"Nah, you won't. Not on the trip you're going on. A three-month cruise through the South Pacific; I can't imagine how wonderful that would be."

"Let's not forget the extended land portions in New Zealand and Australia. Little Jacob will be staying with his father and grandmother in Manhattan, so I know he'll be well taken care of."

I paused to blink back some tears. It had been two years since the divorce was final, but there was still a part of me that wished Gabe could share this great experience. At least we were still friends.

Our marriage, which had always been rocky, never recovered from the Melfia's invasion into our lives and my husband's inability to protect us. Once again it was Magdalena to the rescue, and that was once too many for him. Soon after Little Jacob's safe return to the PennDutch, Gabe moved across the road to the kooky convent, and six months later he was back in his native Manhattan. But enough of those thoughts.

"Anyway," I said, "I decided to hike the Southern Alps and

see Milford Sound. And I've always had a thing for Ayers Rock. Isn't that odd?"

"Forgive me, Magdalena, but nothing's odd when it comes to you."

"Hmm, I think I'll choose to take that as a compliment."

"As well you should." Agnes found room for three butter cookies simultaneously in her mouth.

"And you, dear," I said, "you utterly gobsmacked us with your performance on *America's Most Talented*. Who knew you had the pipes? Is that the word?"

"Yeth."

"I mean, I knew you sang in your church choir, but not like *that*! Agnes, I'm not just flattering you when I say that you sang "Memory" better than Babs, and I heard her sing it in person. Right here at the inn. And then you kept winning every week—all of Hernia was agog. Oh, and the final performance, when you sang "Time to Say Goodbye"—I don't mind telling you, dear, that I wept."

"You did not," Agnes protested, spraying me with cookie crumbs.

"I most certainly did; I wept that it wasn't me winning the million-dollar prize."

"Now *that* I believe. But what I still can't believe is that humongous flat-screen TV in your bedroom."

I sighed. "As you know, I never used to watch TV until Gabe made me watch your first performance on YouTube on his computer. That's when the Devil got into me."

"It's not a sin to watch TV, Magdalena. There are even special channels devoted exclusively to religion."

I glanced around the kitchen. We were alone, except for our consciences.

"Monday night," I whispered, "I watched a rerun of *Two and a Half Men*. What a potty mouth Charlie Sheen's character has!"

"Why didn't you turn it off, then?" she said. "Or, better yet, change the channel to something more uplifting?"

"Are you kidding?" I said. "I enjoyed every moment of it."

Without warning my very best friend in the whole wide world threw her arms around me and gave me a buttery kiss on the forehead. When she released me, it took a couple of seconds for me to regain my equilibrium.

"Magdalena," she gushed, "I'm going to miss you more than I'd miss white bread if it were taken away. Will you write?"

"You know I get writer's cramp easily; how about I call instead?"

"Okay," she said, and fled outside. It was the last I would see of her for a very long time.

I took the plate that held the butter cookies into the adjacent dining room. The cookies themselves didn't even make it as far as the table. No doubt about it they wouldn't have made it out of the kitchen, had there not been a sign on the door that read: KEEP OUT.

The cookie culprits were a pack of teenage boys, but the crowd that filled the public rooms of my inn was composed of a wide mix of the friends, neighbors, and relations of Doc Shafor. It was officially the old geezer's ninetieth birthday, and the party was my present to him.

To say that Doc was a lech is a bit like calling Mozart musically inclined. The old coot lived to seduce the fairer sex, *moi* in particular. If I had a dollar for every time he'd proposed to me, I wouldn't be envious of Agnes for winning *America's Most Talented* (although the truth is, I have plenty of money). Doc has even dated and, in fact, almost married Ida. I heard from the horse's mouth that they even consummated said relationship, which I think is just too icky to contemplate. The only thing commendable about the old goat's lifestyle is that he is interested only in mature women. Silly little things with nary a dimple of cellulite, or sign of a crow's-foot, need not apply.

Not seeing Doc in the dining room, I pushed through the throng until I got to the den. And voilà! There he was, holding court whilst sitting in Great-great-great-granny Yoder's hand-carved rocker. Frankly, a person has to be slightly off his, or her, rocker to spend any time in this chair, because it is terribly un-comfortable, built as it was back in the days when to enjoy one-self was considered a sin. Mankind was meant to suffer (it's all there in the Book of Genesis).

"Doc," I said happily.

"Ah, Magdalena, the fairest maiden in all the land."

There followed a chorus of protests from the assembled spin-sters, but I held up a silencing hand. "Doc, I believe that I no longer qualify as a maiden, given that I am fifty-six years old and the mother of an eight-year-old child."

"Magdalena, you will always be an honorary maiden in my eyes. Come, sit with me." At that, the flirt-*meister* pulled me onto his lap. His *lap.*

"Doc!"

"Relax, Magdalena. This will be the last time I'll ever get to see you."

"No, it won't; I'm only going to be gone three months—unless I take a yen to living in Japan. We'll be stopping in Osaka on the way back to San Diego. That was a little joke, by the way."

"Got it. But even if you come straight back, you're going to have to share your travel stories with me up at Settler's Cemetery."

I stiffened. "Doc, are you sick?"

"I'm old. My time has come, and I know it. Some folks are just blessed that way."

"That's crazy talk, Doc. Only God knows when we're going to die."

"Animals know, Magdalena. Sometimes days ahead. I was a veterinarian for sixty-two years, remember?"

"But you're not an animal!"

"My mama died when she was ninety. She predicted her own death a full nineteen days beforehand."

I jumped to my feet and fluffed my skirt. "You're not your mother," I said angrily. "You're the most randy man in of all of Pennsylvania. Why, you're supposed to ask me to marry you! That's the tradition, or don't you remember?"

And that *was* the tradition. Doc had been begging me to marry him for decades—and yes, shame on him, he did it even when I was married.

"Sorry, Magdalena, but all traditions have to come to an end. If you like, you can sit back down on my lap, and we can try to end this party on a high note."

"Doc!"

He winked. But despite his pretense at virility, the dear man died that night in his sleep. I joined the cruise two days late because of Doc's funeral, but considering it was a three-month cruise, a couple of days was no big deal.

Incidentally, approximately two hundred people mobbed the open house in honor of Doc's ninetieth birthday, but only ten people showed up at his funeral—and that included me.

I am not a sentimental person. Still, saying good-bye to Freni hurt about us much as giving birth. I thought I'd said my final good-byes after she and her husband, Mose, had helped me clean up after Doc's party, but of course I saw her again at the funeral. Afterward I walked her to the family buggy.

"If something happens to me on this cruise, Freni, I have written instructions for them to plant me wherever I am. If I'm at sea, they're to toss me overboard."

"Ach!"

"Well, there's no use spending any of Little Jacob's inheritance on shipping me back in a box. I don't want to have an open-casket funeral in any case. I think the Jews have it right."

"Stop this talk of dying. You will return from this cruise and drive me to attraction."

"That's not quite the vernacular, but hey, if it works, I might have a second career."

"Riddles. Always the riddles."

"Hmm. In that case, since I'm famous for asking them, let me ask you another: which high school English teacher married a doctor in December, but despite her promise to call her poor lonely mother at least once a week, doesn't live up to her obligation?"

Freni shook her head, and as she lacks a neck, her smocked black travel bonnet jerked eerily from side to side atop her stout torso. "It is indeed a shame that you cannot call all the way to California on your cell phone," she said.

"Excuse me?" I said.

"Have you tried calling Alison from the kitchen phone?" Freni said. The nerve of her for being so practical!

"That's not the point," I wailed (and this is truly the last time). "A daughter should call her mother, not the other way around."

"Yah, perhaps. But times are changing." She attempted a shrug. "Maybe it is not so important—this who calls who."

"It's easy for you to say that times are changing. You're Amish, for Pete's sake. Nothing changes for you."

We'd reached the buggy, and from that vantage point, we had a fabulous view over the picnic area and the little town of Hernia. Straight ahead was Lover's Leap, over which the Maniacal Mantis had tried to toss me. Fortunately my sturdy Christian underwear had saved that day.

Farther out I could see the rooftops of some of the Victorian homes in the older part of town, and an indentation through the trees that most certainly demarked Main Street. I'd spent a lot of time on Main Street, particularly in the police station—both inside the holding cells as a prisoner, and in my official function as mayor. Across the street from the station is Yoder's Corner Market. It was there that I gave birth to Little Jacob, with only the sleazy Sam to act as midwife. Sam! Now he was someone I was going to miss—in the sort of way one misses a splinter that has gradually worked its way out of one's skin.

"Magdalena, do you wander off in space again?"

"*What?*" Freni had surprised me by stopping off on her way home from the cemetery. Her agenda was to make sure that I called Allison.

"Isn't that what the handsome Dr. Rosen used to say?"

"Something like that. What were you saying, dear?"

"I was saying that even for us Amish there is change."

"Is that so? Give me an example?"

"The bishop has decreed that we are to change our hemlines by one inch. Maybe this is not such a big change, but it is still a change, yah?"

"An inch? Woo-hoo, Freni, sexy-wexy." I know, it was dreadfully naughty of me, but sometimes I just can't help teasing her.

"No, no," she cried. "We do not make them shorter; we must all make our hemlines *longer*! The bishop thinks that our church has gotten too liberal from seeing all the tourists in their skrimpy clothes."

"*Skrimpy?* Do you mean—" My ringing phone gave me the perfect excuse to take my foot out of my mouth. "Hello?"

"Mom? It's me."

"Me who?" I was kidding, of course. The voice belonged to Alison, my ex-pseudo-stepdaughter, and now just plain daughter, one hundred percent, no adjectives needed or wanted.

"It's Marie Antoinette," Alison said without missing a beat. "I seem to have lost my head; you haven't chanced upon a strange one lying about, have you?"

"Hmm, is *that* what it was? I'm afraid I threw it on the compost heap."

"Mom, I want to share something with you before you leave on your trip. You'll be the first to know, but we don't want you to share it with anyone else right now, because it's a little early in the game. Can you keep a secret?"

"Is Barbara Hostetler the best daughter-in-law in the whole wide world?"

"Ach," Freni squawked in my other ear.

"Is Auntie Freni there now?"

"As big as life and twice as ugly."

"Mom, I hate that expression."

"Yah, me too," Freni said.

"Apparently, dear, your auntie Freni has the hearing of a serval cat—you know those big-eared, long-legged beauties one sees in films about Africa? Anyway, do you mind terribly if she listens in on the extension?"

Alison has turned into a genuinely kind young woman, despite the bad example I may have set for her. "Sure, Aunt Freni, you can listen in, but you can't tell anyone either. So, can *you* keep a secret?"

"Does your mother bleach her mustache?" Freni said without missing a beat.

"*What?*" I said. "No fair!"

"That's okay, Mom," Alison said kindly, "I've been hoping you would for a while now."

"You *have*?" I said. "It's that obvious?"

"Well, just when the light hits it a certain way. Mom, don't get upset; I read somewhere that lots of women your age have this problem. Have you ever considered using a depilatory?"

Frankly, I was as embarrassed now as I was that time I had *the* sex talk with Alison. It had been necessitated by a life change in her body that was both exciting and scary—at least for me. It was most definitely an event that called for a celebration. (Incidentally, I believe that in this day and age, when there are so many teenage pregnancies, we should refer to this monthly cycle—at least privately—as "the blessing" and not "the curse.")

"Freni," I said, "now would be a good time for you to go pick up the phone in either my bedroom or my office."

The dear woman padded off, but not before reminding me that Amish women didn't believe in altering their bodies in any way. What God gave them, that's what he intended for them to keep—well, sort of; they did trim their nails, didn't they? I posed this contradiction to Freni over the extension.

"Ach! Must you always argue, Magdalena?"

"It's my nature to do so," I said.

"So now I get mushy, yah?" Freni said. "I think that I will miss this nature."

"Oh, that's sweet," Alison said. "Okay, are you both sitting down?"

"Yah," Freni said, "your mother's bed is very soft."

I pulled up a hard kitchen stool and plunked my tired patooty down. "Yes, go ahead, dear."

"One of you is about to be a grandmother," Alison said.

"*Ach du lieber!* My Jonathan is with child again?"

"I think that would be *Barbara*, dear," I said, losing my patience. "As much as you adore your Jonathan, he isn't capable of getting pregnant."

"Uh, Mom, it isn't Barbara either."

Sometimes I can be slow on the uptake, and this was one of them. After all, Alison had used the word "grandmother," a term I had never even associated with myself, not even in my wildest daydreams. After all, I was the mother of an eight-year-old, full of vim and vigor, practically in the prime of my life.

Okay, so perhaps I'd already reached my "sell by" date, but I still had a long way to go before I got to my "expiration" date, and we all know that some things are still good a ways beyond that. A grandma! *Moi?* But if that was what I was, then grandmothers still had it—whatever "it" was. Being a grandmother just meant that a new baby was coming into my life, that my joy would be multiplied, and that my daughter and her husband were about to be blessed—and sleep deprived—beyond anything that they could have imagined.

"Then it's you," I said. "Oh, Alison, I'm so happy!"

"*Mazel tov!*" Freni said.

We talked for the better part of an hour. When we hung up, I whooped and I hollered. I swooped and I spun in circles, like the crazy woman that I am.

Meanwhile, Freni, who was watching from the safety of the doorway, beamed.

Photo by Penny Young

Tamar Myers, who is of Amish background, is the author of the Pennsylvania Dutch mysteries and the *Den of Antiquity* series. She lives in North Carolina with her husband. Visit her online at www.tamarmyers.com.